BY SARAH ADAMS

The
ENEMY

The
ENEMY

A NOVEL

SARAH ADAMS

DELL BOOKS

NEW YORK

2024 Dell Trade Paperback Edition

Published in the United States by Dell, an imprint of Random House, a division of Penguin Random House LLC, New York.

Originally self- published in the United States by the author in 2020.

DELL and the D colophon are registered trademarks of Penguin Random House LLC.

LIBRARY OF CONGRESS CATALOGING-IN-PUBLICATION DATA
Names: Adams, Sarah, 1991– author.
Title: The enemy: a novel / Sarah Adams.
Description: Dell trade paperback edition. | New York: Dell Books, 2024.
Identifiers: LCCN 2023046616 (print) | LCCN 2023046617 (ebook) |
ISBN 9780593871737 (trade paperback; acid-free paper) |
ISBN 9780593871744 (ebook)
Subjects: LCGFT: Romance fiction. | Novels.
Classification: LCC PS3601.D3947 E54 2024 (print) |
LCC PS3601.D3947 (ebook) | DDC 813/.6—dc23/eng/20231124
LC record available at https://lccn.loc.gov/2023046616
LC ebook record available at https://lccn.loc.gov/2023046617

Printed in the United States of America on acid-free paper

This book contains an excerpt from the forthcoming book *The Off-Limits Rule* by Sarah Adams. This excerpt has been set for this edition only and may not reflect the final content of the forthcoming edition.

randomhousebooks.com

2 4 6 8 9 7 5 3 1

Title page art by lolo2013 © Adobe Stock Photos

Book design by Sara Bereta

To the person who's contemplating getting a tattoo.
This is your sign to get it.

A NOTE FROM SARAH

Hello, reader! Although this book is very much a romcom and written in a way to uplift and leave you feeling nothing but happy and hopeful, it does contain heavier elements. For those who need a little extra assurance before they begin reading, I have provided a content warning below. However, please be aware that the content warning DOES include spoilers.

XO Sarah

Content warning: Please be advised that *The Enemy* portrays themes of healing after experiencing a partner cheating and body image insecurities, as well as mention of parental loss at an early age. This story contains mild cursing and implied sexual intimacy.

The
ENEMY

CHAPTER 1

June

It's been twelve years since I've seen him.

Twelve years since his smug face leaned down to kiss me, stopped just before our mouths met, smirked, and then turned and walked out of my life forever. That day, I stood stunned and awestruck. I wish I had smashed his toes. Instead, I closed my eyes as he went in for the kill. I cringe, remembering how I tilted my chin up, feeling a chill trickle across my spine at the thought of him kissing me after spending our whole high school experience trying to kill each other. I acknowledged defeat the moment my eyes fluttered shut. I hate that he won our war back then.

But tonight . . . *tonight,* I resurrect the battle.

And victory will be mine.

No longer am I that naïve little graduate, excited for a kiss from the enemy. I'm now thirty years old and majority owner of Darlin' Donuts—one of Charleston's top hot spots. My best friend, Stacy, and I opened the bakery three years ago, and we have been enjoying a nice bit of success ever since.

Not only am I the southern queen of the gourmet donut business, but I'm turning down men calling me up nightly for a date. Okay . . . nightly is a stretch. But it's definitely somewhere around three times a week. Twice a week. Once a week. Above average, okay?

Point is, I've got a lot going for me now. Career success. Tons of friends—because family makes the best friends, am I right? And I'm at least four inches taller than I was in high school (read: two inches). Best of all, I've perfected a killer winged eyeliner and paired it with a little black dress that has had men eyeballing me from across the bar all night long.

Sorry, boys. You can look, but you can't touch.

In short, I've made sure that tonight—the night I come face-to-face again with my archnemesis—I look the best I've looked in my adult life. Because mark the words coming out of my red lips: Tonight, I will crush Ryan Henderson under my black stilettoed feet.

He will see all that he has missed out on and weep on the floor, clutching my legs, begging me to give him the kiss he left behind all those years ago.

And FINALLY, I hear the door squeak open. I wait, measuring the seconds passing by, the *click, click, click* of a woman's high heels drawing nearer.

Just a little closer.

Ugh. She passed me, choosing the far end of the row like a normal person. Why did I have to choose the middle?

"Hey there!" I call out. "Why don't you take the one beside me?"

Her clicks come to an abrupt halt, and suddenly, I'm aware of how creepy I sounded.

Because . . . yeah, currently, I'm sitting on a toilet with my fancy little cocktail dress hiked up to my hips and the telltale prickles of a woman who has had no choice but to sit on a toilet seat for far too long shooting down my legs.

"Uh, I think I'm okay with this stall." The woman is undoubtedly shooting off a frantic text to her date saying if she's not out of here in five minutes, it was the woman in the middle stall who killed her.

I laugh, trying to sound as little like a serial killer as possible, because any minute now, Ryan Henderson will be arriving at the party, and I need to be out there to see his ugly face first. (I'm assuming he's ugly because it helps me sleep easier at night.)

"Sorry, didn't mean to freak you out! I'm normal, I swear. Just out of toilet paper over here and was hoping you could slip me a roll."

"Oh." Her voice is still far away. She's not convinced I won't do something creepy if she comes near my stall.

Meanwhile, I'm sitting over here, air-drying on the porcelain throne, worrying I'll never feel my feet again, while Miss Barbie Heels makes up her mind.

I sweeten the pot because, apparently, I'm a black-market toilet paper dealer now. "There's five bucks and a half-used tube of red lipstick in it for you."

That got her moving. Moving right on out the bathroom door. Apparently, red isn't Barbie's lipstick color of choice, and she's decided she would rather risk a bladder infection than get near me. If I hadn't left my phone on the table like a potato, I could have texted Stacy and asked her to come bail me out. But noooo, I had to prove that I'm not obsessed with my phone like the rest of the world and leave it on the table.

Still, Stacy should be receiving my telepathic BFF distress signals. I've been in here forever. She should be worried that I've either been kidnapped or am suffering from some serious stomach trouble. Both of which would warrant an appearance from someone who claims to love me like a sister.

Stacy is also the reason I am having to be reunited with the man

I hate more than menstrual cramps. She and her fiancé, Logan, were high school sweethearts, and after over fifteen years in a relationship (yep, you heard me right) they are finally tying the knot. I would be over-the-moon excited for Stacy if Logan hadn't gone and asked Ryan to be his best man.

Although I think it's debatable, Stacy says it's customary for the best man to attend the groom's bachelor party—which is what is happening tonight. Actually, it's a joint bachelor and bachelorette party, because Stacy and Logan are one of those annoyingly in love couples who do everything together. They share a Facebook profile, order the dinner portion of every meal so they can split it, and even book overlapping doctors' appointments. So it was really no surprise when they announced they were joining their parties together. We're all having one fancy bar crawl, and I can think of at least one hundred things that could go wrong tonight. But all of them happen to Ryan.

1) I slip a laxative into his drink.
2) I squirt superglue on his seat before he sits down.
3) I set his car on fire. (Don't worry, I'll wait until he's out of it . . . maybe.)

I could go on and on, but you get the picture.

I can't, for the life of me, understand why Logan and Ryan have stayed close friends even after graduating and living in different states. Sometimes I wonder what Ryan has been up to this whole time, but I don't dare ask Stacy because I implemented a strict "no mention of the devil" rule a long time ago, and I refuse to break it. Both Stacy and Logan know that even the slightest slip of Ryan's name gets them put in the friendship doghouse for an entire week. Am I being petty? Yes. Absolutely. But I'm okay with it.

I've had twelve blissful years of Ryan-lessness. Well, almost blissful. That time, five years ago, when my fiancé cheated on me and I had to cancel my wedding sucked. Other than that, though, it's been twelve years of success without worrying that Ryan will somehow swoop in and overshadow me. And if I could ever get off this toilet, I could go rub all my newfound success in Ryan's face.

Thankfully, I hear the door open again, and I sit up straighter, determined not to mess up my lines this time. Fate is on my side as the woman chooses the stall beside me. Deciding not to risk it with chitchat, I cut right to the chase. "Umm. Hi. I don't mean to startle you . . . but the thing is, I've been in here for a while, and I was wondering if—"

I cut myself off when a hand shoots under the stall wall, clutching a bouquet of toilet paper. "Yeah, yeah, here you go."

Yes! Finally! See, now this is a woman I can appreciate. Soul sisters. Women who understand each other! I briefly consider giving her my tube of red lipstick and asking her to exchange numbers, but I decide against it.

Once all my business is complete, I emerge from the bathroom like I've been lost at sea for ten years. *It's good to be back in the world. Are the Kardashians still famous?*

I make my way down the dark, slender hallway toward the bar. The music pulses through my chest, and my heels pound the floor with the sure strides of a six-foot-tall *Vogue* model on the catwalk rather than the five-foot-two southern peach I am.

Right now, I am all confidence—high on my own determination as I step out of the hallway into the trendy sports bar. I have no time to scan the room before I'm grabbed hard by the arm and yanked to the side.

"Ow! What the—"

"He's here," Stacy whispers loudly into my face. And *WOW* has she already had a lot to drink or what? I'm going to need to slip her a Tic Tac.

"Who's here?" But I know who she's talking about. I'm just getting into character with my false disinterest.

"Didn't you get all my texts?" She sounds frantic. It makes me laugh a little because I know that even though this is our first stop of the night, she's already a little tipsy. Stacy is a lightweight. And when Stacy gets tipsy, she turns into the star of a reality TV show. Which reality show? It doesn't really matter. A drunk person is the driving force in all of them.

"No, I left my phone on the table."

Stacy looks appalled. "Why'd you do that?"

"Because I was proving that I— It doesn't matter. How long has he been here?"

"About five minutes. He's standing over at the bar."

Nerves zing through me because this is it. After twelve years, my archnemesis is once again standing in the same room as me, and I fully intend to squash him.

My little black dress is hugging my curves, and my loose-wave, honey-brown hair is tickling my spine. I've been saving this dress for exactly this occasion. It has a high neckline but low-cut open back, making it the perfect combination of sexy and sweet. The mullet of dresses, if you will. *Business in the front, party in the back.* Even better, the slender long sleeves cover almost all of my shoulder tattoo, leaving only the tiniest sliver of pale-yellow sunflower petals to peek out over my shoulder blade.

I take in one deep breath before turning around and scanning each man at the bar. I search. I search again. I search *one more time* because . . . "He's not here."

"Yes, he is," Stacy says in a matter-of-fact way that gives me a sinking feeling. "He's right there." She points toward the bar, and I whip my head around to her.

"No. He's. Not," I say through my teeth. "I don't see any ugly men with greasy hair and rotting teeth!" I'm doing that thing where

I'm yelling in whisper form with a smile still plastered to my face. It's scary.

Stacy doesn't back down from my intensity. She gives a look that says *this ends here and now*. "That's because Ryan is not ugly or greasy."

"But you said he was!" I sound so desperate now. I'm seconds away from breathing into a paper bag.

Stacy shakes her blond head, and if I wasn't completely freaking out right now, I would tell her how pretty her new highlights look. "Nope. *You* always assumed he was, and I just never corrected you."

"Why! That's the kind of thing that you correct a girl about."

Her eyes go wide, and her mouth falls open. "You've got to be kidding me! The last time I tried to mention anything remotely complimentary about Ryan, you took my fifteen-dollar glass of wine and poured it into the restaurant's ficus!"

I did do that. And I stand by it.

"Now! Like it or not, Ryan is here, and he's not ugly, greasy, or unhygienic, so it's time to put on your big girl panties and woman up."

Right. She's right. This pep talk was good. I nod my head in agreement, trying to get hyped like those football players before they run out of the tunnel. I feel a new adrenaline coursing through me—an electric shock to my system that triggers my brain to switch into high alert. Because suddenly, the game—or rather, the opponent—has changed.

"Which one is he?" I go shoulder to shoulder with Stacy as my eyes cut fire across the bar.

"The navy suit with Miss USA draped over him."

Of course.

Of freakin' course.

CHAPTER 2

June

As if he can feel my eyes on him, Ryan chooses that exact moment to look over his shoulder. The room tunnels as his gaze locks with mine. I inhale sharply, feeling punched in the gut. Gone is the boyishness of his face. Gone are the lanky arms and legs. It's still Ryan staring me down, but Ryan the man. Ryan 2.0. Ryan maple glazed and covered in sprinkles.

When he realizes it's me, he turns his body out to face me, leaning one elbow against the mahogany bar. The jacket of his slim navy suit protests at the strain and pulls tightly against his broad shoulders. He's wearing a white dress shirt with the top button undone, showing a small triangle of skin that whispers he spends a good amount of time in the sun. His dark brown hair is mussed and wavy like tides in the ocean. Confidence drips off him and zaps all mine away.

Suddenly, my dress is too small. Too noticeable. I'm worried that the stick-on bra cups I'm wearing are going to peel off from all this sweat and plop down on the floor between my legs like I birthed them. Is red even my lip color? This was supposed to be my power outfit. My Trojan horse. If I looked hot and powerful, I'd feel hot and powerful inside. It's not working, though, so I have no choice but to fake it.

I shoot out an invisible SOS to all the *boss babes* of the world and beg them to telepathically send me their strength. When Ryan's mouth tips into a smirk, I don't smile. When his dark eyes skim over me, I don't flinch. And when he straightens to his full height, refastens the middle button of his suit jacket, and begins stalking toward me, I don't drop to the floor and hide under the table. But I really, *really* want to.

"Oh, shoot! He's coming over," says Stacy. "Listen, there's a lot you should know—"

"Shhhh," I hiss back at her. "I have to use all my energy to look confident and irresistible." I haven't broken eye contact with Ryan yet, and although I don't like that he just saw the frantic exchange between Stacy and me, I'm glad he knows I'm not running from him.

My stomach jumps into my throat as he gets close, and I think I might be sick. I *hate* that I was expecting Elmer Fudd, and instead, I'm getting Adonis. He's closing in on me now, and so is the music, and the rapid pounding of my heart, and Stacy's French manicure. I rip my arm from her dramatic grip and break eye contact with Ryan only long enough to give Stacy a look that says *Don't embarrass me!* She recognizes the warning, because she's given it to me often. It's how we keep each other from becoming the next meme circulating the internet.

I turn back to find Ryan right in front of me, hands in his pockets, smirk dialed up to one thousand, and his gaze burning a hole through my face.

Mistake number one was looking away from Ryan.

Mistake number two was ever underestimating my greatest opponent.

Ryan's eyes used to be the color of mud. Now, they are deep pools of hazelnut spread rimmed in 90 percent dark chocolate piping.

"June Bug," his voice rumbles at me—southern drawl a little less than it used to be, but somehow sexier and . . . NO! No. No. No.

This is not how this was supposed to play out. I am the successful one. The one who fought tooth and nail to become an entrepreneurial success. The one who had to jump in the air while squeezing myself into the highest-powered shaping underwear I could find so I could stun my nemesis with my faux smooth form. How am I supposed to crush him under my stilettos if he's towering over me like that?

"Don't call me that name." My hands fist at my side.

We are engaging in a standoff now. We might as well be outside of a saloon in the middle of a dust storm, because both of us have our hands on our pistols, just daring the other to flinch.

"Soooo," says Stacy with an uncomfortable chuckle, looking between us. "Ryan, you obviously remember June."

Neither one of us says anything. Neither of us smiles. Well, I should say, *I* don't smile. Ryan still has that wolfish smirk etched on his mouth. I hate him so much. It's like he's reading my mind and laughing at me because he thinks he's already won.

"Okay, well, I'm just going to go . . . somewhere far away from here." Stacy shuffles off toward the bar where Logan and the rest of the party is gathered.

And now it's just me and Ryan all alone in the corner of this dark, loud bar. The perfect place to murder someone and get away with it.

"Listen, June—"

Nope! No way does he get to start this conversation and claim the upper hand right out of the gate. I learned to never let Ryan be the first one to speak during our junior debates. He might have won most of those, but he's not winning this one. Trojan horse, here I come.

I inch closer to him, square my shoulders, and poke his firm chest. "No, you listen, Ryan Henderson. I can see it in your eyes that you still think you're better than me. But guess what? You're wrong, buddy!" I really wish I hadn't said *buddy,* but I do like my enthusiasm. "I am not that same little girl from high school who let you push her around and didn't push back."

Ryan interrupts my epic monologue with a chuckle, trying to steal my thunder. "In what world did you not push back?"

I ignore him, resisting the urge to settle the sharp point of my heel on the top of his shoe and press down, and instead, continue on, thunder unstolen. "I might've tipped my chin up for you back then, but not anymore. I am a grown woman who has scraped and worked my ass off to open my own bakery and establish a brand that is recognized across all South Carolina. I am a force of nature, so don't mess with me this week unless you want me to cancel your birth certificate." I take a step back and finally let a smirk touch my lips. "But who knows? Maybe if you're nice enough, I can give you a position scrubbing dishes in my kitchen."

I'm on fire right now. Somewhere in the world, Taylor Swift is feeling a tingle down her spine because of this "Bad Blood" re-enactment. I feel like I could run a marathon or lift a truck from all the adrenaline coursing through my veins.

That is, until Alex, one of Logan's other groomsmen, walks up and claps Ryan on the shoulder and says the words that make my blood run cold. "There you are, Mr. Big-time Chef! I'm surprised to see you here. Thought you'd be too much of a hotshot now to give us common folk a week of your time."

I'm sorry, what?

My rapid breathing left over from my heroic speech is dying out now and is replaced with a ringing in my ears. I hesitantly meet

Ryan's gaze. There's a quiet smile on his lips. A knowing smile. "It's no big deal. I was due a little time off."

"Ha!" Alex looks at me with a big dopey smile like I'm in on the joke. "Since when is becoming a Michelin chef not a big deal?"

Ryan still hasn't looked at Alex. His eyes are locked on me, a predatory glint sparking in his dark-chocolate orbs.

"Michelin chef?" I ask, legs wobbling.

Alex squeezes Ryan's shoulder. "I'm happy for you, man! Logan was just telling us how you're the youngest chef to earn three stars. That's ridiculous."

Just bury me now.

Ryan is a chef?! Of course he is. I just made a complete fool of myself telling the man how successful I am, and here he is, brazen with three of the most prestigious culinary stars in the industry. *Isn't that fun?* How do I always seem to come in second place to this man?

Alex's smile dies when he notices the homicidal look I'm giving Ryan, and without saying a word, he just backs away. *Smart man.* It's high school all over again where Ryan and I stuck to our own sides of the hallway, and people stared anytime we had to pass each other because there was always a chance of someone drawing blood when we got too close.

Except Ryan isn't sticking to his side. He steps forward—invading my personal space—and leans in close to my ear while resting his hand on the side of my bicep, creating a romantic illusion to anyone looking on. Even though I don't want to, I drag in a deep breath of his heady scent, which is both cool and spicy. I stay frozen like an animal in the wild that knows it's being hunted. His breath grazes the side of my face, and I hate the way I still feel affected by him.

I will not tip my chin up.

"Thanks for the job offer, June Bug, but I think I'm good. Oh, and by the way"—his voice drops into a gentle whisper—"you have toilet paper stuck to the bottom of your heel."

I cut my gaze down just in time to see Ryan use his fancy leather dress shoe to pull the toilet paper out from beneath the stiletto I was supposed to crush him under.

CHAPTER 3

Ryan

"What did you say?" asks Noah Prescott, the restaurateur on the other end of my phone who's trying to get me to sell my soul for the next three years. "I can't hear you over all that noise. Where are you?"

"Hold on. Going outside." It's amazing and frightening how fast an accent rushes back to a person when they go home.

I push my way through the crowded sports bar to the front door, disliking how people keep bumping into me, sloshing their drinks onto my shoes. It's around 1:30 A.M., and we are at our fourth (and last) bar of the night. The air smells like sweat, tequila, and regret. And let's just say that everyone in our party is less than sober, but none less sober than June Broaden.

To be honest, I had come into town with the full intention of making a fresh start with her. I planned to bury that hatchet and put the water under the bridge. We haven't spoken since high school, which I thought would have been plenty of time to let our old animosity fade.

I was wrong.

When June's green eyes locked on me, I saw her hatred burn brighter. Nothing has faded. It's somehow intensified. And just like that, I was eighteen again, faced with the woman who makes my skin crawl—but mostly from how much I want her. Her cheeks were flushed, eyes narrowed, and I could see she had no intention of burying the hatchet. Nope, she threw down the gauntlet. This old flame between us is still kindling, and I want to kiss her now more than ever.

After our high school commencement ceremony, I almost did. I came within an inch of June's perfect lips before reality crashed over me. I couldn't kiss her on graduation day—not after all our years of dueling. Not when I knew I would pack up later that night and catch a red-eye flight to France, beginning my stint at Le Cordon Bleu. It would have been a cruel form of torture finally tasting June's lips and having to leave them behind for good.

It was better to leave things as they were and part as enemies rather than lovers.

What sucks about all this is that, even after all these years, my situation hasn't really changed that much. June still hates me, and I'm still only in town temporarily. After this wedding, I'll head back to Chicago and either sign a contract to be the executive chef in the new gourmet restaurant Noah is opening, or I'll go bury myself in the other ritzy kitchen I've already been working in for the past four years.

"Can you hear me now?" I ask Noah, feeling a little too much like the guy from those cellphone commercials.

"Yeah, that's better. Where are you?"

"At a friend's bachelor party in Charleston."

"Ah, that explains why I was hearing so many female voices in the background."

I shove my hand in my pocket to keep it warm. Wintertime in Charleston is nothing compared to winters in Chicago, but it's still chilly enough right now to make me want to hike my shoulders up to my ears to hide my neck from the cold.

"Nah, it's not like that. It's a joint bachelor and bachelorette bar crawl with his fiancée and her bridesmaids."

Noah makes a sound of disgust. "That sucks. She's already taking the poor guy's freedom away; did she have to take his bachelor party too?"

Yeah, I don't like Noah either.

"Were you calling for something specific, Noah?" I don't even bat an eye at the fact that he's calling at this time of night, because I've heard that Noah works hard all day and night. He doesn't need sleep and seems to think the rest of us don't either. Which, in his defense, is mostly true. The restaurant industry is cutthroat. Gotta stay ahead to stay alive.

"Oh, yeah. I was just wanting to let you know I've officially secured the investors for Bask, and they all agreed you are the chef they want running the kitchen. We'll center the whole dining experience around you and your culinary style. So all that's left is for you to sign those papers, and we can get the ball rolling with marketing."

I pinch my eyes shut because (1) I'm exhausted from barhopping all night, pretending I'm the kind of guy who does this all the time, (2) I'm not sure I even want this job, and (3) through the window, I can see some guy in a salmon-colored shirt two sizes too big for him slide up on the barstool beside June and strike up a conversation. She's been ignoring me all night, but she's awfully attentive to Mr. Izod right now.

I turn my back to the window so I can focus. I know Noah is offering me the job of a lifetime (I know it because he's reminded me of it at least fifty times since offering it to me) and that I'd be a fool to pass it up. He's started three other restaurants in various parts of the country similar to the one he's trying to get me to sign onto in Chicago. Those other three restaurants have all won Restaurant of the Year awards, and I'm sure this one will do the same. Noah has turned the restaurant business on its head by reinventing the way people view their eating experiences. Because that's exactly what his restaurants are—an experience.

And apparently, my silence is tipping Noah off to my hesitation. "Ryan, don't pass this up. Bask will launch your career into a whole other realm."

"I thought that's what the Michelin stars were supposed to do."

He scoffs. "Those are only the tip of the iceberg."

I hate when people say phrases like that. What does it even mean? If you want me to sign the next three years of my life away to work grueling hours in a high-stakes restaurant game, give me a PowerPoint presentation of the exact ways it will benefit me. Don't hit me with frilly meaningless answers like "tip of the iceberg" because I'm not a freaking glaciologist. And yeah, I'm grumpy. It has nothing to do with me looking over my shoulder and seeing Izod Man touching June's shoulder. Just a coincidence.

"I need a little more time to think about it," I say to Noah.

He lets out a sigh, and I can picture him running his hand through his thinning hair. Because that's what this business we are in does to a man who's only in it for the love of money—takes your hair and leaves you with a unique eau de cologne called *Le Douchebag Suprême*. And although the life of a chef and a restaurateur are different, they have a few things in common: long days that often bleed into the next, high-stress work hours, and the constant need to please the unpleasable. It's all worth it if you love what you do.

I'm just not sure that I do anymore . . .

"Fine. Tell you what, I'll give you until the end of the week to decide. But I can't keep the investors happy for long. I've heard them mention Martin's name more than once. They're planning to offer him the position if you pass it up."

"End of the month," I counter.

"What?"

"I want until the end of the month to decide."

"You've got to be kidding me? We both know you're going to take it, so what do you need to think about? Is it salary? Because we're already offering you an obscene amount of money, but I can go back to the investors—"

"It's not the money. I just need some time." My voice sounds clipped and final. I'm annoyed that he's trying to talk like we're buddies and I'd confide in him. We've brushed elbows over dinner a few times with mutual acquaintances, but we're not friends, and I'm not about to pretend we are. In fact, the only friend I have is in that bar right now doing flaming rum shots with his fiancée.

My eyes shift from Logan and Stacy over to the bar where June is sitting with another cocktail in her hand. She shouldn't be drinking any more. The woman was already tipsy two bars ago. I wonder if it's my presence that's making her knock 'em back? Is it because I still get under her skin? That thought makes me smile.

Because she still gets under mine.

"Tell your investors they'll have my answer by the end of the month. And don't go behind my back and make a deal with Martin, because we both know he's not as good as me and his name won't carry the restaurant nearly as far as mine will."

"Ryan—"

I hang up before he gets another word in. And yeah, it might seem like I'm a bit of a cocky jerk, but that's because I am. It comes with the job description. You don't climb as high in life as I have by kissing everyone's feet. I've learned that if I want to be successful in my industry, I have to make people respect me.

Which is why I'm not sure that I want that job. I'm just the slightest bit tired of being an a-hole.

The door to the bar opens, and Logan sticks his head out.

"Ryan! I didn't bring your sorry butt all the way to Charleston just so you could talk on the phone all night. Get in here!" His words are all slurring together, and I know that tomorrow he's going to be hating life.

I put my phone in my pocket and go back inside the bar. The minute I step foot inside, nearly every woman's head turns to look at me. Well, all but one.

Logan hangs his arm over my shoulder, and his breath rams into me like a four-hundred-pound linebacker. "Fun party, right?! I'm having a killer time, bro." Anytime Logan is drunk, he talks like an eighteen-year-old frat boy who sneaks watermelon wine coolers. He raises his glass into the air. "Best bachelor party ever!" he yells and then *woooos* at the top of his lungs right beside my ear. I'm deaf now.

He continues to hang on me as we make our way around the bar. "Where's Stacy? I think we need to get you back on that leash of yours."

"She went to the bathroom." Logan then abruptly stops and catches my arm to get me to stop walking. His face is so serious now I'm worried he might be about to hurl all over me. "Ryan, bro"—he never calls me bro—"have I ever told you how much you mean to me?" Oh, good. We've entered the heartfelt portion of his drunkenness. I need to get him home before the next phase hits: Naked Logan.

"Yeah, yeah, we're besties. Let's go get you some water."

He shakes his head. Clearly, he's not said all that was in his heart. "I'm serious, man. If there's ever anything I can do for you. Just name it. Seriously. Like, do you need my shirt? It's yours!"

And yep, he's unbuttoning it. I guess "Naked Logan" is already in motion.

"Stop taking off your shirt." I grab him by the shoulder and start dragging him toward the table where a few of the other groomsmen are huddled and drunk-swiping through Tinder to-gether. One guy is about to send a message to a woman that he will most definitely regret in the morning, so I snatch his phone and pocket it. He frowns and protests, saying something about me being a killjoy.

I spot Stacy's bridesmaids across the room, all writing their numbers on the bar's wall in Sharpie. This is not a "draw on the wall" sort of bar, and I'm pretty sure they are seconds away from being kicked out.

But I knew this would happen. That's why I cut myself off after one drink. Someone needs to be the voice of reason in the group. That, and because I haven't partied since I was in my early twen-ties. Life hasn't exactly given me any downtime to go out late with friends. I'm not even sure I know how to let loose anymore.

"Sit," I say, depositing Logan in a chair. He looks up at me, and now he's a pouty toddler who's just had his lollipop ripped from his hand. "I'll go find Stacy and then call you two a ride." A few of the guys at the table boo me. "Looks like I'm calling everyone rides."

In the next moment, the music cuts off, and I hear someone blowing into a microphone. I turn around and spot June up on the karaoke stage, mic clutched between both her hands, smiling like her mouth is numb from dental surgery and she's halfway under the effects of anesthesia. She still looks every bit as cute as she did at the beginning of the night, though. If not a little more, because now she's taken off her high heels and loosened up. She looks more like the girl I secretly crushed on in high school, and it's making my stomach twist.

"Helllloooo, ladies and gentlemen! Who wants to have fun to-night?!" she yells into the microphone. My ears bleed when a sharp whine tears through the speakers. Everyone else in this bar is so far gone, though, that they don't notice. They hoot and catcall like Lady Gaga herself has just stepped onto the stage.

"Good!" June rips the mic from the stand and paces. She actually looks pretty natural up there. "'Cause we're gonna party ALL NIGHT!"

No, we're not. The bar closes in thirty minutes.

"But first"—her eyes cut right to me for the first time since the beginning of the night when I removed the toilet paper from her shoe—"I want to introduce you all to my friend, Ryan Henderson! Come on up here, Chefy!"

I should have known she had something planned. What does she think will happen? I'll go up there and she will stick the mic in my hand and trick me into singing and embarrassing myself in front of everyone? Apparently, she doesn't realize that she's about four more drinks in than me.

I smile and shake my head no at her, trying not to make a big scene.

June stumble-sways to the right before catching the mic stand to balance herself again. "Oh, come on, don't be a party pooper, *Mr. Darcy*!" It makes me laugh that June still calls me Mr. Darcy. She's been doing it ever since I tried to keep my best friend away from her best friend in junior high, aka "pulling a Darcy" from *Pride and Prejudice*.

The bar erupts with drunken encouragement. A beautiful redhead in a skintight dress sidles up next to me and wraps her arm around mine. "I'll go up there with you if you're shy." *Yeah, no.*

I extract my arm and look back up to meet June's seething expression. Seething that I'm not budging or because of the pretty redhead?

"Sorry. Not gonna happen," I call out, trying to settle the crowd.

"Go on, Ryan! Sing with June," Stacy yells after returning from the bathroom and planting herself on Logan's lap.

But June doesn't want to sing with me. This is all a part of the war she started back up tonight. She's looking for a way to humiliate me. To knock me down a few notches. And even though I came here intending to bury our old feud, seeing her again makes me want to play along. I loved dueling with June back in the day. It felt like flirting back then, and it feels like it now. So, I'll join her battle, but I won't play by her rules.

Game on, June Bug.

I lock eyes with June and take off my jacket with a smirk. Her smile falters as I walk toward the stage, because she can't believe how easily she has won this round.

The back of my neck heats from the bright lights as I approach the stage, and she takes a step back. I don't bother with the stairs and, instead, take one big step up—directly in front of June. She looks like a trapped animal now with big alert eyes. I walk closer and take her by surprise when I wrap my jacket around her shoulders. She was anticipating danger and got warmth instead.

"What are you doing?" she asks, looking down dramatically to the jacket. Her mind is moving too slow to figure out what's happening.

"It's cold outside, and I don't want you to freeze when we leave." I put my arm around her, escorting her from the stage so she doesn't face-plant. The second we are off the stairs, she rips away from me and stumbles backward.

"Everyone wants a performance, and if you're too good to sing at karaoke night, then I'll do it!" It's adorable how powerful she thinks she looks right now. I could pick her up off the ground by my index finger and thumb and place her in my pocket.

"You can perform next time. Right now, it's time to get you home safely."

"Ugh! I *need* to karaoke!" is what I think she was trying to say. But really, it came out like "*Hiineedtofereokie!*"

"Can you remember your address?" I say, guiding her toward the table where Stacy and Logan are watching with drunken-confused expressions. They're trying to figure out what new game this is too.

I toss Alex's phone back on the table in front of him and retrieve June's heels. Stacy beams up at us as we walk past her. "BYE, JUNIE! I love you SO much."

No one will remember this night tomorrow.

June sways heavily, so I tighten my grip around her shoulders. She's seconds away from passing out on the ground, and I care about her too much to let her catch Ebola from this nasty floor. Also, Izod Man has been eyeing her all night. I don't trust him one bit not to follow her out of here. This bar crawl is officially over, and I'm going to make sure June is safely placed in her home.

"LOVE YOU, RYAN!" Can you guess who yells that at me right before I leave the bar? Yeah, it's Logan. Apparently, I'm not the only one who shouldn't be drinking heavily in his thirties.

"Night, everyone. Logan, call an Uber for you and Stacy," I say before I scoop June up in my arms and carry her out of the bar as she yells that I stink the whole way to the door.

CHAPTER 4

Ryan

I get June into my car after a long trek to the parking lot. I'm sweating even though June is wearing my jacket. This woman has zero care for the workout I just endured carrying her to my car, because the second I start it, June opens the door and jumps out. She chases a plastic bag floating on the wind through the parking lot, nearly getting hit by a car before I manage to catch her. When we are once again situated safely inside the vehicle, I buckle her up and give three-sheets-to-the-wind June a pointed *stay put* look. She giggles and slumps over in her seat.

I can't help but wonder if June always drinks this much. But somehow, I know the answer is no (probably because she was already tipsy halfway through her first one). I think I'm the reason for her overindulgence tonight, and I want to find out why.

She's docile now. A tiger shot with a tranquilizer and about to pass out against the window. I need to find out her address before she's so far gone that we both have to sleep in this car until she sobers up and can tell me where to go. June leans her head against the glass, balls her hand up under her chin, and lets out a whimper. It's a pitiful sound. My jacket is still around her shoulders, swallowing her whole. Her mascara is a little smudged under her eyes, and there is only the faintest tint of red on her lips now. She looks like she's gone through the wringer, and I doubt that this is the look she intended to portray tonight when she was getting in my face with how successful she is. Still, I like that I get to be the one to take care of her like this—also that I'm the one to make her come a little undone.

I've been doing nothing but running through the paces of my life these past twelve years. I go from achievement to achievement, turning over stones and trying to find *something* under them. I don't know what that something is yet because I've never found it. I just keep moving to the next stone.

But seeing June again tonight—sensing that spark ignite between us again—it has me pausing. It feels like my heart is trying to kick back to life. And I know she's aware of it too. Evidence being that she has drunk herself into oblivion just trying to keep busy and avoid making eye contact with me all night.

Yeah, but I saw you stealing glances at me, June.

Something is there. I feel it. I just need to play her game and peel back the layers of her hate to find it.

When I ask for June's address, she mumbles a few incoherent words and swats her hand in my direction like she's trying to get me to shut up so she can sleep. I give up and let her pass out. Reaching into her purse, I pull out her phone and open the maps app. Luckily, she has her address saved under *home,* and I start the directions.

Ten minutes later, I'm pulling up in front of a small white bungalow. I cut the engine and walk around the car to help June out. She stumbles a bit, her legs moving more like spaghetti noodles than functioning limbs, so I pick her up and carry her to the front door. I pause outside the bright, teal-colored door and realize I have no idea if she lives with anyone or not.

Surely, if she had a boyfriend, he would have come with her to-night? And I know she's not married, because you better believe the first thing I did when I saw her again was assess her ring finger. Well, it was *almost* the first thing I assessed on her.

I could kick the door to see if someone answers, but I've always enjoyed being a risk-taker, so I'll take my chances. I set June on the ground beside the door. Her head rolls back to rest against the siding while I scoop up her clutch and start digging through it. Annnnnd I've sailed right past *gallant knight* and pushed straight into *creepy guy*, because I take my time, making a mental note of the contents I stumble over. There's nothing exciting, though. Some gum, her credit card and ID, a tube of lipstick, a hair tie, a guy's phone number (*oops, it flutters right out of my fingers and into the wind*), her cellphone, and keys.

After unlocking the front door, I scoop June up again and carry her through, amused at how much she would recoil at the idea of her greatest enemy carrying her over the threshold of her home like a syrupy-sweet couple, fresh from the wedding chapel. I consider placing a band on her ring finger just to mess with her when she wakes up.

Once we're inside, I use my foot to shut the door behind us, plunging us into darkness. Truthfully, at the start of this evening, I might have briefly imagined taking June back to her place at the end of it. Needless to say, my fantasy looked MUCH different from this.

I flip a switch and turn on the lights. June's house is simple but comfortable. I like it. It's completely opposite of my apartment in Chicago. Where mine is all dark furniture, hard surfaces, and a sprawling view of the city, June has a plush yellow couch, a midcentury coffee table, a thriving fiddle-leaf fig tree that proves she remembers to water it, and picture frames full of her smiling with friends and family.

Also . . . wait. Is that a throw pillow with Nick Lachey's face on it? Yep. Definitely is. More disturbing, I think there's a blanket folded up on the end of the couch to match it. I'd go check, but honestly, I'm scared. I'm not ready to find out that June is a secret Nick Lachey mega-groupie and has been clipping letters out of magazines to send him creepy fan mail all these years. Better to assume there's a reasonable explanation and move on.

Besides seeing Lachey's face on way too many surfaces, the whole vibe in here makes me want to kick off my shoes, unbutton my cuffs, roll up my sleeves, sink into that couch, and sleep until noon tomorrow. It's an urge I can't say I've ever had when looking at my black leather couch. But something tells me that if I did sleep here tonight, I would wake up in the morning to June hovering over my body with a butcher knife. So instead, I make my way through her house, passing a bathroom, an office, and a kitchen before finding her room.

I turn on the light and smile at the ruffled coral throw pillows on her bed. No man lives here. And there wasn't a single framed photo of her with any dudes, so I don't think she has a boyfriend. I think I'm cheating in our game right now. I'm behind enemy lines, getting an eyeful of her battle plans.

And if June's plans have anything to do with the lacy blue bra I see hanging on her bathroom door, I'm a goner. But I'm also a gentleman, so I don't look at that bra above four times before I set June on her bed and make my way to her dresser. I pull out a cotton T-shirt and some PJ shorts and toss them onto her lap. She's still sitting up, but her eyes are shut, shoulders sagging.

"Put those on and yell when you're dressed."

Her heavy eyelids crack open, and she frowns. "I don't like you."

"Yeah, I got that." I shove my hands into my pockets.

"I don't think you do." Her words are still slurring heavily, but I understand her perfectly. Her hair is hanging over one of her shoulders, and she's sitting on the edge of her bed, wearing my suit jacket like a blanket. It looks way too good on her. "I haaaaaate you."

"Why?" I ask, knowing I shouldn't but also unable to resist getting this unfiltered truth.

She lifts a shoulder and drops it. "Because it's what we've always done. Hate each other."

She's right, and the realization makes me oddly sad. June and I fought over everything in high school. We had no choice but to be around each other often since our best friends were dating, but we made it a point during those forced hangouts to annoy each other as much as possible. If June wanted to go to the movies, I convinced everyone we should go bowling. If I planned a New Year's Eve party, she planned a bigger, better one. If Stacy and Logan convinced us all to have a *friends dinner* (meaning just the four of us), I would bring a date to rile June up. All of this, plus at least a hundred harmless pranks.

Yeah, thinking back, I wasn't the nicest guy in the world to June. The thing is, my pestering was never done out of spite. It was the only way I could get her to pay attention to me. And I wanted her attention on me.

"But worst of all . . ." Her sleepy words break through my thoughts. "I tipped my chin up to you, and you walked away."

"Tipped your chin up? What are you talking about?" I step a little closer.

She falls onto her side to bury her head in her pillow. The hem of her little black dress hikes up an extra inch, and suddenly, it feels wrong standing here in her room without her sober permission— wrong to see her picture frames, and her throw pillows, and hear her honest thoughts. I'm an uninvited guest, staying late to a party I wasn't even invited to in the first place. I needed to get her home safely, and I did. Time to go.

I cross the room to stand next to June's bed and pull her comforter up over her. Looks like she's going to be sleeping in that dress tonight.

I'm just about to leave the room when June's mumbling words stop me. "On graduation day, I wanted you to kiss me, but you walked away."

Wait, what? My head spins. Her hatred for me now is because I didn't kiss her that night? Does that mean she didn't hate me back then? Was she just playing the same game I was?

After I've lingered beside her way too long, and maybe even brushed her hair out of her face, I let myself out. But I continue to wonder what life would have been like if I hadn't walked away.

What if I'd kissed her that day?

Would I be sleeping next to her tonight?

Would I be happier than I am now?

*What if*s ping around my brain for the rest of the night like an annoying screen saver where the words never reach the corner. No matter how hard I try, I can't convince myself I made the right decision all those years ago. And even worse, I still can't tell if I'll make the same decision again a second time.

All I know is that June says she hates me. But I don't hate her. In fact, I think I'm just as wild about her as I was back then. Maybe it's a mistake, and maybe I'll think more clearly in the morning, but I want June's attention again. And it turns out, the strategy is exactly the same as it was in high school.

I've gotta get under her skin.

CHAPTER 5

June

I am going to murder my best friend.

Go ahead and zip me up in an orange jumpsuit and lock me in the slammer for life, because Stacy Williams is dead to me.

Was she out of her everlovin' mind to plan her bachelorette party on a Sunday night? Meaning, the night before MONDAY—the day that I have to wake up at five in the morning to open the bakery. (For those of you doing the math at home, that's only about two and a half hours after I stumbled into my bed.)

I hate her. I grumble it fifteen more times before I bring myself to squint my eyes open, and *good heavens,* that's one spinning room.

How did this even happen? I haven't had more than two drinks in a night since my early twenties. I'm usually very careful, especially knowing I have to open the bakery the next day. But last night, having Ryan only feet away from me did strange things to the rational thinking part of my brain. I was too nervous to eat and lost count of my drinks (did I mention I never do that?). The combo was brutal and life-changing. Life-changing in that I will never touch another cocktail again.

Women hung around Ryan like the world was suddenly being depleted of oxygen and he contained the superspecial, never-ending supply behind his lips. Everything he said garnered a barrel of laughs. The man should be a stand-up comedian for how funny everyone seemed to think he was. If the conversation just barely turned to something that wasn't worship for His Majesty, some little *darling* would pull it right back to him and then stare at his special oxygen lips while he spoke.

Ooooh, Ryan, you're a chef! Ryan, what's it like running a prestigious kitchen? My, what big muscles you have, Ryan!

I don't know if it's the tequila trying to make its way back up or the thought of Ryan that's making me want to barf, but the nausea is real.

Finally bringing myself to open my eyes, I realize I'm hugging a man's gray suit jacket, and I fling it to the ground. Memories assault me like I've just put a beehive on my head. Ryan brought me home last night. *STING.* He came in my house. *STING.* Put me in my bed. *STING.* Covered me with a blanket. *STING, STING.*

And . . . oh no. I admitted to wishing he had kissed me!

Now I'm really going to be sick. Oh, but no worries. There is a wastebasket beside my bed with a fresh trash bag in it, because RYAN put it there, knowing I'd be out-of-my-mind hungover today. *Cool.* Cool, cool, cool.

My head is throbbing, and my body feels like a semi has run over it, hit reverse, and then taken one more pass. Honestly, I wish it had. Then I wouldn't have to face Ryan the rest of this week.

All I want to do is lie here in my bed and wallow all day long, but I can't. Although I thought ahead to have Stacy's shift covered, I didn't anticipate myself trying to drink the entire contents of four bars in one night and still thinking I'd be in tip-top shape this morning. Somehow, this is all Ryan's fault. It feels good to throw the blame on him.

Tossing off the covers, I force my legs off the side of the bed and sit up straight. I immediately spot another clue that my nemesis was in my house. Two little aspirin pills lay innocently beside a full glass of water, taunting me. Sure, it could have been a friendly gesture: *I hope you feel better soon, June!* But I know Ryan. This is his way of saying *I win again.*

I don't even want those pills—don't even need them!

But when I stand and cross the room at the pace of an injured snail, I turn back and down the aspirin like my life depends on it. Ryan will never know.

Twenty minutes later, I still feel (and look, mind you) like the Grim Reaper, but I've wiped the caked-on mascara out from under my eyes, brushed my teeth for a solid two minutes, and signed a contract I scribbled out onto an old receipt, stating that I will never drink again. I also attempt to scrub off all my regret in the shower. It doesn't work. With every minute that passes, I realize I despise my actions from last night more.

After dressing and applying a fresh coat of makeup to hide the new circles under my eyes, I make my way to the kitchen. More clues are littered around my house, and I want to scream. There is a fresh pot of coffee on my counter (*How did he get the auto brew feature to work? I've been trying all month!*) and my favorite mug sitting beside it. There's an innocent photo of Nick Lachey printed on the front, but when you fill it with hot liquid, his shirt disappears, revealing his glorious, chiseled six-pack. *Best magic trick ever.* But that's beside the point.

All these little "acts of kindness" are nothing but Ryan setting the stage.

Telling me he's the boss.

Reminding me of my indiscretions.

Just to spite him, I fill a different mug, take a sip, and *dammit,* he makes incredible coffee! Of course he does. But Ryan doesn't matter to me anymore. I don't have a crush on him. I don't think he's hot. I DON'T. And I only smelled his suit jacket one time to see what gross cologne a spawn of the devil wears. Okay, I smelled it twice. Three times. FOUR, GOSH!

Unable to stomach all the reminders of Ryan scattered around my house, I take my coffee out on the front porch to enjoy it in peace. I tiptoe toward the patio seat, trying to sip as I walk without sloshing any coffee on myself, when my foot bumps into a package I somehow missed yesterday. It's little and taped up with a familiar washi tape, tipping me off immediately to who sent it.

I pull out my phone, and although it's early, I dial my mom because I know she'll already be up. I settle myself on the porch chair and pin my phone to my ear as I tear into the box, pushing the polka-dot tissue paper aside and extracting the gift.

"Well, morning, darlin!" Mom says with a chipper tone that I can't help but grin at. Here's the thing, I'm southern, but my mom is country. Ask anyone in the South and they will tell you there's a big difference. Her family is from Kentucky, where you never pronounce the *g* sound on the end of a sentence, and when you've had enough to eat, you're "full as a tick on a hound." She's like sunshine poking through a rainstorm.

"WHERE did you find this sweatshirt?" I ask, holding up the most amazing article of clothing that's ever been created.

I hear Mom clapping with excitement on the other end. "It's the best, isn't it? I bought it a month ago, and it's been torture waitin' for it to get to you. I found it in a little Etsy shop called *90s Hot-tees*. Get it?"

You know those moms you see on TV that seem too good to be true? The ones you watch, feeling jealousy grow inside your chest because *no one that amazing really exists*? Well, she does. Her name is Bonnie Broaden, and she is my five-foot-nothing southern firecracker mom with teased-up blond hair, toenails that always match her purse, and just enough progressive opinions to make you question everything you thought you ever knew about this particular stereotype.

Only a mom like mine would commit to a five-year-long inside joke, buying up every unique piece of fan merchandise devoted to the king of 1990s hot guys: Nick Lachey.

Five years ago, when I called off my wedding at the last minute with the weak excuse of *it just didn't work out,* I expected my family to be angry and full of questions. But my mom took one look at my puffy, bloodshot eyes, asked if I wanted to talk about it—to which I responded with a firm no—and then never questioned me again. She took care of canceling the venue, returning my wedding gifts, and contacting all the guests to let them know that Ben and I would no longer be getting married—all without ever demanding a single reason why. Sometimes I look back and wish I had told everyone the truth right away instead of hiding behind the excuse that we weren't right for each other, but it just hurt too bad at the time to say the words out loud.

On the day of my supposed-to-be wedding, Mom showed up at my doorstep first thing in the morning, giant cup of coffee in one hand and a massive gift bag in the other. When I opened the bag and pulled out a huge fleece blanket with the image of my high school celebrity crush, Nick Lachey, printed across it, she said, *I figured if you're not gettin' married today, you might as well have your favorite man in the world to snuggle with.*

And that was that.

From then on, every holiday, every birthday, and sometimes when she knows I've had a hard week, I find presents like this one on my doorstep.

Today's treasure, though, is my all-time favorite. It's a white cotton grandma-style crewneck sweatshirt with a picture of the band 98° in their red zipper jumpsuits with text down the side that says TURN UP THE HEAT!

Basically, it's better than gold, and I'm going to be the most popular girl at school. Well, actually, I'll probably be trolled in the grocery store by thirteen-year-olds because I'm a grown woman and shouldn't be wearing boy band apparel from the '90s, but I don't give a shit. I will risk humiliating remarks from teenyboppers because I adore my mom and these trinkets of love she sends me. They are our thing. Our secret code. Our BFF bracelets, if you will.

Sometimes I feel guilty that she's given me all this uncondi-tional love, and I still haven't told her what happened between Ben and me, but the more time that passes, the harder it gets to rip those memories out of the steel vault I locked them away in. They are better left sealed away where they can't hurt me anymore.

Or . . . at least where no one is able to see that they hurt me.

After I finish gushing to Mom about the sweatshirt, we talk about the bachelorette party. I tell Mom a happier version of the night, tiptoeing around the part where I accidentally got ham-mered and made a fool of myself (even cool moms don't want to hear those bits). But mostly, I use all my energy avoiding any men-tion of Ryan and how he's ridiculously hot now, and successful, and brought me home safely, and made me coffee, and put aspirin be-side my bed. *Ugh, the jerk.*

When you say it all together like that, it paints him as the knight in shining armor just like he wants. It's his tactic—I know it—and I will not aid his campaign of complete world domination.

Once I finish talking with Mom, I pull on my sexy new sweat-shirt (*That's right, fellas—I'm single and totally ready to mingle*) and go back inside. Unfortunately, Ryan is still on my mind. I need to get him out. So, only to prove to myself how much I really don't care about Ryan, I find the clutch I carried with me last night and dig through it, intending to pull out my secret weapon: random guy's number.

Sure, I don't remember what he looks like . . . I think he had brown hair? And I don't remember if I told myself to throw his number away or call him first thing in the morning, so I think I'll split the difference and text him. A fun dinner date with a cute guy is exactly what I need to remind myself that Ryan means nothing to me anymore.

Except the phone number is not here. It's been replaced with a note from a psychopath.

He was a tool. You can thank me later.

I won't thank him later. I will replace his shampoo with Elmer's glue later.

I pull into the parking lot of Darlin' Donuts around six A.M., see my employee Nichole's car, and thank my lucky stars that I no longer have to do the graveyard shift. Perks of being an owner: I never have to work from three A.M. to six A.M. prepping the dough if I don't want to—which I never do. Having to be here at six is bad enough. And honestly, right now I would give this whole bakery up to the highest bidder if it meant I could just go home and sleep. *Five whole dollars?! Sure, why not! Can I go home now?*

Too bad it's so early that I don't even pass anyone on the street to give them the purchasing option. Plus, there's already a space for sale across the street from us. Pretty sure if someone was in the market, they'd snatch up that little shack in a heartbeat. And I must really be hungover to keep dwelling on this ridiculous hypothetical.

Instead of being relieved of my bakery-owner duties, I'm forced to nurse my head all morning as I'm rolling out dough, resisting the urge to toss up my cookies at the smell of donuts in the fryer.

Sometime around ten o'clock, after the morning rush has faded out and we are nearly sold out of our most popular donuts, I see Stacy enter the bakery. She's wearing sunglasses and a baseball cap, and her blond ponytail is waving down her back with leftover curls from last night. She looks like a celebrity trying to fly under the radar.

"You're brave, showing your face around here," I say as she approaches the counter.

"Ugh. I feel like someone tried to kill me but then decided to keep me alive just enough so they could continue torturing my body slowly and painfully."

"Really? I feel amazing."

"You do?!"

I don't have the luxury of wearing sunglasses to aid my pounding head, so Stacy has a front-row seat to my icy glare. "No! I got two hours of sleep before I had to wake up and open the shop. I swear, I'm never touching alcohol again. It's prune juice for this grandma from now on."

Stacy has the audacity to laugh, because apparently, she's hoping to get punched today. "It's your own fault. No one forced those last few Jell-O shots down your throat."

"No, it's your fault for planning a bachelorette party on a Sunday night!"

Stacy shrugs a shoulder. "Sunday nights are less busy."

"Yeah, no kidding. No sensible person wants to show up to work hungover the next day."

"Don't be mad at me because you lost your cool around Ryan McHotChef."

I point a finger at her. "First, you can come up with a better nickname. Second, you're already on thin ice, ma'am. Keep it up and you'll need to give your heart to Jesus."

"You sound just like Bonnie."

"Thank you."

She chuckles and rounds the donut counter to stand next to me. *Brave move.* "Okay, time to get your panties out of a wad, because we need to talk." Something in her voice makes me feel like we are about to break up. And I say so. I'm not encouraged when she sighs and takes off her sunglasses.

"Oh gosh. You *are* breaking up with me?" My voice is high-pitched and panicky.

She gives me a tense smile that does nothing to ease my anxiety. "No way, you're stuck with me forever." She pauses, and I can feel the giant *but* coming. "But . . . you'll just be stuck with me from afar from now on."

What! She really is breaking up with me! Oh gosh, does this mean I have to box up all the stuff she's given me (I've stolen) and return it? She'll have to pry that green jumper from my cold dead hands, though.

"Stacy, you're freaking me out. What's going on?"

"I'm sorry. I thought about telling you sooner, but I decided that a long, drawn-out goodbye would be too hard. Ripping off the Band-Aid is better for both of us."

"I will shake you, woman, if you don't tell me why the hell you're ripping Band-Aids off me."

Stacy's face crumples as she rushes to me and wraps her arms around my shoulders so forcefully that I make an involuntary *oof* sound. We're holding on to each other for dear life when the truth spills out of her. It's all blubbering nonsense, but since we've been friends for so long, I understand every word.

"Logan got a job in California. It's his dream position at a great hospital, working under the best thoracic surgeon in his field. We talked about it for so long, and he told me he didn't want to take me from my dream job, but then I realized . . . I don't think this bakery ever has been my dream. It's yours, and I love you so much that I've just wanted to help you bring it to life. But now that that's done, you don't need me here anymore. So I told him to take the job. We're moving after the wedding."

"After the wedding!" I say, but it comes out like one long whine. "So soon."

"I know. I'm so sorry, June. I don't want to leave you, but it's going to be really good for Logan and me. *Doyouhateme?!*" Her words are nearly indiscernible at this point.

Mine are no better. *"Areyoukiddingofcourse Icouldneverhateyou!"*

I tell her I want the best for her, and we continue to hold on to each other and cry for another few minutes. I'm just grateful that no one has come into the shop during this soap opera. *Here, try our newest donut: french vanilla with a hint of "my best friend is leaving forever" tears.*

Finally, we peel off each other and wipe our faces with the backs of our hands. Sniffles are our only words for another minute before I ask, "So, what about the shop?" I look around like it's our child and I'm trying to decide if I want to let Stacy have it every weekend or just on holidays.

When she doesn't answer right away, I look back up at her. Her face crumples again, but I give her a look that says *Keep it together, woman*. She takes a deep breath, and when her tears are under control again, she says, "I'm going to sell my half. I'll be useless trying to help run the company from California, and it'll be nice to put that money toward buying a house."

It's official. This day sucks. First, I wake up swaddled in Mr. Darcy's suit jacket with the sinking realization that I'll have to see him all week, and now this? I want to go back to bed so I can wake up again and realize it was all some terrible boozy nightmare.

"But who are you going to sell it to? No one will be as good a partner as you are."

"Actually . . . I was thinking *you* should buy me out."

"Me?" My eyebrows hit the ceiling.

"Yes—you. No one loves this shop as much as you. You should be full owner."

"Full owner?" The words settle on my tongue like battery acid. Every decision would fall to me alone. Every failure. Every missed opportunity. *Me. All me. Alone.* "Nah, too much of a headache. I don't want to bury myself in the upkeep of this place." I try to sound nonchalant and even pick at my fingernail while I say it so Stacy isn't tipped off to the panic welling inside me.

"What are you talking about? You're practically running it yourself already. You're the idea woman; I just smile and nod and stand here as eye candy for the clients."

Not true. I mean, yes, the eye candy part is true, but the rest is false. Whether she knows it or not, Stacy is my rock. She's the one who keeps me from making terrible decisions, doing too much too soon, and quitting when things get hard.

Because, here's the thing, I've already tried to run a company on my own, and I failed. When Ben and I were still engaged, he helped me start a little flower truck business. It was cute, and I thought it was my dream job. I had visions of hipsters everywhere, lining up in their floppy sun hats and crushed denim jeans to purchase one of my bouquets.

It thrived for about three months. And then Ben cheated on me, and I canceled our wedding, and the entire business fell on my shoulders, and I let it go down the toilet. But no one knows Ben cheated on me. No one knows I found the text evidence of his affair in his phone. And no one will find out, either.

Why should I backtrack now? My life is good. Secure. I've even been thriving in the dating scene thanks to my only-one-date rule.

Basically—it ensures I keep things fun and light and don't get too attached to anyone again. If someone asks me out, I go and have an incredible time. But that's it. No second dates.

And luckily, my family never makes me feel bad for being the only one still single and not having anyone to pose with for Christmas photos. Instead, the conversation goes something like this: *We'll get a family shot of Jake and Evie and the kids, and then June, darlin', we'll take your photo over there next to the Christmas tree in your cute sweater. Smile extrabig!*

My Christmas cards from the past five years look like I've given up on the human race completely and married that Christmas tree, but oh well. *Douglas Fir makes a wonderful spouse.*

But anyway, I just didn't have a desire to keep my flower truck going. And sure, maybe the depression played a big part, but what if that wasn't the reason? There are more situations in my life that point to my "give up when things get tough" personality. I dropped out of college three credits shy of graduating to go to cosmetology school, and then I dropped out of cosmetology school to spend a summer in London "finding myself," but then I had to come home because I ran out of money and clean underwear.

This donut shop is the longest success I've ever had, and I know it's all because of Stacy. If I didn't have her . . . well, I don't know what would have happened by now. I'm happy in my single life, but owning a business is the one area of my life where I refuse to go it alone again.

Over the next ten minutes, I try convincing Stacy of all the reasons I don't want to buy her share of the company without actually telling her the real truth. That I'm a liar. Not as tough as I look. That I still feel a little broken from Ben. That I don't know how to trust myself anymore.

Finally, Stacy relents, and we agree that we'll put out feelers for any interested parties and interview potential candidates. Then she flattens my already deflated heart to a pancake when she admits that she already has two meetings with potential buyers lined up for Wednesday who she found through friends of a friend. *WEDNESDAY!* As in, two days from now!

That's not nearly enough time for me to sabotage Logan's new annoying job in California while simultaneously finding him an equally prestigious position here that will pay even better than the other. I mean, who even wants to live in California anyway? Blue skies? *Psh, hate them!* Seventy-degree temperatures year-round? *Gross!* The potential of seeing a famous actor around any corner? *Boooorriinngg.*

It's no use, though; Stacy is set on it. And after listening to her talk about the house they've been looking at online, and how they will live closer to Logan's parents and start trying to have a family since they will have help nearby, and the school systems, and the restaurants, and the ocean, and the other obnoxiously wonderful things that I can't even argue with, I relent and give her my blessing in the form of another bear hug.

She's really leaving. *I'm about to lose my best friend.* I feel like another piece of me is breaking off.

"Okayyyy," she says in a mopey tone as she's slowly making her way back to the door.

I tell her to hold on so I can turn on sad music over the speaker. And because she's the best friend a girl could ever have, she complies without question. I turn on that terribly sad song "I Will Remember You," and once it's blaring over the speaker, I nod for Stacy to leave.

She gives a pitiful smile. I give her the same one in return. A lone tear streaks down both of our faces as she turns around and walks out the door. It's the end of an era. I might never see her again.

Just before the door closes, she stops it and peeks her head back inside. "Oh! Don't forget about the dress fitting at four!"

Oh, right. She's still getting married here at the end of the week, and there are, like, a million tasks we still have to do together before then.

"Yep! Ride together?"

"Sure! I'll pick you up here at closing."

"Kluvyoubye."

Then, she's gone, and I let the sad music drown my soul once again, thankful that Ryan isn't here to make it worse. And will someone *please* tell me when I'll stop thinking about him?

CHAPTER 6

June

"All right, take off your clothes," says Ms. Dorothy as if I'm used to hearing that phrase on the regular.

"Right here?" I look around the seamstress's empty shop and, despite its vacancy, don't relish the idea of stripping in public. "I think I'll just go in the dressing—"

"Phooey, nonsense!" says the million-year-old seamstress, pulling the shirt right off my body and tossing it somewhere across the room. "The curtains are covering the windows, and the rest of the wedding party isn't due here for another fifteen minutes. None of those boys will see your boobies if we hurry."

My eyes go wide. "Boys?"

Ms. Dorothy is mercilessly peeling the jeans off my hips, and Stacy is holding in her laughter so hard that tears leak down her face. I swear, she looks like she's going to burst a blood vessel from all that repressed laughter when Dorothy tosses my jeans to the far end of the room—right next to the shirt I wish I was still wearing.

"Actually, it's only Ryan coming," Stacy says, chuckles bubbling through her words. And now I understand why this scenario is so funny to her. "He's the only other one that needs any alterations."

"Oh my gosh! You're kidding!" Suddenly, I feel stark naked standing in the middle of a seamstress's shop in my bra and panties. I hurry to cover myself with my hands as if that will keep Ryan from seeing all of my bits if he were to show up early.

Ms. Dorothy thinks I'm only being shy in front of her. She bats my hands away from covering my boobs. "Oh, stop that. I'd kill to have my body look like that again. You ought to parade it around the square right now instead of hiding it behind your hands."

I don't care to be the grand marshal for that parade, though. I lunge for the midnight-blue bridesmaid gown and have to pry it from Dorothy's wrinkly hands. But let me tell you, this old woman is strong, because she is not letting this dress go without a fight. Maybe she wanted to measure me before I put it on? I don't know, but it feels like she's trying to force me to be confident in my own skin through immersion therapy. Guess what? It's not working.

Finally, Dorothy releases the dress with a huff. "I forgot my pins in the back."

She strides off and I whip my head in Stacy's direction. "Quick, shove me into this thing!" My eyes are frantic, and I look like someone just announced an impromptu sack race that I'm now the most eager participant of. I'm hopping and shimmying into this dress as if a million dollars are on the line. Really, though, my ass is on the line.

I'll die before I let Ryan's greedy eyes get a peek at my rear end.

Stacy is doubled over laughing. Really, I've never seen her crack up so much. She thinks the prospect of Ryan sauntering in here and seeing me in my underwear is hilarious. Have I said how much I hate her?

"I'm going to cut up your wedding dress like a paper snowflake if you don't help me zip this up!"

She does, but she takes her sweet time, laughing harder with every tiny inch the zipper rises. "There, you're decent again." She wipes her eyes and looks a little disappointed that the situation didn't play out like she was imagining. "I've never seen you move so fast! I swear"—she pauses for more laughter—"it looked like you just discovered your superspeed powers or something."

"Hilarious," I say, deadpan.

I catch my breath when Ms. Dorothy emerges from the back and proceeds to turn me, poke me (with a pin twice), and admonish me for squirming over the next ten minutes. I can't stand still, though. The devil will walk through the front door any minute, and I *refuse* to be standing here with my hands in the air like I'm surrendering in our war. I plan on being long gone before Ryan arrives.

"Alrighty, I'll take in an inch on either side, and you'll be good to go. Should be ready for you to pick up in two days. You can take it off now." She's reaching for the zipper again, but I sidestep her and make a break for the dressing rooms.

"I'll toss the gown over the door for you," I say, and Ms. Dorothy frowns. I'm starting to wonder if she and Stacy are in on some sort of quest to embarrass me in front of Ryan. It's ridiculous, of course. They would never do that.

But still . . . I lock the door to the dressing room.

I turn around and look in the mirror, almost not recognizing the woman staring back at me. This gown fits like a glove, hugging, lifting, and accentuating all the right places. I silently thank Stacy for not being one of those brides who chooses an ugly dress for her bridesmaids. *You all get bright-orange dresses with fifteen pounds of added ruffles! Enjoy!*

No, this dress is nothing short of lovely. It has a sweetheart neckline and dainty spaghetti straps. The bodice is made from a stiff material that is tight and flattering, but this skirt has layers and layers of soft sheer fabric that cascade like a waterfall from my waist to the floor. It looks as if I should be going to, rather than a wedding, an award show with a red carpet where photographers shout my name.

Ms. Dorothy's scratchy voice cuts through the stall door, and I jump a mile off the floor. "Almost done in there?"

I hurry and unzip the dress before sliding it off and tossing it over the door. I watch the fabric disappear and hear Ms. Dorothy shuffle off.

Turning back to the mirror, I play with my hair, getting ideas for how to have it styled for the wedding while I wait for Stacy to toss my clothes over to me. But now that the dress is off, a familiar discomfort creeps up my spine. My eyes fall from my brown hair to my chest. Not much to see there. My boobs are . . . nothing to write home about. I assess my hips next, noticing the cellulite on each side. And then I start angling my body, trying to find the perfect pose, because maybe if I suck in my stomach and stick my leg out just right—

No!

I breathe in deeply and unclench my stomach. I pull my leg back in line with the other and relax my shoulders. I look at my breasts and my curves and I tell Ben to *get out of my head.* Because that's what this really is about. I never struggled with how I looked to this degree until after he cheated on me. Until after what he said to me . . .

For the last few years, I've really hated being naked. Hated being anything less than perfectly put together if I'm being honest. It's a lot of the reason I have an only-one-date rule. And why I don't sleep with anyone on those dates. If I never let anyone get close, they can't hurt me.

Not attracted to you anymore.

My ex's voice is still too loud in my head, and I *hate* him for it. No matter how hard I try, I haven't been able to stop asking myself the same questions over and over. *If I had trained more at the gym— not let myself get so comfortable around him, would it have stopped him from cheating on me? Why wasn't I enough for him?*

But then, a healthier part of me surfaces from his callous words and actions and reminds me that *he* wasn't good enough for *me*. That I deserve a man who loves me for me—in every form. And each day that I get further away from Ben's toxic influence, I'm able to grab that version of myself by the hand and see her beauty.

But I would be lying if I said the insecurity is gone completely. I'm fighting through it. I'm fighting for myself. And I'm learning to look in the mirror at every part of me and *love her*.

"Shoot!" Stacy says. "Ms. Dorothy, I completely forgot to have you look at my slip. It's about three inches too long for my dress and peeks out the bottom. Let me go grab it from my car."

"Never mind that. I'm taking this dress home to work on tonight, so help me carry these things to my trunk, and I'll get it from you out there."

And any minute now, my clothes will rain down on me like manna from above. Except, I hear the chime above the door, followed by the sound of it shutting behind them.

"Stacy? Ms. Dorothy?" I call out to the empty room.

Well, shoot.

I have two options: (1) stand here shivering until they return or (2) make a run for it and retrieve my clothes with my newfound superspeed powers.

Ha ha, like I would ever pick option two! No way; I've seen all the movies, and the second my booty is in full view of the front door, Ryan will enter. No, thank you. I'll turn into a human Popsicle before I let that happen.

Just then, the door chimes again, and I sigh a breath of relief. "Stacy, you jerk! You left me in here naked without my clothes! Just for that, I get to wear your red dress to the rehearsal dinner."

I wait for her teasing laugh, but instead, a rumbling voice comes that makes my world tilt. "You're naked on the other side of that door?"

My stomach drops through the floor. *Ryan*. Does he have some sort of radar that goes off when I'm in the middle of a humiliating moment? Maybe if I just stay really quiet, he'll think he was hearing ghosts.

"June?"

I hold my breath.

"June, I know you're in there."

Shoot. I need to throw him off my scent. "Umm, *no hablo . . . eagles.*"

"Your Spanish is just as bad as it was in high school."

Time to bring out the big guns. I assume my very best ghost voice this time. "Whattt do you meannnn? I'm just a ggghhoossttt." Someone sign me up for a part in *A Christmas Carol* because I nailed that ghost voice.

"So you're a Spanish ghost now?" He sounds closer. I swear, if he looks through that crack, I will find a pair of trimmers and shave a stripe right down the center of his gorgeous hair.

"Yessss—I mean . . . siiiii." It's in this moment that I think I might have finally cracked under the pressures of life.

Ryan is quiet for a minute, and I'm hoping that maybe he left. But that's ridiculous because I never heard the door chime. I would give anything right now for a magic blue genie to pop out of a lamp and give me three wishes. For the first, I'd selflessly ask to end world hunger. For the second, I'd give Ryan a permanent green booger that always hangs out of his nose. For the third, I'd beam him away to the farthest speed-dating service and lock him in for a million years, forcing him to go round and round a table of prying women until he loses his mind.

I peek through the crack in the stall door and find that Ryan has moved across the room and is leaning his shoulder against the adjacent wall, gaze cast down to his crossed boots. He's facing away and wearing a plain white T-shirt that stretches across his back muscles flawlessly. Those dark jeans make his butt look way too good, and I'm not even a butt-admiring type of girl; however, even I can admit that *his* is something to behold. He's also wearing a baseball hat, and from this position, I can see the ends of his hair curling out the bottom. He looks relaxed and effortlessly sexy, and I want to kick him.

"So why are you naked in there?"

I step away from the crack in the door. "I'm not naked. I'm wearing my . . . underclothes, but that rude woman stripped me out of my dress before she and Stacy left me in here to rot."

"*Underclothes?* Are you in the nineteenth century?"

"I wish I were, because then YOU would be a gentleman and offer to bring me my T-shirt and jeans."

His low chuckle rolls over me. "I'm definitely not that."

"Ugh. I hate you."

"I know. You told me that last night. Repeatedly."

My face flushes at the memory of him driving me home, carrying me into my house, tucking me into bed. I hope to goodness that he won't bring up what I said last night, but of course he does, because he's evil. "You also told me a few other things last night. My favorite was that you wished I had ki—"

"Stop! I remember what I said. It was the alcohol talking last night, nothing more." I hope lightning doesn't strike me. "Now, will you shut up and give me my clothes so I can come out?" I hear his footsteps, and hope blooms in my chest.

"So what you're saying is, you're stuck in there until I give you your clothes?"

I don't like the mischievous lilt to his voice. Not one bit.

"Uh . . . maybe. Why? Are you going to set fire to the building? Try to smoke me out so you can see me in my underwear?"

He chuckles. "Nope. Even better."

CHAPTER 7

Ryan

I hear June audibly swallow. It makes me smile. "If you want your clothes back, you're going to have to answer a question for each article of clothing."

"You little sh—"

"Ah-ah-ah. I wouldn't be rude to the host of the game if I were you."

She groans. "Why are you just as annoying as an adult as you were as a teenager? I thought men were supposed to grow out of their obnoxious phase."

"Most do. I chose to grow *into* mine."

I find it interesting (and disappointing) that June still hasn't realized that I only teased her so much back then as a way of flirting. More than once I contemplated confessing my feelings for her, but her hatred felt like an insurmountable obstacle. There was no use telling her I was wild for her, because I'm fairly certain she was wild for my blood—spilled all over the pavement with a chalk drawing outlining it.

"Ryan . . ." says June. "Do me a favor? Eat glass, will you?"

"Oh, come on, June Bug. Can't take the heat of a few get-to-know-you questions? Fine. You could always just come out and get your clothes yourself."

There's a long pause followed by the sound of her forehead banging against the stall door. "What's question number one?"

I grin. "Number one. How much have you missed me on a scale of one to ten?"

"Negative fifteen. Next question."

I toss one of her socks over the door. "Number two. What's your biggest fear?"

"That I'll have to see you again tomorrow."

I put my hand over my heart even though she can't see me. "Wow. That one hurt."

Her fingers raise above the stall's wall and she wiggles them. "My other sock, please."

After throwing it over, I lean back against the wall and fold my arms, preparing my next question. "If I had asked you out in high school, would you have said yes?"

This should be a movie moment. One of those scenes where she laughs and admits that she would have said yes in a heartbeat. Needless to say, that doesn't happen.

Instead, she lets out a bark of laughter and says, "Absolutely not. Because number one, it would have ended up being another one of your pranks. And two, I was too good for you back then." I can hear the smile in her voice and imagine her sticking her nose up at me.

I toss her shirt over. "Then tell me this, June Bug. If you're so much better than me, why are you still single?" I'm smiling in the silence, waiting for her zingy comeback, but the more time that passes, the more my smile fades. "June?" *Shitt.* I'm not totally sure, but I think June is sniffling in there. I press my ear against the side of the stall to listen closer. "Are you . . . crying?"

A sharp sniffle. "NO. Just . . ." She's definitely talking through tears. "Ugh, Ryan, can you for once do something nice for me and just give me my damn clothes?!"

The urgency in her voice shocks me. June—the bold, give-it-right-back woman—has a tremble in her voice that I'm pretty sure is because of tears streaming down her cheeks. I feel horrible. The worst of the worst. What I thought was good-natured teasing is making her full-on cry. I didn't mean the question seriously. If anything, I was just trying to fish around and find out about her dating history. Somehow, I managed to strike a very sensitive nerve—one I would have never intentionally hit.

Without hesitation, I toss June's jeans into the stall. Neither of us speaks during the time it takes for her to dress, because I'm not sure what to say, and I don't think she *wants* to say anything. But I do manage to run this scenario over again and again in my mind at least fifteen times and wonder how it tore her up so quickly. I would have expected June to march out in her underwear and kick me in the crotch for saying something that hurt her feelings before I expected her to cry. But it's becoming more and more clear that June is not the same girl I used to know. She's a woman who has a history I might never get to learn about.

A moment later, the door to the stall flies open, and June barrels out—more representative of the woman I was anticipating than who she was in that changing room. Gone is the vulnerable June from a moment ago. She squares her shoulders and levels me with white-hot anger.

"I told you not to mess with me, Ryan, and I meant it. We're grown adults now, and you need to start acting like it!" She pokes me hard in the chest, but I don't sway. I wonder if she'd be mad if I ran my finger across the bridge of her nose, drawing a line through her freckles. The blaze in her eyes tells me I shouldn't try it unless I want to lose a finger. "But you know what else? My worth isn't tied to whether I'm in a relationship or not! Even all on my own, I'm still better than you."

She's throwing tough words at me now, but I can still hear the same shake in her voice from earlier. She's like a kid trying to convince her friend that she's not afraid of monsters anymore while still sleeping with all the lights on. And it's the tremble in her voice that makes me think there's more to June's story—more to those tears and hatred—than just me.

I look down into her bright-green eyes and realize I need to change my tactic. She meets my gaze and lifts that defiant chin of hers into the air, but her façade is no use—I can clearly see the hurt now. It's hurt I didn't put there, and I want to find out who did.

She pokes my chest firmly again. "And one more thing! If you think—"

I interrupt her by gently wrapping my hand around her wrist, preventing her from stabbing me with her finger another time. "You're right. I'm sorry about all that just now. I shouldn't have acted like we were still teenagers. It won't happen again." My truth must shock her, because I see June's shoulders drop. My grip on her wrist is featherlight, giving her all the chances in the world to move away, but she doesn't even try.

I really shouldn't be this concerned about winning June over, though. I should be giving all my attention to considering Noah's restaurant and whether I want to be a part of it. But I'm not. I can't bring myself to spare it even a second of my thoughts. Last night, I fell asleep thinking of ways to make June smile. I just want *one* aimed at me. Just one and I'll be happy. I've never been on the receiving end of one of her smiles, but I'm determined to get one by the end of this week. It's not that I'm head over heels in love with the woman already, but I feel a pull to her. A need to spend time with her. Be close to her. I can't shake it.

I look in June's eyes and see a million conflicting emotions flying through them. She's a human slot machine right now, and her eyes are rotating emoji icons. *Daggers, hearts, crying face, smile, purple devil.*

She blinks her long dark lashes. "Just leave me alone from now on, Ryan."

A second later, the door chimes, and June and I both swivel our heads to see Stacy storm into the shop. She shoves her phone into her pocket and huffs out a sigh. "You're never going to believe who I just got off the phone with." She pauses when she sees us standing so closely.

June immediately rips her hand back and steps away. "My earlier sentiments still apply. Eat glass."

Stacy blinks. "What did I miss?" She then shakes her head and waves her hand. "No, you know what? I don't want to know, because my whole life is falling apart and I can't deal with your bickering right now. My caterer and most of her staff for the rehearsal dinner just came down with the flu! There's no way they'll be over it by Friday night."

I lift my hat up off my head and scrape my hand through my hair before replacing it. That's my way of preparing to say no to what I'm sure Stacy is about to ask me.

"What! No way," says June. "Is there anyone else we can hire?"

Stacy shakes her head no, but I doubt she's even tried to hire anyone else. "Not on this short notice. Everyone else I've reached out to is booked solid."

I narrow my eyes. "Who else have you tried?"

She shrugs a shoulder but doesn't meet my eye. "Just some locals. Doesn't matter. You've never heard of them." *Beep. Beep. Beep.* My lie detector is going off. "Anyway, it doesn't matter because I know who I want to have cater it."

I shut my eyes tight, bracing for impact.

"Please, Ryan. Please, please, please. You're pretty much the best chef in the country! It will be such a treat for everyone if you make the food."

I don't bother hiding my groan. "It's so last minute. I don't even have a kitchen."

Stacy is tugging on my arm now. "Oh, come on. There's only going to be about fifty people there. A chef as good as you doesn't need much time to prep, right? And you can use my kitchen. Or June's!" She's just trying to butter me up.

"I think you might be confusing me with a fairy godmother. All chefs need time to prep."

"Well, well, well," says June, sounding like a middle-school bully who's cornering me on the playground. She's going to steal my lunch. "Who knew catering a rehearsal dinner would be too hard for Mr. Bigshot?" She has her hands on her hips and is smirking at me. It's cute.

It also gives me a new idea.

I smile and take a step toward June, locking eyes with her but addressing Stacy. "Tell you what, Stacy. I'll do it."

June narrows her eyes, but Stacy squeals. "Really?! Thank you, Ryan! You're the b—"

"But only if June lets me use her kitchen and assists me."

If there was a record playing right now, it would grind to a screeching halt. "What? No," says June, her hands falling off her hips. "I'm not helping you." She looks to Stacy. "I'm not helping him."

I shrug and turn to face Stacy. "Sorry, I tried. I can't do it without help, though. It's too much work by myself."

Stacy's face is so forlorn it's laughable. She turns big round puppy eyes to June. "Juuuunie—"

June flashes her a no-nonsense look and takes one big step away. "No, don't start that."

Stacy rushes up to her and drops down to her knees, clasping

June's hand inside her own. "My darling, June. Love of my life. Soul sister from another mister. Please help Ryan! I'll never ask you for anything again."

"I doubt that."

"I'll give you my house."

"You're renting."

"My kidney."

"Don't need it."

"My car."

"It's older than mine."

Stacy sighs and stands up. "Fine. I didn't want to have to do this, but . . ."

June's eyes go round, apparently understanding what Stacy is threatening. "You wouldn't."

Stacy stands and faces me with a determined look. "Ryan, have I ever told you about the time that June peed—"

"*Stop!* Fine, I'll do it, sheesh."

A smug smile spreads over Stacy's mouth as she whips around to throw her arms around June's neck. "Love you!" She then kisses June's cheek so hard that it makes June's lips smoosh to one side.

"Well, I like you a little less now." June smooths down her shirt, and I try not to let my eyes linger on her curves.

Stacy laughs. "I'm your favorite person in the world. Don't deny it."

June just groans.

"What about me?" I say. "No kisses for the man who will actually be doing the catering?"

Stacy winks at me. "We'll just call it even for when you tried to break me and Logan up in seventh grade."

Savage. I can respect it.

Stacy pulls her phone out of her pocket and starts dialing as she walks toward the door. "Meet me at the car, June. I'm calling Logan to tell him the good news."

I turn my gaze to June and find her already studying me. Her full, bubblegum lips are slightly pinched together, and I can't tell what's going through her mind. She looks oddly thoughtful—contemplative.

"What are you thinking about right now?" I ask her.

"Which kitchen utensil I'll use to kill you."

My stomach clenches when I see a hint of a smile in the corner of her mouth. She turns away, trying to keep me from seeing it, but it doesn't matter. I know it's there, and that's worth something.

CHAPTER 8

Ryan

"Still no girlfriend back in Chicago?" Logan asks after the bartender slides our beers in front of us.

I shake my head and take a drink. "No time."

He laughs. "I don't think that's actually the problem."

We've been friends since birth because our moms were long-time best friends. And even after choosing different careers, going to schools in different countries, and then settling down in different states, we're still just as close today as we were as kids.

Logan has walked with me through every major event in my life. My buzz cut in eighth grade, the first time I made out with a girl freshman year (he wasn't there, but you better believe I recounted it to him in such detail that he felt like he was the one who kissed Tory Hayes), and also when my mom died junior year. I don't like thinking back to that time—even after all these years, it hurts. My dad passed when I was five, so I never really had any memories of him, but my mom and I were more like friends than mother and son. And no one can prepare for a car accident.

Logan's mom, Molly, was my mom's best friend and is also my

godmother. So, when Mom passed, I went to live with Logan and his family for the rest of high school. He's seen me through my best and my worst days (the buzz cut being among the worst). And that's why, now, I think of Logan as my brother. He calls me on my shit, and I let him because he seems to know my motives better than I do, anyway.

I set my glass down and turn my full attention to Logan. "I work six, sometimes seven, days a week, and usually until midnight. So it kinda feels like the problem to me."

Logan laughs. He's shaking his head at me. My answer wasn't the right one, apparently. "You want to know the actual problem?"

I lean against the back of the barstool and resist the urge to clasp my hands behind my head. "Yes, please tell me why I don't have a girlfriend, *oh wise one.*"

"Women love you . . ."

"Ah, yep—there's the problem. Can't believe I didn't see it before."

He holds up his hand. "Let me finish." I nod for him to go ahead. "Most women you meet like you right away. Take those three ladies, for instance," he says, nodding to somewhere over my shoulder. "They've been undressing you with their eyes since we sat down, but I have a theory . . ."

I glance back, and yeah, a small group of women have their eyes locked on me. Their targets are set, and I probably have a little red dot in the center of my forehead.

When I accidentally make eye contact with them, all three ladies sit up straighter and toss their most welcoming smiles at me. I don't want to be rude, so I give them a tight smile and lift my glass in a silent toast.

"Aha! See. Theory proven. Beautiful ladies are smiling at you, and you immediately go back to scowling at your glass. You hate it."

"What's your point, Logan?"

"I think you hate their attention because you've mentally already checked out on everyone besides one woman. The one woman, in fact, that you've never been able to get over, who would rather slap you than kiss you. I think you like June, and you also like that she doesn't fawn over you like everyone else."

Damn.

I think he's right.

June challenges me around every corner and *I love it*. She's someone who doesn't care about my looks or my job or social status—she's going to call me out if I'm wrong every single time. But she's also so funny, and beautiful, and smart. She's absolutely someone who would make me want to come home from the restaurant early at night. And I don't think I've ever had that feeling with anyone else.

"Why haven't you visited her before now?" Logan asks, raising his brow and catching my attention again.

I rub the back of my neck. "I don't know. It never seemed like the right time."

"But you've thought about visiting her before?"

"I mean . . . yeah. I've wanted to see her. Does that shock you?"

"No. So why haven't you?"

"I've just been focusing on my career and . . ."

"And what?" Geez, he's inquisitive tonight.

I sigh before I speak again, because there's nothing I hate more than admitting my feelings when they make me sound like a coward. "I guess, I knew she wouldn't be happy to see me. It was hard to convince myself to face a woman that I crushed on for years that only hated my guts in return. I like that she challenges me, but I don't like that she hates me."

"Well, in all fairness, she's always thought you hated her too."

Logan downs his drink, and I want to keep talking about June and find out what she's been up to all these years, but he closes up the subject, and it feels weird to force it. So, instead, the conversation moves to his and Stacy's plans for the future. I do a pretty good job of avoiding any thoughts of June until Logan tells me they are moving to California after the wedding and Stacy is selling her half of Darlin' Donuts. My mind is all too happy to race back to June, and I wonder if she's feeling crushed right now. I know how much Stacy means to her.

Maybe I'll go by her place and see how she's doing. Although she'll probably just think it's some kind of trap and I'm actually only there to set a mouse loose in her house. I did that once in high school, so her guess wouldn't be all that misguided. But then I look down at my phone and see that it's almost eleven o'clock. Too late for house calls.

"Are you going to go after her?" Logan asks.

"Will you stop reading my thoughts? It's annoying."

He chuckles. "Then stop wearing your feelings on your face. You're smirking like a villain. The only time I ever see you look like that is when June is around. So, are you going for her?"

"Is it terrible if I say yes?" Even without Logan answering, I know the answer is yes. Awful. Bad idea.

I still have to decide if I'm going to take the job in Chicago. If I do, I won't even have any time for June. I'll barely have time to eat and sleep. Is that what I want? I've been working my butt off to get to this exact place in my career, but it doesn't feel like I thought it would now that I'm here. Turns out, it's lonely at the top.

"Terrible? No. Unlikely that you'll succeed? Yes. The way she's talked about you over the years, I'd think drowning puppies is your favorite hobby."

I laugh. "I don't doubt it."

"Besides, June has a 'one-date' rule, and I don't see you agreeing to that."

Well, this just got interesting.

I frown. "One-date rule? What are you talking about?"

"She won't go out with anyone more than once. One date and then it's *sayonara.*"

"No way."

"I'm dead serious. Stacy and I thought it wouldn't last long when she first announced she'd never date the same man twice again, but that was five years ago, and she's still going strong."

"Why?" I ask, not certain how I feel about this news.

Logan picks up a handful of peanuts and tosses them into his mouth. "To keep herself from getting hurt again." He pauses his chewing and meets my gaze. Now he's a chipmunk—frozen with wide eyes and cheeks stuffed with nuts. "Oh shit. I shouldn't have said any of that."

Hmm. Now that's something. And exactly what I've suspected. For a while now, I've been suspicious that there is some sort of "no talking about June" policy in place, but I could never be completely certain. Logan just confirmed it, though.

Lucky for me, he's the easiest walnut to crack.

"Shouldn't have said what?" I run my finger across the condensation on my beer glass. I'm relaxed. Nonchalant. No big deal.

Logan swallows his massive bite. "Nothing. Forget it."

I swing my casual gaze to Logan's face and let it rest there. My smirk is easy-breezy as I lay my arm down on the bar, getting comfortable.

Logan's shoulders sink. "Come on. Don't do that."

"Do what?"

"Make me tell you this secret."

I shrug. "No one's making you tell them anything. I'm just enjoying a beer with a friend . . . a friend who looks like he's got a lot on his chest."

Poor Logan. He's pressing his lips together because he's an unopened soda bottle, and I'm shaking him up. Most men have to wrestle with their friends for an hour before they can get the truth out of them. I just stare at Logan, and he crumbles like a cookie, because he hates keeping things from me. I'm surprised he's been able to harbor this secret all these years.

But tonight, I'll get it out of him.

We enter a staring contest for two minutes. By the two-minute-and-ten-second mark, a bead of sweat drips down Logan's forehead, and I know he's moments away from spilling every secret he's ever had.

"She was engaged five years ago!" Logan blurts and then immediately slumps over like he's just dropped a fifty-pound weight.

I, on the other hand, have been punched in the gut. *Engaged.* I had no idea. I mean, it makes sense. She's thirty, incredible, and gorgeous.

But for some reason, I'm still surprised. "Engaged? What happened?" I ask, but Logan looks torn again. "Oh, come on. We both know you're going to tell me, anyway. Just spill it."

"Fine. But if Stacy asks, you were holding me in a headlock, and I had no choice."

I roll my eyes and nod my agreement, but Logan holds out his elbow. He looks as serious about sealing this promise with our secret oath as he did when we were six and first established it. I look around, making sure no one is watching, and then tap my elbow against his. There. It's done. He now has the right to give me a swirly if I break our agreement.

"None of us really know," he begins. "One day, Ben was June's world, and the next, she was sending out a group text the week of the ceremony that said *Wedding is off. It didn't work out.* She claimed she felt suffocated in the relationship and that she'd lost touch with herself. But Stacy thinks it was just a cover for something that June didn't want to talk about. She's always been a pretty private person, so it makes sense."

I grip my empty glass, and I think it cracks a little. I'm not totally sure why I'm having this reaction. Maybe because, like Stacy, I think there's more to the story? I remember the tremble in June's voice earlier this evening, and my mind starts working through possible scenarios of why June would have called off her wedding. "She ended it the week of the ceremony?"

Logan nods. "Yep. Strangest thing."

I make a *huh* noise and focus my attention on the liquor bottles behind the bar, processing one uncomfortable realization after another. She almost married someone else. I could have lost my chance with her forever. I should have come back sooner.

After a few quiet moments, I tap the wooden bar five times with my middle finger—each tap further solidifying the decision I'm making.

Logan's chuckle has me turning my head to look at him. He's smiling and shaking his head at me like he thinks I'm a complete sucker—a man about to buy a knockoff Rolex from a street vendor, thinking it's the real thing. "You're going after that second date, aren't you?"

I smirk. "I do love a challenge."

"Especially when it concerns June."

I pull a twenty out of my pocket and throw it on the bar to close out our tab. "Especially then."

As I walk to my car, I feel my phone vibrating in my pocket. It's late, so I really don't even need to look at the caller ID to know who it is. Still, I register the name *Noah* flashing across my screen and then ignore the call.

CHAPTER 9

June

"June, open up!"

I shoot up from my pillow and briefly wonder if that gas station attendant found out about the candy bar I stole when I was eleven and is coming to perform a citizen's arrest.

"No! I'm too tired to go to jail right now," I yell back.

He's a no-nonsense kind of guy, though, because he bangs on the door again. "Come on, open up."

When I finally shake off the last remnants of sleep and remember that it's been nineteen years since I stole that Snickers, I pick up my phone and scowl at it. Is the entire world against me getting my beauty sleep?

"It's six-thirty in the morning. It's too early to deal with you. Go away!" I lie back down and pull the covers up to my chin, making a warm cocoon.

I think I got rid of him, because everything is blissfully quiet. One of our employees is opening the shop today, so I don't have to get ready until 10:30. I plan on squeezing every bit of sleep out of this morning that I can.

I nuzzle my head back into my fluffy pillow. *Good, pillow. I love you, pillow.*

"Morning, Sunshine."

"AH!" I scream and yank the covers all the way up over my head. There is a man in my house. A MAN IN MY HOUSE!

And then I hear a familiar chuckle, and it makes my stomach squeeze. *No, no, no.*

"How did you get in here?!" I screech from under my blanket tent.

I hear footsteps in my room. How dare he come in here!

"I used the key under your unicorn gnome. Stacy told me where to find it when I couldn't get you to answer your phone."

Yeah, I have a unicorn gnome. And although I tell everyone I bought it because my twelve-year-old niece begged me to, I actually just bought it because I thought it was adorable and wanted to look at it every day. One perk of not being married: I can put unicorns wherever I want them.

"Well, put it back and go away! You're not allowed in my house."

"I've already been in your house, remember? When you told me you want me to kiss you."

"No. I told you I wished you had kissed me in *high school*. Big difference, buddy!"

"Why are you calling me *buddy*?"

"Because I don't like you. It's dramatic emphasis."

I feel my mattress sink down at my feet and realize that that jerk is sitting on my bed! I scrunch my legs up to my chest, because I'm an armadillo now—rolling up into a protective little ball. How dare he invade my house before I've had a chance to brush my hair and put my makeup on. No one sees me without it. No one.

"Come on, get up. We've got a lot to do this morning." He's trying to yank the covers off my face, but I have a Ms.-Dorothy-tight grip on them, and they don't even budge.

"Stop it. Leave me alone." I take off one of my socks and peek my hand out from under the covers to throw it across the room. "Fetch, boy!"

He chuckles. "Why are you hiding under there? Are you naked again or something?"

"You wish." I inch the covers off my face and clutch them over my braless chest. I'm wearing a yellow camisole and sleep shorts. Not too inappropriate but also not something I feel like letting Ryan get a peek at.

It's then that I'm hit with the full force of Ryan's attractiveness. It's not fair. Not one bit. I don't see even a hint of sleep crud in his eyes. No bedhead. He's wearing a crisp, navy-blue T-shirt, and his hair is nicely tousled with some kind of matte hair product. Even worse, he smells incredible. Like, make-you-want-to-sell-all-your-belongings-and-run-off-into-the-sunset-together *incredible*. He's gorgeous. Evil people shouldn't be gorgeous.

I, in comparison, have drool crusted on my mouth.

He doesn't notice the drool, though. I watch his dark eyes fall to my shoulder and stop. The corner of his mouth quirks into a grin. "You have a tattoo." His voice is kind of gravelly, and it does things to my insides. "Can I see it?"

I don't know why, but I nod my head in approval. And then, even worse, I twist around so he can see my shoulder better. He leans forward a little, and I stay still—completely frozen—because Ryan Henderson is sitting on my bed with me, and I can't fully bring myself to hate it.

My body and my mind are bickering. They don't agree on a single thing right now.

Ryan doesn't touch my sunflower-covered shoulder, but I feel the heat of his gaze across my skin as if it were his fingers. My toes curl. His nearness is too much. Too loaded. Too intense. I shoot out of bed faster than a bottle rocket, race into my bathroom, and shut the door. I'm breathing fast, and my eyes are wide like a deer who barely made it across traffic without getting hit.

What's happening to me?

"You said we have a lot to do today?" I yell through the door, and it's ridiculous how squeaky my voice sounds. "I don't remember signing up to be your assistant." I throw on my (Stacy's) olive-green cotton jumper before I remember I DID technically agree to be his assistant.

Wonderful. I should have just let Stacy tell him I peed my pants on a roller coaster. *Big whoop.* I'm sure women in their twenties pee themselves on a double loop-de-loop coaster all the time. Well, maybe not so much a roller coaster and more like a scrambler . . . with my niece . . . who had no problems controlling her bladder. So, never mind, spending the morning with Ryan is probably a better outcome.

"Right," says Ryan, sounding as if he's wandering around my room. "Think of it less like assisting and more like grunt work."

I finish tying the straps of my jumper over each of my shoulders, throw my hair into a bun, and swipe on a base layer of makeup before opening the door. Ryan is standing in front of my dresser, looking at the picture of me with Sam and Jonathan (my niece and nephew) at the beach. I'm not sure if he knows I'm watching him or not, but he smiles softly at the photo.

My brows pinch together because I'm not sure what to make of this Ryan. There's a part of me that realizes it's been a long time since high school. We've both grown up. We've both lived a lot of life and become completely new people since we were last sticking chewed gum to the bottom of the other's desk. More than likely, Ryan is not the same teenager who sabotaged all my dates, toilet-papered my bedroom, and put a lizard in my backpack.

On second thought, I'm not quite ready to let go of my hatred yet.

"Quit snooping around my room," I say, going to his side and laying the picture frame face down. He doesn't get to know things about my life.

He turns that soft smile to me. "Do you have two secret children I don't know about?"

"Yes, they live here and here." I hold up both of my fists and raise my middle fingers.

He doesn't look offended like I had hoped. He chuckles and gently folds down my birds until his big hands are covering mine. "I think you need some coffee."

Why is he doing this? Being so touchy-feely? And doing that strange thing with his face? On most people, it's called a smile. But on Ryan, I don't trust that it's something so nice.

I consider telling Ryan I gave coffee up just to spite him, but he's right. I do need coffee. I need it funneling into my mouth from one of those beer hats at all times.

A grunt is the only snarky reply I can think of until I get a hit of that aforementioned coffee. I jerk my hands out of his hold and head toward the kitchen, wishing I didn't feel so annoying. I've never treated anyone like I treat Ryan. Even when I broke things off with Ben, I never acted snarky and disagreeable.

I turn my head and find Ryan opening my fridge.

"What do you think you're doing?"

"Making eggs." He reaches in and pulls out the carton.

"No, you are not." I cross the kitchen and take the eggs from him and put the carton back in the fridge. "I don't eat breakfast."

It's true. I don't even sneak one of our own donuts until after lunch.

He shakes his head at me and reaches in for the eggs again. "You should. Maybe you'd be less angry all the time." I grind my teeth into dust as Ryan sets the eggs on the counter and starts looking in all my cabinets. He pauses with his hands on the handles of the open upper cabinets and looks at me over his large shoulder. "Do you not own a mixing bowl?"

I roll my eyes. "Of course I do." I push him out of the way with my hip. I won't let my hands touch him. They have a mind of their own, and I'm afraid that if they feel his hard body, I won't be able to pull them back off. From then on, I would have to go with him everywhere, my hands plastered to the six-pack that, no doubt, lives under his shirt. "But I'm not a million feet tall like you, so I keep everything down here." I open a lower cabinet and wave my hands in front of it, making the classic ta-da gesture.

Once the mixing bowl situation is settled, I pour my cup of coffee and hop up onto the counter to watch closely (because I'm keeping a steady eye on the enemy, not because I think he's sexy) as Ryan goes to work making us breakfast. He takes out an egg, taps it on the counter, and cracks it open with one hand. He does this with five eggs before washing his hands and going back to my fridge to pull out a bell pepper and cheese. My eyes follow him around like the head of the CIA has assigned me to investigate his every move. Like they are suddenly concerned chefs making morning omelets might be starting a nuclear war.

Ryan makes himself at home. He's forgotten I exist and that this is *my* kitchen he's taking over. I sip my coffee while Ryan pulls out a knife I've only ever used to wield as a weapon and starts chopping the bell pepper at a frightening speed. He's humming, and his tan forearms are flexing as the knife continues to slice and dice. Finally, he lays down the knife and scoops the veggies up to pour into the egg mixture and dumps it all into the hot skillet on the stove.

Now he's got a hand towel draped over his shoulder and is flipping an omelet, and the veins down his arms are popping, and my mouth is watering, but it has absolutely nothing to do with breakfast.

After Ryan tosses our omelets onto plates, it occurs to me that I have a three-star Michelin chef making me breakfast in my kitchen. "What are you really doing here, Ryan?"

He hasn't spoken to me or even glanced in my direction since he started cooking, so I sort of just thought he forgot I was here. But when his eyes find me right away, I realize he never lost track of me once. He's been just as aware of me as I am of him.

"Making you breakfast before we plan the menu for Friday night."

I shake my head and set down my coffee beside me. "You don't need me for that. You're a chef."

He folds his arms and leans back against the counter, keeping his eyes fixed on me. "You're right."

"So, why then? I want the truth. Is this some kind of trap or way for you to mess with me like you used to?"

He gives me a sad tilted smile and shakes his head. "After all this time, you still don't see the real reason I messed with you back then?" The string connecting us pulls tight.

I force myself to swallow. "Because you hated me."

He pushes off the counter and walks toward me, one slow agonizing step at a time, until he's close enough to pin me in. His hands land on the counter beside my hips, and I forget how to breathe. "Has it never occurred to you that the only reason I picked on you in high school is because I was into you? Or that messing with you was the only way I could get you to look at me?"

My heart is beating so hard right now I'm afraid if I open my mouth, it will leap right out. I settle with slowly shaking my head.

He smiles, and his eyes fall and settle on my mouth. "June, I'm not your enemy." Those dark eyes hold my mouth for five heart-beats before they pop back up to meet my gaze. "I never was."

For a minute, I think we're going to kiss. But then he pulls away, picks up our plates, and carries them to the table.

I, however, can't move. I'm numb—inside and out.

His words seep into me like a dry, brittle sponge slowly being dipped in water.

I'm not your enemy. I never was.

But that can't be. What he just said *can't* be true. Because if it is . . . that means, all this time, I thought he hated me, and he thought I hated him, but really we were both into each other. It means we could have been kissing in high school instead of biting at each other like wild dogs. We could have gone to prom together. He could have brought me milkshakes after my tonsillectomy. I could have held him when his mom died.

I would never have met Ben.

But no . . . *no, no, no.* Ryan had his chance to kiss me at graduation, and he didn't take it. If he really liked me, he would have. What he just told me changes nothing. So what if he crushed on me back then? So what if we are attracted to each other now?

We both have different lives, and his happens to be all the way in Chicago. Plus, I still have my one-date rule. I'm not ready to let go of it yet, and when I do, it definitely won't be for someone like Ryan Henderson. No, I just need to make it through this wedding week and then wave to him as he drives away, retreating back to his important life. Everything will go back to normal.

I slide off the counter and make sure my legs still work before I straighten my shoulders and march into the breakfast room. I don't sit down when I make it to the table. Instead, I lean over and level Ryan with a glare that would scare the head of the Mafia. I throw my hand behind me, not breaking eye contact with Ryan, and point to the kitchen. "What you just said back there changes *nothing*. And for the rest of the day, we will discuss nothing but food and menu items. Understand?"

He's not threatened. He's not shaking in his boots like I want him to. He wants to take my picture and post it with the hashtag *cute*. "Fine. Whatever you say, boss."

And then his smile tilts, and I'm worried I'll never be in control when it comes to Ryan.

CHAPTER 10

Ryan

True to her word, June makes sure we never discuss anything personal all morning. She barely looks me in the eye. After scarfing her breakfast down and draining two cups of coffee, she fetches a pencil and notepad and taps the lead against the paper in a Morse code that says *Let's get this over with and then get out.*

I'm not quite ready to comply yet, though. Instead, I feel like seeing how much I can learn about June without her realizing I've squeezed personal information from her. "Tell me about Darlin' Donuts," I say, and she narrows her eyes at me. I raise my hands in surrender. "It's just a business question."

June is skeptical as she searches my face for the hole in my lie. She can't find it, though, so she gives in and spends the next twenty minutes talking nonstop. It's ridiculously hard not to smile and give myself away as I watch her talk about her bakery.

Her eyes light up, and she smiles when she recounts to me the day they bought the shop and how it was filled with dead mice and rotting holes in the walls. Her brother, Jake, is an architect and helped her redesign the building, fitting it for a new industrial kitchen and shop front with seating. She goes on and on about how they designed the bakery to look both vintage and modern, mixing bright pastel pinks, yellows, and turquoise with thick, intricate crown molding.

I listen and nod approvingly through the entire monologue, acting surprised when she tells me they have a peg wall behind the counter that spells out D.D. where they hang each of their signature donuts every day to showcase their flavors. I smile as if I didn't already know about it. As if I don't also know that her booths are tufted in a blue-green velvet and the floor is speckled marble. I have to act surprised so she doesn't find out I've been secretly following the bakery's Instagram account ever since Logan accidentally informed me about Darlin' Donuts a few years ago.

I don't actually *follow* her account or like or comment on any photos, so she has no way of knowing that I've been keeping up with her. But every night when I fall into bed, the first thing I do is type @DarlinDonuts into the Instagram search bar and stare at whatever photo she's posted that day, hoping to see a glimpse of her face in every reflection.

I don't tell her any of this for two reasons: (1) I don't want her to hit me with a restraining order because she suddenly thinks I'm her stalker; and (2) it sounds an awful lot like I've been pining away for her since high school—but honestly . . . I have been a little bit. But I've also been busy and content in my life, working so hard that I barely have time to think about anyone or anything but the career ladder I've been climbing. You don't become the world's youngest three-star Michelin chef by sitting on your ass and dreaming of a woman far away. *You think of her while you're working instead.*

But it's really been in the last few years that I've thought about June more than normal. Logan and Stacy visited me in Chicago, and Logan let the news of the bakery slip. Stacy kicked him under the table, and that was when I was first tipped off about the "no talking about June" policy. I didn't press it in the moment. But I did manage to get the name of her bakery before Logan left, and I then proceeded to think about June every day for the next three years.

Actually, yeah, *I do sound like a stalker. Great.*

But the thing is, June has become a comfort to me from far away. An enigma. A figment of my imagination and someone that I've let myself dream of reuniting with for so long that I've been afraid to actually see her again. The more time that passed without me coming to visit, the more I talked myself out of ever seeing her again. I couldn't imagine there being a scenario where the real June measured up to the one I had created in my mind.

Except, here she is. And she's worlds better than the June of my fantasies. She's beautiful and spunky, and yet soft as butter behind all those sharp thorns.

In the middle of her business talk, she accidentally tells me about the time Justin Timberlake came into the bakery and how she was so nervous she spilled an entire tray of donuts onto the floor. This leads to her telling me about how sometimes she drinks too much coffee and it makes her hands jittery. Which leads to the story about the time she tried to cut her own bangs after drinking three cups of coffee, creating a new system in her family for identifying a date in time known as BBB and ABB (Before Bad Bangs and After Bad Bangs). And how the only thing that could calm her down after seeing her jagged bangs in the mirror was a trip to Taco Bell because fast-food tacos always make her feel better.

June realizes that she's been talking about her life and promptly seals her mouth up, leveling me with laser eyes because I tricked her again. And that's that. No more personal talk. We spend the rest of the morning fine-tuning what we want to make for the rehearsal dinner, and then she kicks me out an hour later with barely a second look.

After I'm back at the hotel, I work out in the gym to clear my head of June, and when that doesn't work, I take an ice-cold shower. When I'm out, I wrap a towel around my waist and check my phone. I have three text messages in a new group chat.

> STACY: Hi guys! Friends dinner tonight at our place for old time's sake?
> LOGAN: I don't know why Stacy added the question mark. It's not an option. This is a mandatory friends dinner. Be here at 7:00 or be removed from the wedding party.
> UNKNOWN NUMBER: Is that a promise? I'm kinda getting tired of doing all of Stacy's bidding anyway:)

And just like that, I have June's phone number.

I immediately save it in my phone and then get ready to shoot off my reply when another text comes through.

> JUNE BUG: But for real, I'll be there. But I plan on eating all of Ryan's dessert so he doesn't get any.

I pull up out front of Stacy's house and notice June's Jeep already in the driveway. I take a deep breath because I feel something close to butterflies in my stomach, though I refuse to call them that because it's got to be the most emasculating feeling to claim.

I get out and slam my rental car's door a little too hard. I can't help it, though. As hard as I'm trying to play it cool, all my actions are coming out aggressive and choppy. I'm a tightly wound rubber band, and I'm ready to snap.

After pulling a bottle of wine from the back seat, I walk up the nicely manicured sidewalk and ring the doorbell on Stacy's little cookie-cutter cottage. There's a welcome mat that says *Love lives here*. I read it while I wait for the door to open and throw up a little in my mouth. Somehow, I know that if June and I were a couple, she would shoot me dead in my tracks before she ever let me close to a house with a welcome mat like that.

"Ryan!" says Logan with an odd smile when the door opens. His eyes are wide, and his lips are tight like he's trying to tell me something. Someone teach this man the art of discretion. "Come on in. *Everyone* is in the kitchen." He says that about 75 percent too loud as I pass by him.

I glance back at Logan with a look of suspicion—suspicion that he might have lost his mind in all this wedding planning—and then I head for the kitchen.

I hear June's voice before I see her, and a big wild smile pulls at my mouth. My feet move a little faster, and when I realize I'm showing the same level of excitement as a puppy going somewhere new, I make myself slow the hell down. I round the corner into the kitchen, and my smile falls.

There's a random dude standing near June. He's staring at her even though June is giving all her attention to Stacy, who is stirring a pot on the stove. Dude's got dark-brown hair and a jawline that could be used for measuring perfect right angles, and I immediately decide his brain is the size of a pea. I set the wine bottle down on the counter so firmly I'm surprised it doesn't break. I'm a grumpy toddler, angry and breaking things because I was promised a cookie and I've been given a piece of broccoli instead.

Everyone startles at the sound and whirls their heads toward me. I smirk and say, "Hi," but I'm only looking at June.

Her green eyes briefly take me in from head to toe before she seems to remember something and latches onto the guy beside her. She weaves her arm through his and then around his waist to tuck herself in closer to him, turning a coy smile to me. "Glad you could make it, Ryan. This is Carter."

I don't look at Carter because he's irrelevant to me. I'm fixed on June, and her eyes are glittering at me—taunting. And then it hits me. I know what's happening here. She's bringing back the oldest play in the book. *My* play that I ran too many times to count. She's intentionally breaking the rules and bringing a date to our foursome *friends dinner.* So now I'm the odd man out. It's retaliation at its finest.

I smile, letting the original sting I felt roll right off my back. June is striking back. She's trying to get under my skin.

You know why? Because she likes me.

CHAPTER 11

June

"Well, isn't this cozy," says Stacy once we are all seated around the dining room table. She's not happy with me. She really wanted tonight to be the *friends dinner* we never had in high school. Just four grown adult friends, sitting around the table, eating and laughing, and swapping stories of where life has taken us over the years. But I rained on her parade by bringing Carter tonight. I couldn't resist.

I can't tell you how many times Ryan did this to me in high school. It should feel good to return the favor now. But no, it doesn't, because he doesn't seem like he's affected by it one tiny bit. Is it too much to ask for a little scowl? One itty-bitty jaw clench?

Ryan is Mr. Sunshine, leaning back in his chair and smiling at me and Carter like we just tied the knot, and he can't wait to throw the rice.

"So cozy," I say, scooting a little closer to Carter's side and bumping my shoulder against his. Am I using him? A little. But in all fairness, I *told* him ahead of time that I would be using him tonight. *Plus,* he's getting a free meal out of it. So that's sweet, right?

"How long have you two been seeing each other?" asks Ryan with a suspiciously cordial voice from across the table.

"First date, actually," Carter chimes in, and I want to pinch him under the table to remind him to stick to the script.

"Oh, but we've had our eye on each other for a while now."

Ryan lifts his brows with a delighted smile. "Really? How sweet. Where did you meet?"

"The gym. Stacy, can you pass the rolls?" I ask, adding an extra layer of butter to my smile so it matches Ryan's.

"Ah, where all true love blossoms," he says, and I resist letting my face fall into a scowl.

And so dinner proceeds in exactly this way for the rest of the meal. I don't think anyone is afforded the opportunity to speak because Ryan and I continue to wield our swords across the table, hoping the other will lose steam. I reach for the salt, but he picks it up first so that *he* can be the one to give it to me. He goes for the wine, but I snatch it up first and fill my glass to the brim, taking the last of it. (P.S. Stacy's glare is really scary.)

Ryan is relentless, though, continuing to badger Carter and me with questions about our budding relationship and suggesting vacation spots we should try out. WE GET IT, RYAN. YOU KNOW IT'S A SHAM.

But I don't give in. No way. I'm in charge of this rodeo, so I venture a step further and lean over to lay my head on Carter's shoulder. Now I'm fluttering my lashes up at him as he tells us about his job at the marketing firm, and I hate myself so much it's startling. It's like my spirit slips out of my skin, and for a solid minute, I'm hovering above my own body, watching myself pet Carter and wishing I could pull my own hair to make it stop. My scheme isn't even working. Ryan is not annoyed. He's still smiling. He's still staring at me. And he is still the most attractive man I've ever seen.

My soul zooms back down into my body when I see my phone light up on the table with a text.

MR. DARCY: Why don't you just shove your tongue down his throat?

I hurry and rip my phone off the table before Carter has a chance to see the text. I look up and find Ryan's dark pools searing me. He lifts a taunting brow, and for a split second, I think that maybe I do see a little jealousy there. I glance quickly around the table and confirm that Stacy and Logan are engrossed in Carter's monologue about his boring job.

JUNE: Don't text me.
MR. DARCY: That's fine. I was just trying to see if you saved my number in your phone, anyway.

I immediately flip my phone over like *that* will keep Ryan from seeing the truth. But my phone buzzes again, and I can't help but look.

MR. DARCY: Don't bother hiding it. I already saw that you saved my number. Want to get out of here with me?

Goodness. Has Stacy always kept it so hot in her house? It's a furnace in here. I'm about to spontaneously combust, and no, it doesn't have anything to do with Ryan's texts. Clearly, her AC is broken.

I quickly pocket my phone and shoot up from the table. I guess I did it a little too forcefully, because everyone's eyes fly to me, wide and alarmed. I smile softly and excuse myself to go get a little more ice for my water, aka stick my face inside the freezer. Part of me thinks that Ryan will follow me, and a big part of me hopes for it. Why? I shouldn't be feeling this way.

In the kitchen, I stew. Anger is bubbling inside me, and I'm annoyed that no matter what I do, Ryan still has the upper hand. I pace circles like an MMA wrestler waiting for an opponent to step into the ring. Why is he doing all this? He's going to be leaving in less than a week.

Ryan was always a wrecking ball in my life, and it appears that nothing has changed. My skin sizzles when he looks at me. My stomach turns a hundred flips when he touches me. And even though I'm trying desperately to push down the hope I feel growing, I can't seem to smother it.

I wanted Ryan to like me in high school. I wanted him to want me at the bachelorette party. I wanted to dangle a kiss in front of him like a dog bone on a string. And now, it feels like I've gotten my wish. *Poof.* My fairy godmother is somewhere in the world, waving her wand and making all my dreams come true. Now, I just want her to undo it.

Sorry, oops, wrong wish. You thought I said please make Ryan want me? What I said was, Ryan GOSLING. Honest mistake, it's fine. I'll wait while you beam him down for me.

The truth is, I'm scared to death of Ryan Henderson. He's my kryptonite. An arrow that shoots straight to my heart and never misses. I'm too wounded to withstand any hits from him. He'll be gone in a week, and if I let myself fall for him completely, he will crack my heart wide open. It will never seal back together. It's why I have my one-date rule. It's why I pour myself into my work. The game of life is easier when I'm the one moving all the pieces.

After spending a minute gathering my wits, I go back into the dining room and take my seat. Carter smiles his pretty Beach Boys smile at me while finishing up whatever conversation he was having with Logan, and I smile back absentmindedly, because I'm still a little focused on the fact that Ryan was trying to get me to bail on this dinner and go somewhere with him.

". . . Yeah, that movie looks great. Maybe I'll take June to see it this weekend. What do you think, June?"

"Hmm?" I look up, pausing my superfun game of pushing the steak bites back and forth across my plate and dreaming of what Ryan and I would be doing if we weren't here. "Oh, yeah. Sure."

Carter smiles again and reaches under the table to squeeze my knee.

I suddenly wonder what I just agreed to. There's no time to dissect it, though, because apparently my date is a Chatty Cathy and is now driving the conversation across the table.

"So, Ryan, you live in Chicago?" Carter asks, being a better friend at this dinner than I am. I've gone dead silent. Chewing this steak is my only objective.

"I do." Ryan's curt tone has me looking up. His dark eyes are stormy, hiding below his furrowed brows—smirk nowhere to be found.

"And you're a chef?"

"Yep."

"That's awesome. I can barely make ramen noodle soup."

"Congrats?"

Whoa! Attitude alert.

Logan senses it, too, because he clears his throat and asks Ryan to help him clear the plates. Stacy takes the opportunity to tell us why she really brought us here. She lays out a blueprint of the seating chart for the reception. Her hands unroll the paper and smooth out the edges, because actually, she has lured us here under false pretenses of a friends dinner when, really, she only needs help writing out name tags for the reception place settings. *Stacy, you dirty little con artist.* I feel a tiny bit guilty about forcing Carter into this, but he's a good sport and assures me he doesn't mind.

After an hour, I can't take the guilt anymore and tell Carter he can head out. I'll make Stacy drive me back home since she now owes me a million favors for all she's put me through over the past few days. Carter hesitates like any nice guy would but eventually gives in, and I walk him out the door. We reach that awkward moment on a first date (if you can really call this a date) where we decide if we should kiss or not. Part of me wonders if Ryan is watching, and if so, maybe I should lay a big one on Carter.

But I don't know . . . my heart's not in it anymore. Ryan's bad mood soured mine, and now I just kinda want to shoo Carter off as quickly as possible. I settle for letting him kiss me on the cheek and apologize for such a strange evening. Once he drives off, I go back in the house and shut the door. That's that. Another man exits my life.

I turn around and find Ryan standing in the living room. He doesn't look happy, and his already imposing figure somehow feels even bigger. Up until this point, Ryan has been smooth and congenial. Like nothing I could ever say or do would truly fluster him.

He looks flustered now, though.

His scowl is so angry it blisters my skin and pins me to the door at my back. He lifts a brow. His face says, *Well?*

I lift one brow to mirror his.

He takes a step, and so do I.

"Are you two about to duel?" Logan asks from the threshold of the kitchen.

"Go away, Logan," Ryan all but growls.

"No way. In fact, don't move. Let me go get my phone so I can film this." Logan rushes off, and Ryan and I are left here, fighting about I don't know what. We're always fighting about something, though, so it doesn't really matter.

"So . . . you got me back," he says, breaking the silence first. One point for me. "Brought a date to friends dinner." I don't answer. Another point. He steps closer, and a sad smirk touches the corner of his mouth. "How do you feel? I'm guessing not as great as you hoped."

I clear my throat so my words will dislodge. "Why do you say that?"

"Because that's always how I felt after I brought some random girl to our friends dinners. Every single time, my only motive was to make you jealous. But you never were."

I stay quiet still because my emotions are teetering. He's standing there and laying his heart on the line, and I'm on mute. I don't know how I want all this to end. If I stay quiet, nothing is final. Nothing is decided.

"Does he get a second date?" asks Ryan. And when my brows pinch together, he says, "Yeah, I know about your rule. Logan told me." Freaking Logan. "And I want to know if, after five years, *Carter the marketer* gets a second date with you?"

Is that why his mood crashed? My stomach flutters. He's angry because I might be into someone else?

I could string him along. He very clearly is annoyed by the idea of me breaking my rule for Carter, and it's the perfect way to gain an extra point in our game. But I can't. For some reason, I don't want another point. "No. I don't want to go out with him again."

Ryan's face softens, and I think I hear him let out a relieved breath. "Good." He comes closer, and the air ripples between us.

I hold his gaze, lifting my chin. "Good."

He swallows, and I watch his Adam's apple go up and down. "I saw that you moved your name away from mine on the seating chart," he says, and I resist the urge to smile. "I moved it back."

My smile drops even though something in my stomach flutters wildly.

As much as I didn't want it to, his declaration this morning does change things. Ryan has a hold on me, and I'm scared to let him see it. I'm worried I'll be tempted to break my rule for him. But maybe I won't have to. Maybe he'll leave without saying goodbye after the wedding, and that will be the end of us forever. I'll go back to my life of casual dating and keeping busy, so I don't sit still long enough to feel my loneliness. *A girl can only hope.*

"Okay, I got it!" says Logan, rushing back in the room, slightly out of breath. "I had to wrestle it from Stacy because she wanted me to leave you two alone, but I won." He angles his phone at us and must click the record button the second Ryan and I smile at each other, because he just groans and lowers the phone. "That was definitely not worth Stacy's pinches."

Later that night, after I'm tucked into bed and tossing and turning for half an hour, I sit up and grab my phone. Before I have time to think it over, I open up my text chat with Ryan and send him a message that I'm sure I'll regret in the morning.

JUNE: I was always jealous.

And then I literally toss my phone to the other side of the room and bury myself under the covers as if that's going to protect me from Ryan Henderson.

CHAPTER 12

June

How do I put this mildly?

I'd rather jab a pencil in my ear over and over than co-own Darlin' Donuts with the woman sitting across from me.

". . . And the color scheme is all wrong," Heather (the woman naïvely thinking she is nailing this interview) continues after a solid ten minutes of other insults about our bakery. "I think we would do better to market to the corporate world. Sleek and clean-cut, if you will. It wouldn't be that difficult to change your colors over to black and gray. We could get rid of this old bar"—she's referring to the gorgeous antique wooden countertop that was used in a French patisserie in the early 1900s we practically stole from an auction—"and replace it with something metal and clean. IKEA has affordable alternatives."

Deep breath.

"But . . . our whole brand is a crossover between Charleston's old southern-money roots and modern-day trends."

"Exactly," she says, making absolutely no sense and giving me a pitying smile. She feels so bad that I don't see the glaring problems with my bakery, which was featured in *Vogue* as a must-visit attraction in Charleston. "But I think with a little facelift, we can probably do pretty well for ourselves here." *Oh, honey.*

Let this be a lesson for anyone trying to get a job: Do your research before you interview.

"Well, thanks for coming, Heather," I say, concluding the meeting early. "Don't forget to grab a Slow as Molasses donut on your way out."

Stacy hides a snicker behind her hand.

I glare at her. *This is all your fault.*

The moment the door closes behind Heather, I let out a puff of air and sink back against the counter. "Well, she's a no go."

"Really? I thought she was charming." Stacy's voice sounds too innocent.

"Did you pick someone terrible on purpose? You're like a little kid in an inspirational movie, trying to sabotage the sale so I learn my valuable lesson."

Stacy shakes her head and smiles while popping a donut hole into her mouth. The fact that she's not denying my accusation is telling. "I should really be worried about fitting into my expensive dress on Saturday, but I can't bring myself to care. Is that a bad sign?"

Okay, I see. We're going to change the subject now because I was dead-on with my sabotage remark.

"I think it means that you're in a really good place and you're not stressing about the little things. You're marrying your *second* best friend in a few days and it shows."

She smiles softly, and I still find it ridiculously sweet how happy she looks when she thinks about Logan. "Plus even if I outgrow the dress, I think I could wear yoga pants and a stained T-shirt and Logan would still be happy to marry me."

"He'd probably like it better than the dress. Your butt looks great in yoga pants."

She laughs. "So I should just return the dress, right?"

I shrug. "It won't stay on you very long anyway."

We go back and forth like this for a few minutes, and I don't let myself give in once to the sadness I feel under our laughter. I'm going to miss her more than anything. She's my girl. My person. When she's gone, who will make dirty jokes with me?

Her mind follows the same track as mine, because after a minute, her face softens, and she comes over to cup my face dramatically, making my lips pooch out. It's silly. But I love that even in the serious moments of life, she still makes me laugh. "We're not saying goodbye forever. We will talk every day on the phone. Make lots of visits. Everything is going to be fine; I promise." Why don't I believe her?

Stacy's eyes then catch on something over my shoulder, and she makes a *hmm* noise. "You're not going to like what I see out that window."

I follow her gaze over my shoulder, and my heart shoots up into my throat. Crossing the street and heading straight for our shop is Ryan. He's wearing a pair of cargo joggers with black Nikes and a zip-up hoodie. He has the same baseball hat on from the other day, but it's sitting backward on his head, and honestly, I'm so attracted to him it hurts.

Suddenly, I remember the text I sent him last night, and I wonder if I can pack my bags and move to Mexico before he finishes crossing the street. No? Fine. I'll do the next best thing.

I hop up on the counter and slide across to the other side and then race to the front door of the shop just as Ryan is reaching out for the handle. I twist the lock and fling the Open sign around, so now the shop is officially Closed.

I look through the glass up into Ryan's dark smirking eyes and shrug my shoulders innocently. *So sorry, you just missed us!*

"Funny," he says through the glass. "Open up."

I cup my hand around my ear and squint like I can't hear him through the glass. I'm a mime inside a box, and I'm just as surprised by these glass walls as he is. I mouth *Can't hear you* and then point to the sign again.

It's childish, I know. But I don't want him to come in here. This is *my* special place in life, and I'm proud of it. I'm just a little afraid that if I let Ryan Henderson—world-renowned chef—through my door, my confidence bubble will pop. What's a donut shop compared to all he's accomplished?

Ryan puts his hands in his pockets, and his shoulders twitch like he's making himself comfortable. He'll stand there all day, apparently. And a second later, when a woman and her two children walk up to the door, he smiles, and his devil horns pop out. I see a vague resemblance to the boy I went to high school with.

"I'm sorry, ma'am. They're closed," he says with a sunny smile that doesn't fit the news he's delivering.

Her brows furrow, and she looks at the store hours listed on the glass. "Says they're open until three o'clock."

"Oh, we are!" I say through the door.

"Not so soundproof anymore, is it?" Ryan says from where he stands beside the woman. I scowl at him before unlocking the door and cracking it open for the woman and her children to come in. Once they are inside, I hurry to shut it before Ryan can weasel his way in. But he anticipates my move and wedges his foot in the crack.

I will break his foot; don't think I won't.

He puts his baseball-glove-size hand on the glass and opens the door even though I'm using all my strength to push against it. I'm just a little gnat. He swats me away with a single push.

"You're being ridiculous," he says after he makes it inside.

"Takes one to know one." I'm so mature I should win an award.

"Nice. Why are you so jumpy?" he asks, looking down at me and making my skin flush.

I don't have an answer to his question, though. At least not one I'm willing to voice. *You turn me inside out.*

He shoves his hands back into his pockets and gives a chin lift to Stacy, who is waving at him from behind the bar while she waits for the mom and her kids to make up their minds. "Hey, Stacy. This place looks awesome."

She beams back at him. "It's all June! She's the mastermind behind it all."

I don't like the way the spotlight suddenly shifts to me. It feels too bright.

"Ha! Mastermind. *Pshhhh,* no. Barely even." Basically, I just took a bunch of words from thin air and strung them together until it felt like a real sentence.

Ryan shifts his eyes to me, amusement and concern mingling in them. "I'm gonna look around now. Do I need to strap you to that booth while I do, or are you going to be okay walking with me?"

His taunts bring me back to life, and I jump in front of him and spread my arms in a mom-bear-protecting-her-cub pose. "This is my shop. You're not going anywhere in it without me."

"Good. Show me the kitchen."

See, here's the thing. I shouldn't find that statement ominous and sexy. But he's a chef. Like, a freaking good one. So that sentence coming out of his mouth feels like he's just told me, *Show me the bedroom.*

My knees feel like Play-Doh, but I do an admirable job of walking as I lead Ryan back to the kitchen. He walks too close to me, though. Stacy watches us, and she chuckles, shaking her head at me because, apparently, I look like I am actually walking him back to my bedroom. I push through the swinging door that leads to our little kitchen and then hold my hands out in front of me. "Here it is. Where the magic happens." I cringe at my word choice.

Ryan looks over his shoulder with a tilted grin and then stalks around my kitchen like the king of the jungle inspecting another lion's pride. I try to look at the space through his eyes, and just as I feared, it doesn't look very impressive. Tall metal shelves hold clear containers of various ingredients and dough starters. A long silver worktable sits in the middle of the room, sprinkled with flour from our morning of rolling out donuts. I have two industrial-size mixers, lots of extra-large mixing bowls, and several drying carts for after we finish icing the donuts. It's all pretty standard, and I wonder if Ryan thinks it's small fries compared to his prestigious big-city kitchen.

He loops around the worktable, and I don't realize I've been lost in my thoughts until he stops in front of me. "Why do you look so sad?"

"Hmm? I'm not."

He ignores my protest. "Do you not like having me in here?"

"I—I don't know. I guess I'm still getting used to this new version of you."

"What version is that?"

I lean back and grip the counter behind me, hoping to look at ease and not like I'm using the counter to help hold myself up—which is exactly what I'm using it for. "The one that doesn't hate me."

"You mean the one that's into you?" I jerk my gaze up to his. I'm so used to Ryan playing games with me; honesty is just not something I was expecting.

Ryan is into me? As in currently. Not past tense? I suspected it. But there's a difference between suspecting and knowing.

He smiles, and I'm happy to see he still has the same dimple in his right cheek. "Let's talk hypothetical for a second."

"Okay."

"What if I wanted to take you on a date?"

So, on a completely unrelated note to what Ryan just said, what's a healthy heart rate? I'm pretty sure mine is tipping over into cardiac arrest right now. "I would remind you that you are going back to Chicago after the wedding."

"Forget Chicago."

"But it's where you live."

He steps closer, the tips of our shoes touching. "You're bad at hypothetical."

He's too close, and I need some air. I slip away from him and move to the other side of the worktable, pulling my hair up into a bun to let some airflow onto my neck. He turns around slowly and watches, amused. I roll up my sleeves and wash my hands before pulling down a tub of dough and dumping it out onto the counter, ignoring the fact that Ryan's eyes never stray from me.

"Fine. Hypothetically, I would say sure. What would one date hurt?" I say after so much time that he probably thought I had given up on the topic altogether.

"You'd hold me to your one-date rule?"

I pause rolling the dough and look up at him. "I hold everyone to it."

"Forever? You'll never go out with someone past that first date ever again?"

He's not the first person to ask me this. That's why I'm able to answer without thinking. "Not unless that first date is life-changing. Like really, *truly* something, and I know that he's the man I want to spend forever with."

His eyes narrow ever so slightly, and then he nods slowly. "Noted. All right, show me how to do this."

"What?" I ask, pulling my brows together. I guess it really was just a hypothetical, and he's not really going to ask me out. I had nothing to worry about. Super. Wonderful. Perfect.

He unzips his hoodie and hangs it up on a peg beside the kitchen door. And SHOOT, his arms look good when he moves. He has those amazing man veins that wrap around his biceps all the way down to his fingers. And that shirt of his is hugging his every muscle in a way that makes me consider suggesting he take it off so he doesn't get any flour on it. Because, you know, flour is sooooo messy. And who wants to go through all the trouble of dust, dust, dusting it off at the end of the day. See? So impractical. *Strip that shirt off, buddy.*

Ryan turns around and catches me ogling him. "You done?" he asks in a sexy voice that instinctively makes me clear my throat. It's fine, though. I'm so good with all my resolves. So what if Ryan is into me? I don't care. Not one bit.

I narrow my eyes at him and aim my rolling pin at his smug face. "Listen up, Chef. You're in my kitchen now. Insubordinate comments come with consequences."

He lifts a brow.

"Dish duty." I jerk my head toward the sink full of sticky mixing bowls.

I watch warily as Ryan rounds the worktable to come stand on my side, nearly hip to hip with me. I don't want to smile. I really don't, but it's hard. I'm losing my fight against Ryan. I like him near me. I want him near me. And over the next hour, as we work side by side, rolling and cutting dough and flirting with flour like a cheesy Hallmark movie, I feel my heart physically crack a little.

It's both painful and healing at the same time.

Once we both finish and wash up, I try to walk past Ryan to leave the kitchen, but he catches my arm. I stop and look up at him. He smiles softly, making my nerves twist and zing. "Thanks for letting me see this today."

"I didn't really have a choice, did I?" I say, going for a teasing tone, but instead, it comes out breathy and oh-so small.

His thumb glides up and down my arm, and his grin hitches. "Not really, no."

We stand here, frozen in this limbo between what we were and what we could be. He inches closer, and my heart knocks painfully against my chest. I'm worried he can see it trying to burst out of my skin.

"I wish I'd come back sooner," he says as his calloused fingers glide down my arm to rest on my wrist. I look down and wish his fingers would fall to lace with mine, but I can see that he's waiting for me to make the next move.

I fill my lungs with air and look up to him, contemplating letting the truth out for once, when the door to the kitchen flies open.

I jump a mile away from Ryan and pretend to wipe down the counter with the closest rag I can find . . . which is actually my apron. *Nothing polishes quite like stiff canvas!*

My show goes unnoticed, though, because Stacy is oblivious as she rushes in and grabs a tray of fresh donuts from the drying rack. "Are you coming back out?! I think a bus of tourists just unloaded or something, because the rush is wild out there. Grab another tray of Just Peachy on your way out."

And then she's gone, and the kitchen door swings shut.

"Smooth," says Ryan with a taunting grin as he nods to the counter I'm still furiously scrubbing. "She's gone, so I think you can stop polishing." He's loving my discomfort as he moseys over to the coatrack, pulls his hoodie down from the wall, and slides his sexy arms into it. "Well, this was fun, June Bug. Tell you what, since you showed me yours, next time, I'll show you mine."

He taps the wall with his hand on the way out the kitchen door and leaves me wishing I could hate him for that cheesy closing line instead of melting on the floor like I am.

CHAPTER 13

Ryan

"How's the new junior chef working out?" I ask Nia, my sous-chef back in Chicago. She's been running everything while I'm away, and normally, I wouldn't be able to sleep at night, worrying about all the ways my kitchen will be run into the ground while I'm gone, but with her in charge, I know I have nothing to worry about.

"Slow. But he's learning."

"How many times have you made him cry?"

"Only three."

I smile and switch my cellphone from the car speaker back to my phone as I pull up out front of June's house on Friday morning. "Well, that's an improvement."

I cut the engine and look out my window. June's not expecting me, so I don't think she'll be too happy to see my face. I've realized that she likes to be 100 percent in control of every aspect of her life. Which is why I make it my life's mission to uproot her finely tuned plans.

"You're coming back Sunday night, right?" Nia asks as I open my car door and get out.

I pause, taking in June's white bungalow and teal front door. The wooden porch seat looks lonely. Sure, it has a sunshine-yellow pillow on it, making the whole scene look happy, but when I picture June sitting in that chair all by herself, I get the urge to drive straight to Home Depot and pick up another matching one to plop down right beside hers. I'll put a dark-blue pillow on it. It'll be my pillow.

I make a half-hearted grunt noise into the phone. "Yeah, Sunday."

Nia laughs, misinterpreting the cause of my disgruntled sound. "I feel ya. Sunday is too many days away when you're ready to get back to your kitchen. Don't worry, though; I won't let it burn down."

Yeah, 'cause that's really my problem: wanting to get back sooner.

I think if Nia called me tomorrow and said, *So sorry, but I accidentally spilled gasoline all over the restaurant and then lit it up like the Fourth of July,* I would only feel relief. What does that say about me?

Just then, movement catches my eye, and I see June's front door open. She doesn't see me across the street when she tiptoes out with bare feet to grab a package off the front porch. It's only about fifty-five degrees outside, and her spaghetti-strap tank top and PJ shorts provide little in the way of warmth, so she crosses her arms across her chest and shuffles her feet quickly to retrieve the box by the stairs.

June is all curves, tan skin, and wild brown hair. She's real and soft, and suddenly, I want to wrap a big parka jacket around her because I don't want anyone else looking at her. *Mine.* Not sure when I became the jealous type, but here we are.

"Nia, I'll call you back," I say, keeping my eyes on June and ending the call before she replies. She's going to add extra salt to my famous hollandaise sauce because she hates when I hang up on her like that.

June must have heard my voice, because when her hands land on the box, her eyes shoot up to me. And then she frowns, those brows pulling so tightly together they are practically touching. I smile and cross the street.

She backs toward her door, saying, "No, no, no! Why do you keep showing up at my house at the crack of dawn?"

"We need to go to the store to get the food for tonight. But, June"—I'm rushing up the front steps to catch her—"I swear, if you shut another door in my face . . ."

"Go to the store without me, Ryan!" She turns around quickly before I can look at her face.

June is the physical embodiment of Katy Perry's song where I'm concerned. Hot and then cold. She's telling me to get lost, but she leaves the door wide open after she storms inside. One minute she seems into me, texting me she was jealous of the girls I'd bring around in high school, and the next, she's running away like I'm coming at her with fangs bared.

"I don't want to go to the store without you," I say, stepping through the front door and closing it behind me.

She turns around again and tries to dart to her room, but my voice stops her. "June! Wait. *Please.*" She slowly turns to face me, but zeroes in on the floor. Apparently, it's the most interesting floor in the world, because she won't turn her attention from it. "Look at me, June."

"No."

"Why? I don't get why you're so skittish around me sometimes." I understand that there used to be bad blood between us, but that's gone now, and I know it. We had a good time making donuts together on Wednesday. She smiled. We flirted. There's a different reason she's so hot and cold.

"Because you're always showing up when I don't want you to. Would it have killed you to give me even just a five-minute warning?"

"Surprise is the spice of life."

She scoffs at my joke. "I disagree." Now she's shrinking—physically shrinking—under my gaze. Her shoulders are slumping in, and she's crossing her arms and tucking her chin down. It's so opposite from the strong June I know. "Are we done with this chat? Because I need to go."

"Go where?"

"I don't know, Cabo?"

"June."

She finally looks at me—or rather, lets me look at her. Her eyes are literal daggers. "I just want to go put my makeup on, okay? Quit being such a jerk all the time."

"I'm being a jerk? By trying to get you to look in my eyes instead of the floor?"

"You can clearly tell I don't want to, and you're pushing it! So yeah, that makes you a jerk."

She stomps away, and I'm not too proud of it, but my eyes catch on her perfect butt for three full seconds before I go after her. Tiny pictures of Nick Lachey are printed all over her shorts, and he's never looked so hot to me. "You don't need makeup."

A mirthless laugh escapes her. "Gosh, I hate hearing lines like that from men. They're so untrue. You heard it in a romance movie, so you're repeating it."

"Not true. Stop walking for a second," I say, but she doesn't even slow a bit. I'm forced to jog to catch up with her as she races through her room toward her bathroom.

"Ughhh, Ryan, you're like an annoying puppy following me around everywhere!"

"What's gotten into you since Wednesday? I thought we were getting along better."

She puts her hands over her face and sounds way more frustrated with me than the situation warrants. "Ryan, I swear to Dolly Parton that if you do not get out of my bathroom right now, I will burn you with my curling iron."

"That's it." And that's the last thing I say before I scoop her up in my arms. She squeals as I carry her into the walk-in shower.

"What the hell are you doing?! Put me down!"

I get us both in the shower and position us under the showerhead, one hand on the nozzle. "Tell me why you're being so rude or else I blast us both with cold water."

I don't particularly want to douse myself in icy water, but I will if I have to. I have a feeling that everyone in June's life lets her hide away, keep all her secrets pinned up inside so she can hurt privately. Not me. I'm not as nice as them.

"You've lost your mind," she says, but she's not squirming anymore.

"Tell me, or we both freeze."

Her green eyes bounce up to mine, and I see her stubbornness lurking like a shield. She lifts her chin and wraps her arm more firmly around my neck like she's settling in for battle. "Do it. I'm not afraid of a little cold water. And there's nothing to tell. I'm just annoyed that you keep showing up as if I want you around!"

I gave her a chance. I really did.

I wouldn't be surprised if the neighbors call the cops from the scream that June releases when the ice water hits her skin. Unfortunately, she's not the only one getting punished, because I'm the one standing under it holding her.

"Okay, you doused me! Now, turn it off!" She's reaching for the faucet, so I turn us around so she can't reach it. Except—*super*—now I'm taking the brunt of the spray.

"Not until you tell me the truth."

"You're infuriating." She beats my chest as water drips down both of our faces. She's getting heavy, and I realize that my grip on her is soft enough that if she wanted to, she could easily escape. But I don't think she does. In fact, one of her arms is still wrapped tightly around my neck. She's not going anywhere, and part of me wonders if she's hanging on because she wants me to get the truth out of her.

"Please just tell me, June. What happened? I want to know." I look at her eyes and notice that it's not just water rolling down June's face.

Her body sags against me. The final thread of her resistance toward me snaps. "My ex posted on Instagram this morning that he's getting married. I guess it . . . triggered some old wounds. Are you happy now?"

I cut the water off and slowly set her feet on the ground, expecting her to bolt, but she doesn't. We are both freezing, our bodies shaking and miserable, but neither of us moves. Her hair is wet and clinging to her face, much like her clothes are clinging to her body, but I don't look. Because that's not why I pulled us in here.

"Do you miss him?" I ask, but I'm not sure I actually want to hear the answer.

"No. I miss who I was *before* him, though." She pauses, but I get the feeling that she's not done, so I stay quiet. June chews the side of her lip, wrestling with something. She looks torn between the urge to run or stay. She folds her arms up tightly in front of her, and her knuckles turn white as she grips her arms. Finally, she shifts on her feet, and her eyes shoot up to mine. They are giant green pools of tears. "Ryan . . . I . . . I called off the wedding because"—another agonizing pause—"he cheated on me."

Those words act as a detonator in my mind. The name BEN flashes before my eyes, and suddenly, my target is set. I hate this guy.

And I hate him even more when June continues: "And do you

know what happened after I called him out for it and broke off our engagement? He sighed with relief. He *audibly* sighed, and then he said it was probably for the best because . . ." She looks down at her folded arms, shame coloring her expression. "Because he wasn't even attracted to me anymore. Said I'd gotten too comfortable around him."

And there it is. The truth. It sets all the pieces into place, and suddenly, who June is now makes more sense to me. My heart splits for her.

I rub my hands up and down her arms to warm her. She looks at me with water clinging to her eyelashes and her cheeks rosy from the freezing water. And then she shakes her head. "No, don't look at me like that."

"Like what?"

"Pity. I feel small enough for letting his comment affect me like this for so long, I don't need a look of pity too. I mean, *so what*? He didn't like my body anymore. I wasn't pretty enough to attract him anymore. Who cares, right?" I can see that she's trying to strap that armor of hers back on, but I won't let her. Not yet.

I pull her tightly to my chest. "No. You didn't deserve that from him. From anyone. And it's okay to admit he hurt you, June."

She surprises me by melting into me and resting her face on my chest, curling her hands up between us so that I'm fully holding her. I feel her shoulders shake with more tears. "The girl he's marrying now is a blonde and, like, six feet tall."

What June means is, *she's exactly the opposite of me*. There's so much insecurity in her voice, and I can hear the unspoken question of *What does she have that I don't?*

I hold her a little tighter and kiss the top of her head as I try to find the right words. "I could bash on that woman with you right now if that's what you want. I could also list a hundred different ways I think you and your body are perfect. I could tell you that I check you out from head to toe every time you walk away from me, and that, last night, I had a dream about you that would definitely make you blush." She chuckles against me. "But I think what you need is to hear that your ex was a self-serving ass. You're beautiful, June. His words had nothing to do with you and everything to do with his teeny-tiny—"

"Ryan!"

I laugh and squeeze her. "He was a jerk. End of story. It was wrong of him to cheat on you and even worse to make it seem like you were to blame for it. It's not your fault he cheated. It's his loss." I look down and push some of the hair clinging to her face back behind her ear. "But I can't say I'm not glad he's out of the picture."

Her emerald eyes look up at me from beneath her lashes, and for a split second, I think she's going to give in to me. That her heart will melt right into my hands. I hold my breath and look down at her lips. Just as I do, I see her beautiful mouth frown. "I'm not ready yet, Ryan."

"That's okay," I say gently.

She pulls out of my arms softly this time and walks out of the shower. She grabs a towel from the hook beside the shower and wraps herself in it before tossing another over to me. Telling me to hand my wet clothes to her after she leaves, June steps out of the bathroom and closes the door.

As I spend the next five minutes trying to wring the water out of my clothes, I can't shake the feeling that we're running out of time. She's not ready yet, and I've got a life to get back to in Chicago soon. What if when she's ready, it's too late? I'm not asking for marriage or a pledge of her heart. I just want a chance. A chance to see if we are as good together as I think we'll be.

A few minutes later, I emerge from the bathroom with my wet clothes in my hand and the towel wrapped around my waist. I open the bathroom door at the exact moment that she steps, fully dressed, out of her closet. Her eyes land on me, widen to the size of saucers, and her lips part.

She scans me up and down like she's trying to memorize every bit because she plans to paint a portrait of my body later. I clear my throat, trying so hard to keep the cocky smile off my face, but it's useless. She's practically drooling, and I've never been happier.

"Hey, so . . . I'm sorry I pulled you into the shower. Probably wasn't the best way to go about getting information from you."

"Uh-huh." She sounds a million miles away. She couldn't care less about the shower fiasco right now.

I get a little closer and hold up my clothes. "You said for me to give you my wet clothes."

I watch her swallow before her eyes finally make their way back up to mine. She gives me a tilted smile and shakes her head slowly with narrowed eyes. "You play dirty, Henderson."

I can't help but laugh at the look on her face. "What are you talking about?"

"I tell you I'm not ready for whatever it is you're wanting yet, and then you parade your rock-hard body around my house in the buff? Just rude."

"I'm not in the buff. I'm wearing a towel. And you're not exactly turning away to give me privacy."

Her eyes fall to my abdomen again, and then she emits a noise somewhere between a groan and growl and turns to flee the room faster than I've ever seen anyone move. She's *The Flash.*

Once she's out of sight, she yells, "The freaking dryer is down the hall on the right!"

I smile and make my way out of her room when my eyes catch on a tiny piece of yellow paper tucked into the corner of her vanity mirror. It's half hidden behind a picture of her and Stacy, but I recognize it right away. I check the door to make sure June isn't watching before I go pull the paper out of its hiding place.

My stomach clenches when I verify that it's the note I think it is. Seeing it again immediately jolts me back to that day, our tenth-grade year, when I wrote it during homeroom. June had spilled a soda on her white sweater, and everyone teased her endlessly all day. There wasn't any actual bullying, and the teasing was only coming from her friends and boyfriend, but I could still see the humiliation behind her I'm-being-a-good-sport-about-this laughter.

So I passed her this note: *You look cute covered in soda.*

It was the only outright compliment I ever gave her in high school. At the time, I didn't think it meant anything to her. She read it, crumpled it up, and rolled her eyes like she thought I was still just messing with her.

But apparently, it meant more to her than I thought. Enough to smooth it back out and hold on to it all this time.

And now I'm thinking maybe we won't run out of time . . . maybe we'll get it right this time.

CHAPTER 14

June

O h, *Ryan, Ryan, Ryan.*

He thinks he can just waltz around my house in a towel for half an hour—*yes, it took a full freaking thirty minutes for his clothes to dry*—and then I'll be putty in his hands? Begging him for a date? For him to kiss me?

Ha!

He's right.

I'm sitting on the counter after we return from the grocery store, watching Ryan move around my kitchen, trying so hard not to blurt out *just kiss me already*. He's turned on the Black Keys and is humming while he puts produce in the fridge. I can't handle it.

Thoughts of him in that towel with wet hair tousled like every teenage girl's hot-lifeguard fantasy keep flashing in my mind. Do skillets weigh hundreds of pounds? They must for Ryan to have a body as sculpted as he does. His abs are like six perfect shelves. I could store things on them if I needed to.

And his mouth. So *so* perfect. I don't think I've ever considered what makes a mouth perfect before, but Ryan's is the standard. Full but not too full. A nice curve when he smiles that makes his eyes crinkle. Reddish, pinkish, brownish. Gah—I don't even know what that means. It's just good, okay? And I bet those lips would feel sooo good on mine.

When my palms start sweating at the thought of grabbing Ryan and pulling his mouth against mine, I decide it's time to turn my mind to more productive tasks—like aimlessly scrolling through my phone.

I swipe it open and look down, but let's be honest, I'm not really *seeing* what I'm looking at because I've trained my peripherals on the man in my kitchen.

Ryan's voice makes me jump. "So, is there a reason you still follow your ex?"

"Huh?"

I look up in time to see him tilt his head toward my phone—eyes trained on the potato he's chopping. "This morning you said your ex posted about his engagement. I was wondering why you still follow him on Instagram if he hurt you that much?"

"Oh." I set my phone to the side. It wasn't distracting me anyway. "I don't. I just . . ." Oh gosh, I don't want to admit this. To say it's embarrassing is an understatement. But I've already told Ryan something about my life that no one else knows. Might as well get this off my chest too. "I occasionally go check his profile, hoping to see that maybe he's grown a new mole on his face since I last saw him." *Please don't make fun of me.*

He grins. "I get it."

"You do?" He has a quiet smile as he nods.

Chop, chop, chop.

His knife sails over the cutting board, and I get the feeling there's more that he's not saying, so I do a little digging. "You have an ex-girlfriend you stalk on Instagram or something?"

He shakes his head, and his eyes cut to me for a split second before training on the cutting board again. "Not an ex."

I swallow, and my heart races from this new game we're playing. "Hmm . . . interesting. So, it's someone you don't want anyone to know you follow?"

Ryan sets down his knife and walks toward me. My stomach tightens when his gaze fixes on mine before grabbing both my hips and sliding me to the side so he can open the drawer I was blocking and pulls out a ladle. But he's not far enough in his cooking process yet to need a ladle. Busted. He sets the unneeded utensil down beside the cutting board and starts on another potato but doesn't speak.

"So, this mysterious woman. Do you like her?"

"How long do you think this game is going to last? Because I need your help cooking." He doesn't need my help.

Ryan had come up with the most incredible menu for the rehearsal dinner. A Tuscan seared salmon with seasonal vegetables roasted in a red wine sauce and the most decadent chocolate cherry tart for dessert that Stacy immediately vetoed before slapping a worn-out, handwritten recipe into his hand. I've never seen Ryan so dejected as he read over Stacy's desired rehearsal dinner menu: a dish I'd had many times at her mom's house called potato-chipped chicken, old-fashioned mashed potatoes, green beans slathered in butter, and homestyle mac and cheese. I think Ryan wanted to cry. I enjoyed it too much.

"I just want to hear you admit it," I say with a satisfied smirk.

He stops and levels me with a melting smolder. "Admit what?"

Under his attention, my confidence wavers. A minute ago, I was enjoying this game. Now, I see that, in classic Ryan style, he has turned the tables. The spotlight isn't on him anymore. I'm the one who has to say the words out loud that my heart is hoping are true. But they might not be . . . this might all just be in my head.

"Never mind."

"Admit what, June?"

"No, this was silly. Let's move on." I want him to quit looking at me, but he doesn't. I'm angry at myself for pushing this game. I can't take any more hits today, and I've set myself up for embarrassment.

"What do you want me to admit to you?"

You know what? *Fine.* In for a dime, in for a dollar. Here we go.

I pull on my fake courage and meet his blistering stare. "Admit that you've been pining away for me all these years."

The dare floats between us, and the only evidence that he even heard me is when the corner of his mouth lifts the tiniest bit. "June, I've been pining away for you all these years."

His words tip me over. Spin me around. Disorient me until I can't see straight. Ryan's face is serious. He really means what he just said, and his admittance makes my stomach turn inside out. I can't say anything. My tongue is tied up in a neat little bow.

At my silence, he grins and turns back to his work. I should take this opportunity to laugh in his face. I could *finally* win our war. Here and now, I could claim victory and plant a flag in the ground, staking my win. I *should* do that. I don't. "Are you ever going to ask me out?"

I want Ryan to jump or startle at my words, but of course he doesn't. His confidence is what makes him so attractive. "You just told me, about an hour ago, that you're not ready. Something changed?"

Something has definitely changed, but because it feels safer to admit I'm attracted to Ryan than I have feelings for him, I tell a different truth. "Yeah. I saw your abs. It got me thinking that maybe one date won't hurt."

"No, thanks."

"What?" I immediately start picking my shield back up. I should have known better than to think this wasn't all some trick.

He must hear the edge to my voice, because he turns to me and looks me in the eyes. "June, I'm not interested in becoming the next guy in your long string of one and only dates. I like you—I have for a long time—and I'm done hiding it. I want to give us a chance, but one date is not gonna do it for me. So, are you ready to give up your rule?"

Yes.

"No."

He nods but doesn't get upset like most men would. "Okay, then." He takes a deep breath and wipes his hands on a kitchen towel. "Get over here and help me make some mashed potatoes."

Part of me thinks we should keep talking about this. That I should empty my feelings out onto the counter like an adult and tell him I'm scared of him. I'm scared of loving him and him walking away from me. But I can't. The words won't budge.

I slide off the countertop and move to stand beside him as he hands me a big knife that I don't think he would have given me if he knew how few times I've held it before. That fact is clear, though, when I grab hold of the slippery potato and inch the blade through it. *Nice and slow. That's it. Easy does it. ANNNNND one cut complete!*

The knife makes a sound when the blade connects with the cutting board, and I smile, feeling like someone should give me a gold medal. Maybe *Top Chef* is still taking auditions?

"You've got to be kidding me." Ryan's less-than-enthusiastic voice has my head jerking up to look at him.

"What? I did it! Look at that solid cut!"

"I turned a million years old in the process."

Someone likes to exaggerate. "Is speed always your top priority?" I give him a taunting, flirtatious look, but he doesn't take the bait. Still, I see the corner of his mouth twitching. I want to kiss it.

"How do you not know how to use a knife?"

I shrug. "I work with dough all day. Very rarely do I have to use something sharp."

"Okay, well, today you learn." The authority in his voice is doing nothing to lessen his attractiveness.

I'm ready for Ryan to move in close behind me and pick up the knife so he can teach me how to use it. He'll keep his body pressed up next to mine, and his breath will tickle my ear as he shows me how to properly slice a potato. His calloused hand will cover mine, and my whole body will break out in chills from his touch. It will be the sexiest cooking lesson in the world, and we will fog up the windows in my house when he kisses my neck, knife lesson forgotten. He'll probably spin me around and carry me to the couch and—

"June!" He's waving his hand in front of my face, and I blink. "Where'd you go?"

My cheeks flush, and if he notices, he doesn't comment. He's too engrossed in my impending lesson—all business. He holds up his knife and nods for me to do the same. *Super.* I guess I really am getting a lesson in knife work with a gap so wide between our bodies I'd have to stretch just to get our elbows to touch. *How sexy.*

For the next ten minutes, Ryan drones on and on about how the knife should never leave the cutting board, and the blade should rock back and forth, letting me move through the potato faster. Honestly, I'm bored to tears. I couldn't care less about this dang blade. This is nothing like when we were making donuts side by side. Instead, Ryan's brows furrow, and he's serious—joyless.

I pause my practice and look up at him. "You know, I had no idea that you even liked to cook—back in high school, I mean," I say, interrupting his monologue on the various techniques of rocking the blade at different angles.

He freezes, and I see something flash across his eyes. "No? Huh."

"You never mentioned it. Not once."

His attention is back on his work. "Not exactly surprising. We never talked back then unless we were trying to annoy each other." He's right. And now that breaks my heart. So many wasted years.

"Well, tell me now then." I lean my hip against the counter and look up at him. "When did you get into it?"

"June, we have a lot to get done. Let's just focus on getting the dinner made before we have to get ready for the rehearsal."

Oh, I see. He expects me to open up about my life, but he gets to keep all his secrets inside? I don't think so.

"What are you doing?" he asks, sounding close to amusement.

"I'M . . . CARRYING . . . YOU . . . INTO . . . THE . . . SHOWER!" I say with my arms wrapped around Ryan's gigantic body, using all my strength to try to lift him off the ground. Someone please call Superman. He's the only one who can get this job done. Ryan is clearly made of lead. "Make yourself lighter!"

He laughs, turns around, and picks me up by my armpits, setting me back onto my perch on the counter (apparently, I wasn't that much help in the slicing department). I find it ridiculously unfair that he can just move me around like a rag doll, and I can't even push him an inch.

But I'm not so easily deterred. I reach for the sink sprayer and aim it at Ryan's chest, but I don't wait for him to spill his secrets. Nope. I turn on that cold water and blast him like a machine gun of liquid. Otherwise known as a water gun.

His shoulders jump, and he drops the knife onto the counter, but that's the most startle I get out of him. He rests his hands on the counter and takes the stream of cold water like a war hero. Then, slowly, his gaze shifts to me, and I see retaliation in their depths. His dark eyes flash fire.

They say when you get close to death, you can feel it. I feel it now.

I drop the sink sprayer and bolt up onto the counter, jumping off the island to the other side. Ryan is fast, though. He's rounding the kitchen island and racing toward me. I don't know what he'll do when he catches me, and I don't want to find out.

I race out the front door, squealing in a way that I'm not proud of as I run toward my backyard. I feel Ryan close on my heels, and when I glance over my shoulder and find miles and miles of his toned, tan abdomen instead of his drenched shirt, my steps falter. When did he take that off, and how did I miss it?

I land hard on the ground.

A better man would check to make sure I'm not hurt. Ryan is not one of those men.

He dives onto the ground and pins me down so he can jab his fingers into my ribs until I'm practically screaming from laughter. How dare he remember that I'm highly ticklish! I want to murder him. Or run my hands up and down his abs. One of those two things.

Finally, the torture stops, and I open my eyes. He's smiling. A warm, heart-wrenching, let's-do-this-forever kind of smile, and I feel a piece of the ice around my heart break off. I wish I wasn't this girl. The one protecting her heart like it's made of spun glass. He's still pinning me down, but there's a new tenderness in his eyes as he shifts his weight to his elbow and uses his other hand to brush my wild hair out of my face.

"I used to cook with my mom," he says quietly, and both my rapid breathing and smile fade into something softer. "Anytime I had a bad day but didn't want to talk about it, she'd pull me into the kitchen with her, and we'd cook something together. It was our thing. By the time whatever we were making came out of the oven, I had told her everything that was bothering me. And somehow, just having her listen made me feel better." He gives a sad smile. "The day she died, I went in the kitchen and cooked her favorite lasagna. It went in the trash when it was finished because I didn't have an appetite for a while after she died, but that's how I got into cooking. It's how I remember her."

"I didn't know."

His thumb traces my jaw. "Because I didn't tell you."

"I wish I had known back then."

"It's okay. You were nice to me when I was feeling my worst after she died. I think it was the only truce we've ever had."

"Yeah, but still. I wish I knew that about you and your mom— that you liked to cook. That you were hurting more than you let on. I wish I knew you back then."

"I wish a lot of things about that time. If I could go back, I'd do it differently."

But we can't go back. And even if we could, would he really change anything? "If things were different between us back then, you might not have gone to France and become a chef. You would have missed out on doing something you love."

His eyes leave mine for the first time to stray to where his elbow is holding up his weight. "Right."

My brows pinch together. "You do love it, don't you?"

Those deep-brown eyes slide to mine, and I'm not able to read them. He opens his mouth, but before words come out, I hear a car door closing in my driveway. He and I both jerk away from each other and look up into the smirking face of my brother, Jake, and my niece, Sam.

"Hey, June. I see your *enemy* is here."

My face is on fire as I look at Ryan propped up beside me, shirt-less, with a crap-eating grin on his face. I shove him away from me at the same time that I look at my brother and say, "I hate him."

Jake's eyebrows raise and lower as he says, "Yeah. Looks like it."

Just go ahead and add Jake's name to my list of people I'm going to murder.

CHAPTER 15

June

"Sooooo," says Jake while reclining on my couch and stretching his arms over the back. "Do you want to talk about the elephant in the room?"

"No," I say, glancing toward the back door, which Ryan, Sam, and Daisy just disappeared through.

Daisy is Sam's seizure-assist dog and goes with her everywhere. This morning, they had a dentist appointment, and Daisy had to be on her best behavior, so Sam took her into the backyard to toss the ball and give her some fun after a long morning of working. Ryan said he loves dogs and wanted to go, too, but I think he was just trying to give me and Jake a minute to gossip behind his back. Why does he keep getting better and better?

"You two looked *pretty* cozy when I pulled up." Jake is wearing a grin the size of the Grand Canyon.

"I said no. I don't want to talk about it."

"Oh, come on. How many times did you sing 'Evie and Jake sitting in a tree' while Evie and I were dating? I think I get to tease you a little. It's my brotherly duty."

"Where are Evie and Jonathan today?"

Jake laughs. "Nice deflection."

I smile. "I learned it from the best."

"Fine. I'll let it go. She's training a new group of volunteers that will help raise the newest litter of puppies. She took Jonathan with her."

That's how Jake and Evie first met. She runs a service dog organization called Southern Service Paws. Sam has epilepsy and needed an assist dog to help during her seizures, and Jake needed a woman to help him and Sam put their lives back together (though he didn't realize it at the time). Evie helped in both cases. They got married a few years ago and had my little nephew, Jonathan, last year. Basically, they have the kind of life that you want to scroll past quickly on Instagram because they are so cute it makes you nauseous. And jealous. I love them.

"Cool, cool, cool," I say, twitching with nervous energy as I keep glancing back toward the door. I think if Jake hadn't interrupted us, Ryan and I would have kissed. We'd probably still be kissing, and I'm not sure what to do with that realization. I need to talk to Jake about all of this, but I'm too scared. It will make whatever is happening between me and Ryan real.

Jake eyes my bouncing knee with amusement and says, "You sure you don't want to talk about him?"

"Definitely not."

"He's grown up since I saw him last."

"Yep."

"Gained a few muscles too."

I shoot him an annoyed look.

He chortles. "All right, how did the meeting go yesterday?" He's referring to the second interview Stacy had lined up with a potential buyer.

"It went great!" I say with over-the-top enthusiasm.

"Really?"

"Until he told me he'd pay a little more if I'd make out with him before he left."

"Ouch. Did he bleed when you punched him?"

"I didn't want to risk hurting my knuckles before the wedding, so I just left a nice slap mark on his cheek instead."

Jake nods like he's not even surprised. He knows me too well to be surprised by anything I do. "So where does this leave you now?"

"Square one. But I think Stacy is doing it on purpose—lining up bad potential buyers."

Jake frowns. "Why?"

"She wants me to buy her half and become full owner."

I resist looking at Jake. I know what I'll see when I do. He'll be all smiles and encouragement because I think he truly believes I'd be good at running Darlin' Donuts without a partner. I wish I shared his confidence.

"Why don't you?"

Thankfully, we get interrupted, and I don't have to answer the questions that have been haunting me since Stacy first proposed it. *Why don't you? What am I so afraid of?* Really, though, that second question can be applied to two areas of my life. And one of them is walking into my living room with a smile that makes my stomach swoop. Sam keeps stealing glances at Ryan, and I think her stomach is swooping too. Thank god he put his shirt back on.

Jake stands and says he's got to get going. He's leaving Sam with me for the afternoon because he needs to go into the office for a few hours. And *THANK GOODNESS,* because I do not trust myself to be alone with Ryan for several hours after the morning we had together.

Just before Jake leaves, he turns back to Ryan with a big smile, and they shake hands. It's odd to me for two reasons: (1) Jake knows all about the lifelong feud between Ryan and me and looks much too pleased to be shaking his hand, and (2) the last time I saw them together was at graduation, and Jake looked so much older than Ryan. Now, they're just two adults shaking hands.

When did we all grow up?

"It was really good to see you again, Ryan," says Jake, and *what the hell?!*

Given all that I've told him about Ryan over the years, he should not think it's really good to see the man.

"Is it, though?" I ask with narrowed eyes, wondering if maybe Jake is just stalling while one of his friends TPs Ryan's car outside. Is it wrong that I kinda hope for that?

Jake grins. "Of course. Anytime another guy helps protect my little sister, he earns my respect for life."

I look between Ryan and Jake, wondering what I'm missing. "Protect?"

Jake gives Ryan a conspiratorial look. "I'll let you tell her. I've gotta get going." He kisses Sam, pats Daisy's head, and then leaves.

I turn to Ryan with my hands on my hips. He doesn't look intimidated (of course), so I tell Sam to do it too. Now he should be terrified. Ryan has two Broaden girls standing in the Wonder Woman pose, and we mean business.

He looks at Sam, and I can see the moment his chocolate eyes hypnotize my preteen niece. "Your aunt is ridiculous. You know that, right?"

Sam's arms fall at her sides, and she smiles sheepishly from below her lashes. "Yeah. She's pretty silly a lot," says the little traitor, who will never get to borrow my pink lipstick again. And good luck having me cover for you when you're sixteen and out late with a boy! *No more cool Aunt June for you, missy.*

I pick up a pillow and throw it at Ryan's head. "Tell me what you did."

He laughs, dodging my attack. "Let's just say on your sixteenth birthday when your boyfriend's tires mysteriously deflated, it wasn't so mysterious to me."

"I knew you did that! Especially after you were the one to show up out of nowhere and *so kindly* offer me a ride home, but you made Isaac stay and wait for the tow truck!"

"It wasn't just me. Jake helped."

"What?" Tension is growing in my shoulders. "Why?"

"Earlier that day, I overheard Isaac and his buddies in the locker room. They had all placed a bet on whether he could . . ." He pauses and looks down at Sam, who is hanging on Ryan's every word like he's giving the exact directions to Shawn Mendes's personal residence. Ryan looks back up at me and adjusts whatever he was going to say. "Well, they bet on whether he could *deflower* you that night."

My jaw drops, and thankfully, Sam is oblivious. "Why would your boyfriend want to take your flowers?"

Ryan smiles, and his dimple tells me he thinks Sam is adorable. "Some not nice guys really like to take girls' flowers."

"That sounds so mean."

"It is. Stay away from those guys," says Ryan, tousling the top of Sam's hair. Heart emojis fill her eyes. She's dropping into full-blown crush mode.

I stare at Ryan, and he must see the panic building in me, because he asks Sam to go into the kitchen and wash her hands because he's going to show her how to properly cut a potato. *She better get the same boring lesson I got.*

"How did Jake come into play in all this?" I ask the second Sam turns the corner into the kitchen.

"I told him as soon as I found out. His suggestion was that we go beat the hell out of Isaac, but I convinced him to help me slash his tires instead so I could take you home before anything happened. Figured it would be less embarrassing for you than your brother beating up your first real boyfriend. And you broke up with him shortly after, so it all worked out."

Mm-hmm, yeah, he's just talking and going on and on like my perception of him isn't suddenly turning on its end. I need to go lie down. There have been too many revelations today.

I fix my gaze on Ryan, and I take in his strong jaw, dark eyes, long lashes, and the small scar on the apple of his cheek from the pop fly that almost broke his cheekbone sophomore year. I trace a line from his straight nose to his lips and scruffy jawline (yet another sign that he's no longer the boy from high school). I'm taking in every inch of his face because I feel like I'm finally seeing him for who he really is—seeing *him*—the whole picture of Ryan for the first time.

"What?" he finally asks, a cautious look on his face.

I smile and shake my head. "You never were the bad guy, were you?"

The air shifts when a mischievous glint sparks in Ryan's eyes. I stay still as he crosses the room, stops in front of me, and leans toward my ear. I'm bracing for him to tell me I have toilet paper sticking out of somewhere it shouldn't be when I feel his hot lips land on the area just behind my jaw, below my ear. Chill bumps roll down my arms.

And then he whispers, "I was definitely the bad guy. I just wasn't against you like you thought."

I feel Ryan's lips on my skin for the rest of the day and on into the night. Like he left a tattoo on my skin. It's there, tingling and reminding me that everything has changed.

During the rehearsal, I keep my distance from Ryan. But he looks amazing in his black suit pants and button-down linen shirt, so my eyes continuously seek him out from across the room. Every time we make eye contact, I instinctively touch the spot on my neck that I have vowed to never wash again. I'm going to wrap it in caution tape just so no one ever taints that patch of skin again. I've christened it as *Ryan's*.

My stomach does barrel rolls when it's time for me to take Ryan's arm and practice walking down the aisle together. He covers my hand where it's resting on his arm, and I curse myself a million times for imagining myself wearing a white dress and mouthing *na na na, boo boo* to every woman who's ever given Ryan the *I'm-all-yours* look. You better believe I would invite them to our wedding. I'm a gloater.

Point is, this all feels like a dream where real life is hovering just beyond the edges, ready to overtake me at any moment.

Logan and Stacy practice the vow portion of the ceremony, and Ryan's gaze is searing into mine. I want him to look away, but he won't. I widen my eyes in the classic STOP LOOKING AT ME sign, but he just makes a goofy kissy face back at me. I'm so mad at him for making me laugh. For taking a sledgehammer to the cement walls I'd constructed around myself. For making me flush and giggle like a ding-dong in front of this whole wedding party.

After the rehearsal, Ryan tries to make his way to me at every turn, but I avoid, sidestep, and duck behind every potted plant I can find, because the more he makes me smile and blush and tingle, the more terrified I become. I KNOW that whatever Ryan feels for me is fake. Or maybe not fake, but temporary. His life is far away from here, and it's going to call him back in two days. I just have to resist him for that long.

A heaviness grows over me during dinner, but I refuse to let it show, because this is Stacy's big night, and I'm determined to make it as wonderful as possible for her. I will keep a smile on my face tonight even if I have to tape the corners of my mouth to my ear-lobes.

But the only time I genuinely laugh the entire night is when Stacy makes Ryan stand up during dinner. "Attention, everyone! Can we all give a round of applause for having our very own Michelin chef, Ryan Henderson, make all this delicious food for us tonight?"

Ryan's face turns blood red, and I know that he's dying inside at having his name associated with green beans and mashed potatoes. I snap a quick picture, because this is probably the only time I'll ever see him embarrassed. Maybe I'll have the photo enlarged and printed. It will hang over my mantel, and it won't be creepy at all.

FINALLY, the night is over, and everyone begins to leave. I stand from the table and kiss Stacy's glowing cheek, forcing myself to not focus on how much losing her is going to hurt.

"Tomorrow's the day," I say, giving her one last hug.

"Tomorrow," she repeats with a dreamy expression.

I look over Stacy's shoulder and lock eyes with Ryan, sitting at a table across the room. *Tomorrow* takes on a whole new meaning in my mind. Tomorrow is the wedding—the end of the reason Ryan came to visit. Tomorrow, the carriage will turn back into a pumpkin.

Ryan's eyes beg me to let him take me home, but I shake my head.

Enemies or not, I am still June, and he is still Ryan. Our lives have taken different paths, and they don't intersect. I refuse to let a man break me again. No matter how many figurines I could set on his ab shelves.

CHAPTER 16

June

"No," I whisper, staring longingly through my car window at the keys lying innocently in my front seat. "*No. No. No.*" I haven't locked my keys in my car since I was sixteen.

How could this happen? Then again, the tears bubbling up behind my eyes remind me I have had just a tiny bit on my mind lately. And I tend to turn into Space Cadet June when I'm overwhelmed. *Don't think about how overwhelmed you are, June. Don't think about Stacy moving. Don't think about Ryan leaving. Don't think about how you're going to have to run your business with someone other than your best friend.*

I'm thinking about all of it.

Oh god, now my eyes are stinging and my nose is tickling and I just want to get into my car, where I can let it all out in peace.

I lightly pound my fist against the glass—begging it to let me in. "Please just open up," I say in a wobbly voice. "If you do, I promise I won't let your seats get all crumby anymore."

"That's a big promise."

I scrunch my eyes shut. *Dammit.* Of course Ryan would be out here right now while I'm locked out of my car and tears are clinging to my lashes. I didn't want to see him anymore tonight. My heart is all twisty and achy, and spending more time with him is only going to make it worse.

I feel him approach at my back. "You okay?"

"Fine!" I say, not turning around. "Apparently my keys are mad at me and have locked themselves in there."

I'm trying to sound happy and cute, but my voice is cracking with emotion and Ryan doesn't even pretend to miss it.

"June?" I feel him approaching me. "Look at me. Or do I need to carry you into a shower again?"

This pulls a little laugh from me as I turn around to face him. "I swear I don't cry this much normally."

His eyes are soft as his brows pull together. He's unfairly handsome when he's tender. "It's okay if you do."

I have to wiggle my toes to keep the sob building inside my body from leaking out.

"Are you crying—"

"*Almost* crying," I correct, making Ryan grin.

He chuffs out a short laugh. "Are you almost crying because of your keys? Or did something happen?" There's an edge to his voice there at the end. Something that tells me if something happened and it was the result of anyone at that rehearsal, he's going to plow back inside and exact revenge on my behalf.

I'm still struggling to accept this Ryan 2.0. I don't know what to do with him. *Well . . . I know what I'd like to do with him, but that's beside the point.*

I sniff aggressively. No more emotions. "Compounding issues. The keys put it over the top."

He nods slowly, diving his hands into his pants pockets in a move that only stresses his elevated good looks. The man is too beautiful. Might have stepped right out of a Banana Republic catalog for all anyone knows. "Can I help?"

"Do you have magical abilities to pass through glass and metal?"

He pulls his phone from his pocket. "No. But I have roadside assistance and can get a locksmith for you."

"*Oh.*" I blink. "You'd let me use your roadside assistance?" For some reason, this is shaking me more than if he would have admitted to having special powers.

A sad smile curves the side of his mouth. "I don't want to dignify that ridiculous question with an answer."

I adjust on my heels that suddenly feel four sizes too small for my feet. I want to be home. Snuggled up in sweatpants and a blanket, trying to block out anything that makes me feel anxious and funky—aka blocking out Ryan until I know what to do with him.

I glance back toward the church and consider asking anyone else in there for help—but Stacy and Logan are busy entertaining their guests, Jake and Evie already left, and . . .

Ryan groans and rolls his eyes, smiling. "I'm calling them, June. You can fight me about it later."

I don't protest as he paces a few steps away, bringing his phone to his ear, but I do shoot my car one last mean-mug. "Expect extra curbs from here on out," I whisper.

Not even two minutes later, Ryan is pocketing his phone and striding over to me. "Good and bad news. Good news, they're sending a locksmith. Bad news, he's got a couple of calls before ours, so we'll have to wait around for him."

I narrow my eyes and hold up my finger. "You keep saying this funny word. *We.* But I think you mean they're sending someone for *me.* And *I'll* have to wait around for him."

Ryan's grin is outrageous. "Nope. *We* have to wait for him. It's my roadside assistance account and they will only service my family members or someone I'm currently riding with. So for tonight, we're pretending I'm your passenger princess."

GREAT. Just super.

I didn't want to spend more time with Ryan. Because more time with Ryan means more time to like him. And I don't want to like him. He's literally leaving in two days. Plenty of people make long-distance relationships work—but I'm not one of those people. My trust is paper thin. Almost nonexistent.

Suddenly my stomach gives the loudest grumble of my life. It shakes the earth.

Ryan's eyebrows shoot up. "Did you not eat dinner?"

I grimace lightly. "I was too nervous."

Ryan's face goes utterly serious, and I think he's about to comment on my lack of dinner, but suddenly Logan calls to us as he's walking out of the church. "I thought y'all left a while ago!"

"June locked her keys in the car because she was so eager to see me."

I turn and glare at Ryan even though I know for a fact Logan won't believe a word of that. (Even if it's a little true.)

Logan makes his way to us. "Shoot. They're locked in there?"

"Yeah, but a locksmith is on the way," I say, trying to sound more cheery than I feel.

Logan nods slowly, glancing back toward the building for a half second. "We were getting ready to head out, but Stacy and I can wait with you if you need us to."

I don't get the chance to tell Logan I'll be fine, because Ryan interjects. "Nah—she's hungry. I'm taking June to get some food while we wait."

"*You are?*" I ask, but Ryan doesn't acknowledge my question or my incredulous tone.

Logan nods with a loaded look that could be interpreted a hundred different ways. "Okay. See you guys tomorrow then. I gotta pull the car around to the other side of the church and pick up Stacy."

The moment we're alone, I whirl on Ryan. "You don't have to take me for food. I'll be okay until later."

"Sure—but I want to."

"But what if the locksmith shows up while we're gone?" I'm grasping for an excuse that will keep me from being locked in close quarters with Ryan Henderson.

"We'll be back in enough time."

"What if we're not?!"

"I'll know."

I frown. "How? Are you suddenly all-knowing and I didn't realize it?"

"Yes. I'm omniscient. Get in the car, June."

I fold my arms across my chest. "Okay, listen. If I get in that car with you . . . I don't . . ." My gaze drops and I shift on my feet again because these heels are really cutting into my skin now. "I don't want you to talk about being into me or us going on a date or anything that feels as if it belongs in an alternate universe than the one I've known all these years, got it? Because I just . . . I'm having a lot of feelings tonight and I can't take more stress to my nervous system."

Ryan smiles with one corner of his mouth. "Okay, I promise." And then he drops to one knee in front of me.

"Oh my god, Ryan, I just said no feelings and you're proposing!"

The look he gives me—so very flat before he reaches forward and takes my calf in his hand, lifting my foot off the ground. "I'm taking your heels off. I can tell they're killing you."

"They're not—" I start as he works the clasps, but then pause when he pulls off the heel and we both see the blisters where the shoes were cutting into the tops of my feet. *And this, my dears, is why you should never wear new heels to an event without breaking them in first.* I can't help but wiggle my toes with their new delicious freedom. A fresh wave of feelings strikes me with the force of a monsoon. *Ryan noticed I was uncomfortable before I even said anything.*

It's unacceptable for him to be sweet and attentive before he drives off after the wedding and leaves me behind again.

As he stands, my black high heels in his hand, I glare at him. "Next time, maybe just suggest I take them off instead of doing it yourself."

He smiles and leans in closer to whisper in my ear, "No way, June Bug. Get in the car."

In his rental car, we're silent as we pull out of the church parking lot. I expect us to turn onto the main road and drive until we hit some place that Ryan deems suitable to eat, but nearly die of shock when instead, he crosses the main road and drives right into the parking lot of a Taco Bell.

My gasp is over-the-top loud. "His Supreme Chef-ness is taking me to get fast food?"

He cuts his eyes to me briefly. "Just because I make gourmet food doesn't mean I can't appreciate a good drive-through taco every once in a while."

"I'm literally stunned."

"Quit."

"I can't wait to watch you eat this. Can I take pictures?"

He grunts a laugh as he steers us into the line, guided by the neon glowing sign. "Out of context, that sounds extremely dirty."

I lean back heavily against the seat and eye him. "It's just so shocking. What kind of fast-food taco does a Michelin chef get, anyway?"

"Just tell me what you want."

I order three soft tacos with no lettuce, and Ryan orders a Beefy

Crunch Burrito. I'm floored even just hearing those words come out of his mouth. When our food is in hand and he's pulled into a parking spot that faces the road (with a clear view of my car in the parking lot) he sorts through the bag of delicious goodness to hand me my tacos.

"Told you I'd know if the locksmith arrived or not." He grins, gesturing out the window.

I take a huge bite of taco, feeling my nerves and sadness settle into something more comfortable and bearable. I want to say it's the food and my blood sugar rising back to normal levels, but I don't think that's it. It's Ryan. The man I don't want to admit I like as much as I do.

He notices my smile. "Will you tell me why you were crying earlier?"

For a minute, there are only the sounds of our crinkling wrappers in the car, and Ryan doesn't rush me. I look out at the church, where, in less than twenty-four hours, my best friend will get married—completely changing her life and mine as a result. "I'm selfish."

"Try again," he says in a soft tone.

"I am, though. I'm selfish because I don't want Stacy to get married tomorrow. And I don't want her to move away or sell her portion of our business." I leave out that my heart is also wrenching at the thought of him leaving after the wedding. "I want her to stay here and keep showing up every day to the shop and run the business side by side with me."

Ryan's brows pull together. "Yeah, Logan told me Stacy is selling her half of Darlin' Donuts." I nod and he falls quiet for a minute. "Who is she selling it to?"

"Not sure yet. I've had a few meetings already with potential buyers, but I'd rather live in a smelly shoe than own a business with any of them."

"Why don't you buy it then and run it yourself?"

Again with that question. The same one Jake asked me and that I've been asking myself on repeat ever since Stacy told me she was selling her portion. I shrug and ball up my wrapper, going for taco number two. "I can't."

"Why not?" Someone has a lot of questions tonight.

"Because I can't. Can you hand me my second taco?" He moves the bag out of my reach. *"Ryan."*

"No, I'm serious. Why can't you?"

I meet his bold dark eyes. "Because I've tried owning my own business before, and . . . it didn't work out."

"What business?"

I don't want to stroll down this memory lane, but I don't think he's going to let up until I do. "I sold bouquets out of a cute flower truck. It did well for a while and then . . ."

He leans a little closer. "And then what?"

I shoot him a look that says he's prying too much and I don't like it. Ryan doesn't give a shit, though. He keeps that bag of tacos out of reach.

"And then," I grit out through clenched teeth, "Ben cheated, and I spiraled into a bad place for a while, and basically gave up on my business. I had to sell the truck, and it was honestly so embarrassing. I don't feel like going through that again."

I make gimme fingers toward the bag of tacos and Ryan sets it in my lap. "You're allowed to go through rough patches, you know. Those moments . . ." He pauses and swallows. "They don't define the rest of your life. They're just that: moments."

I don't look at him. I can't. Tears will spring out faster than a jack-in-the-box.

He lets me eat my taco in peace for all of thirty seconds. "Want to know a secret?" This has me peeking over at him. "I got fired from the first kitchen I worked at out of culinary school."

I choke on my taco and cut my eyes to him. "WHAT!"

He's grinning—that statement having the desired effect, apparently. "Yep. I showed up, cocky as shit on the first day, and tried to overstep the head chef by wowing the kitchen with my unique flavor pairings—which were opposite of how he'd developed the dishes. He fired me before the end of the day."

"*Ryan,*" I say absolutely gobsmacked.

He's nodding, chewing a bite, and then wipes the corner of his mouth with a napkin. My gaze is drawn to his lips, and I find myself wanting to lean over and kiss that perfect mouth of his more and more by the minute.

"My point is," he begins. "I learned a lot from that day. And you're smart, so I don't need to state the purpose of this story. It's your life, June, and if you want to sell Stacy's half, then do it. But if you don't"—he gives me the softest, most understanding smile I've ever seen—"then don't. Because you have what it takes to run it yourself. That one moment in time doesn't define your future."

The air is full of salty Taco Bell aroma, but my heart is nothing but syrupy sweet mush.

CHAPTER 17

June

The moment my eyes pop open, I think *wedding day*.

I should be happy for Stacy—and I am—but I'm also bummed because I can't help but wonder if Ryan will go home right after the wedding or wait until tomorrow. My stomach sinks at the thought of repeating one of my least favorite days: graduation day.

I know for a fact that Ryan flew out on a red-eye that very night. How? Because I went to Logan's house in search of him later that night. I think my professed plan was to stab him with a butter knife for humiliating me. But really, I was secretly hoping that he would change his mind and finish the kiss he'd started. When I got to the house, though, Logan's mom gave me a sad look and said that Ryan had already left for school.

My first thought was *WHO LEAVES FOR SCHOOL AFTER JUST GRADUATING FROM SCHOOL?*

My second thought was that Ryan had told her to say that so he didn't have to see me again. His version of *Sorry, can't, I'm washing my hair*. It made me hate him more.

For years, I seethed, thinking that Ryan had flicked me off his shoulder like a piece of lint he never wanted to see again.

Now I know he was going off to start his culinary training in France. I wonder if I had known that back then, would it have changed anything? If I hadn't forbidden Stacy and Logan from talking about Ryan the day after the *almost-kiss of doom,* would I have been in love with him all this time instead of wishing on every shooting star for his shampoo to magically get replaced with Nair?

It doesn't matter now.

It's Stacy's special day, and that's all I need to focus on.

I roll over and grab my phone and shoot her a text.

JUNE: Do you hear that sound????

STACY: What sound?

JUNE: WEDDING BELLS!!

STACY: *GIF of old lady dancing in the kitchen*

JUNE: *GIF of a couple French kissing*

STACY: Hey, do you have my green jumper? I need it for the honeymoon.

JUNE: Why? You don't need clothes on your honeymoon.

STACY: June . . . bring the jumper. You've had it for like six months.

JUNE: CRACKLE CRACKLE CRACKLE. Bad service. Can't hear you. Sorry!!

Stacy's out of her mind if she thinks she's ever getting that jumper back. My phone buzzes again, but it's not Stacy this time.

RYAN: Want to get an early lunch later before we have to go to the church?

I throw my phone on my bed and avoid it for the next ten minutes. I brush my teeth. I throw on my running clothes and tennis shoes. I tie my hair in a ponytail and fill up my water bottle, all while avoiding the phone on my bed at all cost. I'm Frodo Baggins, though, because I swear I can hear that thing calling for me from the other room even though the volume is not on.

By now, I've formulated a very eloquent piece of literature in my brain, explaining all the reasons why I can't go with him to lunch. It centers around my heart and my hurts and my fears. I lay it all out in a way that will help Ryan see and understand me better.

And then when that thought scares me too much, I shoot him this little gem.

JUNE: Can't. Sorry.

He doesn't respond. And I jog for twice as long as I normally would, forcing myself to go until my lungs squeeze as painfully as my heart at the thought of losing Ryan again.

It's go time.

I expect "Eye of the Tiger" to start playing when I step into the bridal suite at the church, loaded down with all the essentials for a best friend's wedding day. There's a box of Darlin' Donuts in my hand, a bottle of white wine under my arm, a portable steamer draped over my shoulder, and a pair of new fluffy white house slippers in my other hand for Stacy to wear through the day. Right now, I am the epitome of what every bride wants in a maid of honor.

I am prepared to risk my life to keep away anyone Stacy does not want to see on her special day.

I will bodycheck Great-aunt Mildred if she comes within

twenty feet of Stacy with her overpowering hibiscus perfume and cheek-pinching fingers. And I plan on telling Logan's bratty younger sister that the bridal suite is on the opposite end of the church from where it really is.

Most importantly, I will not let Ryan enter my thoughts even once during the hours leading up to the ceremony. Not once. None at all. Nada. SHOOT, I'm picturing him shirtless with his James Dean smile and lifeguard hair.

But not again.

"IT'S YOUR WEDDING DAY!" I yell as soon as I kick the door open and step into the bridal suite, finding my best friend lounging on the couch in her adorable white silk robe.

Stacy's pretty blue eyes light up, and she jumps onto a chair, raises her glass of champagne into the air, and repeats my battle cry. "IT'S MY WEDDING DAY!" We will paint our faces in the traditional wedding war paint of soft-pink lips, smoky eyes, and softly penciled-in brows.

The rest of the bridal party hoots and hollers, and it's then that I realize the bottle of wine under my arm was not at all necessary. I should have brought coffee instead. Empty shot glasses are lying haphazardly around the room, and these wild bridesmaids are hammered already. How? I thought I was early!

Stacy notices my concerned look and crinkles her nose, hops down from the chair, and comes to help me unload my wedding day ammunition. "Yeah, they apparently got here at, like, eight o'clock this morning and have been partying this whole time."

"You're kidding."

She shakes her head. "Drunk as skunks."

I immediately start making my way around the room and extracting the various alcoholic beverages from everyone's hands. They are wearing pink silk robes, and because of the way they are all gaping open, I wonder why they even bothered putting them on in the first place.

Stacy's expression says she regrets having these girls in her wedding party. She's barely seen them since graduating from college but thought it would be a nice idea to have her old sorority sisters stand up with her on her wedding day. Now, it looks like they'll be doing well to be able to stand on their feet at all.

They all groan and call me eighteen different versions of *Fun Sucker* when I confiscate their beverages, but I don't care. My goal is to protect Stacy today, and if that means babysitting seven drunk party girls all day, then so be it.

We're going to need reinforcements, though. As much as I don't want to, I know what I have to do. Or rather, who I have to text.

> JUNE: Hi. Sooooo any chance you don't hate me too much and would be willing to bring copious amounts of coffee up to the church? I have seven sorority sisters to sober up in five hours.

I wait for a response, not entirely expecting one, but then my phone buzzes.

> RYAN: You damn well know I don't hate you. I'll be there in a few minutes.

My heart flutters, and I tell it to chill out.

"Coffee is on the way," I say to Stacy, hoping to ease the worry lines from around her eyes a little.

She wraps me up in one of her famous hugs that I will miss more than the green jumper I brought to stuff in her luggage. "Thanks, Junie."

I squeeze her back and tell my tear ducts they better get themselves under control because there is no time for meltdowns.

"Oh! I have something for you." She lets go of me to reach into an oversize tote bag, pulling out a manila envelope. I secretly hope it's a scrapbook filled with all our best memories, but I don't tell her because I'm cool and supposed to think scrapbooks are corny. Disappointment floods me when I open it and find a stack of businessy-looking papers.

She taps the envelope, and all the sounds of the rowdy room fade away. "These are all the offers for the bakery. They all seem like good candidates, but I'm leaving it completely up to you to choose since you're the one who will be stuck with them."

"And because you'll be in Mexico for the next two weeks before moving to California."

"And that."

"So basically, you're just making me do your dirty work," I say, because joking is the only thing I can do right now to keep myself from dissolving into a salty puddle of tears.

Stacy knows. She smiles softly and puts a hand on either side of my face before smooshing my cheeks together. "You'll make the right choice. I know it." She lets go of my face to smack my butt as she passes. All I can think about is my conversation with Ryan last night and the mix of hope and fear it spiked in me. It's all I could think about as I went to bed.

Slowly, the sounds of squealing bridesmaids and Justin Timberlake reenter my consciousness, and I turn around to find Stacy tossing me a pretty silk robe. The bridesmaids catcall and taunt me to strip my clothes off. Somewhere, Ms. Dorothy is proud of them.

"Uh, I think I'd rather change in the bathroom." If it were just Stacy, I'd be fine. But I have enough self-awareness to know my body image is fragile and healing lately, and I don't totally trust whatever drunken words will come out of these women's mouths.

"Need me to come with you?" Stacy asks.

I point to the slippers I brought her. "No, you need to slip your feet into those little slices of paradise and relax. I'll be right back."

I head down the long church hallway to the women's bathroom and, once inside, choose the first stall of the row. No more middles for me. Although the sanctuary of the church is newly remodeled and looks beautiful, this bathroom appears as though it's been neglected since the days of prehistoric life. I'm pretty sure it hasn't been cleaned since then either.

I slip into the stall and carefully drape the fine silk robe over the door while I change out of my clothes. Once I've stripped down and hung my clothes over the door beside the robe, I reach for the pink silk fabric, and like a magic trick, it slips off the other side and disappears before my very eyes. There's nothing I hate more than having magic forced on me.

For a split second, I worry that my robe has landed on the gross floor and I'll catch something truly disgusting when I put it on. Then I hear giggles followed by another disappearing act: my clothes.

Someone—the ringleader, Carly, I'm assuming—very maturely shouts, "Time to loosen up, Fun Sucker!"

They hightail it out of the bathroom as if they expect me to chase them like we're back in a college dormitory and I have water balloons stuffed in my bra, ready for a prank war at all times.

Fact: People stuck in their college days are more annoying than ingrown hairs.

I sigh and can't help but wonder what events in my life have led me back to this place of being half-naked in a stall twice in one week. Oh, AND I'm phoneless because it was in my jeans pocket. So, great. *Just great.*

I have no other choice but to leave this stall in my bra and panties and walk as quickly as I can back to the bridal suite, where, instead of holding each woman down to Sharpie something mean on their faces like my gut insists, I will say *Ha ha, very funny!* and then funnel coffee down their throats for the rest of the afternoon. *I know.* #maidofhonorgoals.

The gross cream tile is cold and sticky against my bare feet as I inch my way toward the door. The air feels extra chilly now, and I'm almost certain it's like this because the church officials didn't anticipate needing to make the temperature more accommodating for a woman walking around nearly naked.

On my way to the door, I stop by the paper towel dispenser and crank out a long strand of stiff brown paper and begin wrapping it around my body, mummy style. It's not doing much in the coverage department, and I have to walk like I'm wearing a mermaid fin, but at least it's better than nothing.

I crack open the bathroom door and peer down the hallway in both directions, verifying that the coast is clear. When I step out, the hallway seems to grow in length, but I can see the bridal suite at the far end of the hall and am already relaxing knowing that no one will see me like this.

Except, when I'm halfway to my end goal and clutching the brown paper tightly against my bare skin, I hear a door open behind me. I whip around to see blinding light spilling around a tall form. If I were wearing a beautiful dress, there would be a choir of angels singing behind the imposing male figure. But I'm wearing brown paper towels, so instead, the only music my mind plays is the classic *dum dum dum*.

The door shuts, the light disappears, and I'm able to see that RYAN IS STANDING THERE HOLDING COFFEE AND I'M NAKED! Well, not naked. I'm wearing a slip made of archaic bathroom paper.

Instinctively, I let out a little scream and press the paper tighter to me, hoping none of it gives way suddenly. Ryan does not look away. He's fully clothed (which is the normal look for most people in a church) and staring at me. But he's not just normally clothed; he's doubly clothed. A ridiculously handsome navy suit jacket wraps around his shoulders, and a black button-down shirt is tucked into a pair of slacks that matches the jacket. A slim black tie is knotted around his neck, and his hair is already tousled to perfection in a swoopy look you'd see on a model in a magazine.

"Turn around! Stop looking at me!" I whisper-yell because I don't want to alert the whole building to what's happening out here. I'm backing away from him and still trying to cover all the parts of skin that the brown paper is not hiding.

He starts walking toward me, and I can see that wolfish smile of his. "I don't want to."

"You don't have a choice!"

"It feels like I do."

I can't decide if I want to cry from embarrassment right now or laugh uncontrollably because I'm standing in front of Ryan in a church wearing bathroom tissue. Still, I plead one more time. "Ryan! Please. Turn around."

"Okay, okay." He raises his hands in surrender and turns his back to me. "I can't believe my luck that I get to ask you this again in one week, but . . . why are you naked, June?"

"Again, I'm not naked. I'm in my—"

"*Underclothes.* Yes, I'm aware. Your paper towel dress has lost the upper half by the way." He's walking backward in my direction.

I gasp and look down, grabbing the end of the paper that fell loose and is flapping in the breeze and retuck it under my arm. "This isn't my fault. Those little jerks stole my clothes!"

Ryan stops right in front of me and sets the coffee down on the ground. I watch as he shrugs out of his jacket and then turns back around to face me—eyes closed. He steps close enough to drape the jacket around my shoulders, and I let out a relieved breath when I'm covered again. The unhelpful brown paper falls to the ground, puddling around my ankles. I pull Ryan's jacket tightly around me and will myself not to drag in a deep breath of his delicious cologne.

He opens his eyes, and there's something playful lurking in them. "You know, I still remember the first bikini you ever wore."

His words pull a nervous chuckle from me. One that sounds wobbly and slightly hysterical because all my insecurities left over from Ben are bubbling up to the surface of my skin after having a man look at me for the first time without my clothes on since Ben cheated. "You do?"

He nods, his smirk not so devilish now and much softer. "It was light blue with white polka dots, and that's the day I decided we would play shark and minnow every time we all went swimming together."

I always thought it was because he wanted to prove he was faster and stronger than me. "You caught me every single time."

His smile grows, and I feel like he's looking straight through my soul. "Made sure of it. I hated when I had to let go of you."

"In the pool?"

His gaze holds mine, and he's quiet for a moment. "Then too."

The next thing I know, Ryan's arms are wrapping around me and holding on like he's afraid I might disappear. He kisses my head, and the tenderness of it all tears me apart. "Do you want me to carry the coffee back there for you?"

"No," I say into his shirt. "I can take it."

"Do you want to keep my jacket for a bit?"

"Yes, please." And I plan on trying to wring it out, extracting drops of his sexy scent into a vial that I will only let myself open and sniff once a year after he's gone back to Chicago and I'm a lonely, creepy old maid.

"June?"

"Yeah?"

"You're so beautiful."

And that's the moment my heart cracks wide open. I've never felt more vulnerable and safe at the same time.

I want to say something, but I'm afraid that if I do, tears will come out instead of words. So I let go of Ryan and bend down to pick up the box of coffee from the floor and then pad my way down the hallway to the bridal suite. I don't need to look back to know Ryan is still watching me.

I slip through the door, shut it, and then lean back against it with a dummy smile like they do in those classic '80s movies.

"Uh, that's not the robe I bought you," Stacy says, reminding me that I'm not alone.

Each of the bridesmaids' eyes shoot to me, and when they see that I'm wearing a man's suit jacket, they erupt in squeals and whistles. "I told you loosening up was more fun! Now get over here and pick a name."

"A name?" I ask, hesitant to know what their next form of torture—I mean, amusement—is.

"Yeah," says Carly (ringleader). "We wrote down the name of each single groomsman on a slip of paper and put them in here." She shakes a little bag in my face. "We each draw a name, and whoever you get is your man for the night. No tradesies."

I look at Stacy, and she just rolls her eyes, regret of ever asking these women to share her special day written unapologetically across her forehead.

"No thanks," I say, turning away and going to busy myself with pouring Stacy the first cup of coffee and adding two sugars just like she likes it. There's no way I'm going home with some guy just because I draw his name from a bag. Not to mention how disgusting it is to do this behind the guys' back—not even giving them a say. It's giving off objectifying vibes and I don't care for it.

"Okay, I'll go first," I hear Carly sing.

"Who do you hope you get?" asks another bridesmaid.

"I think you know."

"Ryan?"

Hearing his name makes my heart stop. Wait. Somehow, I forgot Ryan's name would be in there. He's single. He's a groomsman.

"Duh. He's so hot." Carly dips her hand in and pulls out a sliver of paper, and I don't even remember turning around, but I have, because I'm holding my breath, watching and waiting for her to read off the name.

She smiles deviously. "I got Ryan!"

My eyes shut tight, and now I feel sick to my stomach. I'm filled with a distinct desire to yell *STOP* and demand that someone push the pause button on life and just give me a moment to think. I just need a second to process. To decide. To weigh all my choices and figure out what I want.

But I don't get to do that because now the bridal suite door is opening again, and a whole parade of wedding day entourage is entering. Hairstylist, makeup artist, mother of the bride, and Logan's bratty sister, who managed to wiggle her way in while my guard was down.

I have no choice but to push thoughts of Ryan aside, let whatever happens happen, and focus on Stacy. It's her day. I will not rain on her parade. And Ryan . . . well, maybe he'll go home with Carly tonight and save me the trouble of having to figure out if he's worth my feelings or not.

CHAPTER 18

Ryan

Logan and Stacy are married.

They tied the knot about an hour ago, and now everyone has moved on to the reception. I don't know much about décor, but even I can admit this place looks like something right out of a movie. They spared no expense on this reception. A blanket of string lights hangs above the dance floor, massive flower bouquets sit in the center of each table, there's an open bar, and a dessert buffet boasts anything with sugar you could imagine.

Everyone has been feeding off the romantic energy, dancing close, stealing kisses from their significant others; and June has stayed as far away from me as she possibly can.

Ever since the incident in the hallway, she hasn't looked me in the eyes. I think she's embarrassed by it, but I have no idea what she thinks she needs to be embarrassed about. She literally has a body that makes me want to change both our names and move to some remote island where no one will ever be able to interrupt us so I can devote the rest of my life to showing June just how much I appreciate each of her curves.

Unfortunately, I'm not the only one who's been appreciating her curves. Ever since the bridesmaids showed up to take photos before the wedding, I've had to listen to every male in this wedding party go on and on about June. *Her green eyes are hypnotic in that blue dress. Man, that tattoo on her shoulder is sexy.* And a whole lot of other comments that I don't care to relive.

And right now, they are all drooling as they watch her dancing with Stacy in the center of the floor. I don't like it. I feel like forming a human blockade around her for the rest of the night—arms spread and stance wide, murder glaring at anyone who dares look past me. *No one gets a peek!*

I'm being a meathead, but I can't stand the way these slobbering fools stare at her. Like they're imagining that pretty dress falling to the floor at the foot of their bed. The longer they stare, the more tension grows between my shoulder blades.

And *wonderful.* When did I become a jackass who wants to keep my woman locked away so no one else gets a chance with her? She's not even MY woman. She keeps making that fact painfully clear.

"Who do you think picked you?" Groomsman Number One says to Groomsman Number Two. I've been sitting at this table on the edge of the dance floor with the other men from the wedding party for about five minutes—which is five minutes too long. Alex is the only guy I can tolerate of this bunch, and he's on the dance floor, swaying with his girlfriend.

A few minutes ago the guys brought up that they overheard the bridesmaids talking about some hat of names. Apparently they're all drawing a name and trying to get that guy to take them home? *I'm too old and tired for this shit.*

"I don't know, but I hope it's Carly," says Groomsman Number Two while wagging his eyebrows like a douchebag.

Number One pipes in now. "I think Katie drew mine, because

she's been all over me since pictures." He does that thing where he leans back in his seat and rests his elbow over the back of the chair beside him so he can display his chest and arms to the other "weak links" of the group.

"Katie's cute, though. You don't want to hook up with her?" asks Number Two.

I've only been half listening. Most of me is too busy paying attention to June dancing like an adorable weirdo on the dance floor. But this new development in the conversation grabs my attention and makes me want to groan, because suddenly I realize why Carly has been stuck to me like Velcro all night.

She drew my name, and now I'm expected to sleep with her? *No thanks.* Her name isn't June Broaden, so I'm not interested.

Number One pulls my attention back. "Nah, I was hoping June would have picked my name. Dude, she's ridiculously hot."

My hands ball into fists under the table.

The guys all collectively laugh.

Groomsman Number Three speaks up. "Yeah, right! Take our word for it, June's not leaving here with anyone."

Suddenly, I'm deeply invested in their conversation. "Why do they need to take your word for it?"

"Because we've all tried and failed," says Number One.

My stomach drops. "All of you?"

They each nod, but Number Two answers, "You know her one-date rule, right? She's a legend around here. We've all gone out with her thinking we'd be the one to get that sacred second date, but nope." He loosens his tie and slips it off his neck. "She's really strict. Barely managed to land a kiss on the cheek after my date."

"Ha! You lucky duck," says Number One. "She wouldn't let me get my lips anywhere near her."

Number Two chuckles lightly. "Sucks. I had a great time with her on our date. She's funny and chill. I was actually hoping to get that second date."

Yeah, I already know all this about June. I also know she's a spitfire, looks beautiful when she first wakes up, has zero qualms about holding a slippery fish so she can shove it in your locker, and has the most sensual pillowy lips I've ever seen. These are just a few of the reasons I'm so into her. And why I stiffen when Carly pulls out the seat beside me and sits down.

"So, Ryan. We haven't gotten to talk that much." She leans in too close, settling her hand on my leg. "Wanna find somewhere more private where we can chat?"

I remove her hand from my leg. "No, thanks. I'm good." *And don't touch my leg.*

Carly's eyes widen like she's never been turned down before in her life. Actually, maybe she hasn't. But I don't appreciate that I've been entered into a game I was never asked if I wanted to participate in to begin with.

She huffs out one short, offended sound and then gets up to walk away, clearly seeing in my face that I'm a dead end.

Groomsman Number One shoots up from his seat and goes after her. "Hey, Carly, wait up!"

I turn my eyes back to the dance floor. June gives a blinding smile and laughs as Stacy pretends to reel her in like a fish. Now she's shopping for groceries and waxing the car. She's one of a kind. And you know what? Not someone I'm going to let slip through my fingers again.

I stand up, pull my phone out of my pocket, and dial Nia as I round the table toward the dance floor.

"Hello?"

"Nia, you're in charge a little longer. I'm not coming home Sunday."

"Wait, what? Ryan wh—"

I end the call because I'm on the dance floor now, and June has just spotted me. A song with heavy bass is blaring over the speakers, and everyone is jumping and pumping their fists in the air like they are at a club. But when June spots me, she freezes—dead center of the floor, a statue among chaos. Music, lights, and people are swirling around her, and she keeps perfectly still.

I push through several people—including Jake and Evie, who I'm pretty sure will not enjoy seeing what I do next—and when I make it to June, her glittering eyes go wide. I don't hesitate. I don't slow down. I snake my arm around her waist and cup her jaw with my other hand. She takes in a sharp breath, and I feel her heart hammering against my chest.

"Are you about to kiss me?"

"If you're okay with that."

She nods, eyes round as saucers as I lean down and press my lips to hers, heat rushing through my body at the first touch of our mouths. Commotion is happening all around us, but I don't care or notice. I've been waiting twelve years for this kiss, and all I can focus on now is how June feels pressed up against me, how her body melts into mine as my mouth explores hers. There's not even the slightest bit of hesitation from her.

She responds move for move, pressing up on her tiptoes, breathing in deep, and clasping her arms around my neck to pull me in closer. She doesn't want me to stop. My lips part, and I taste the mint Chapstick on her bottom lip. It's just a kiss—it shouldn't undo me completely, but it does. Desire grips me from all corners. The taste of her, the smell of her, the feel of her, it all pulls me in and spins me around her finger. And just as June's hand grips the back of my head, I remember this is all happening in the middle of a crowd.

I peel my mouth away from hers and take in her face. Her lips are red and swollen, eyelids slowly fluttering open until my favorite color of green pierces me.

"I changed my mind," I say over the music, running my thumb along her jaw. "I want that date."

June blinks and swallows before she says, ". . . Okay."

CHAPTER 19

June

"That was some serious lip locking on the dance floor last night," says Jake over the phone as I'm folding clothes on my bed. I use the word *folding* loosely.

"*Lip locking?* Are you in a '90s Mary-Kate and Ashley movie right now?"

"What do you want me to call it?" I'd rather him call it nothing, because I'm not thrilled that my big brother saw the best kiss of my entire life as it was taking place.

But Jake and Evie were at the wedding, so they saw the whole thing. Everyone did. Everyone except for Stacy and Logan because they were too busy staring at each other with googly eyes. But the moment Ryan and I parted, the whole dance floor exploded with whistles and applause. My face will now be a permanent strawberry. Stacy thought the applause was for her and Logan. I'm good with her thinking that.

"Oh, I don't know . . . it's just a wild idea, but you could call it a kiss?"

He laughs, and then I hear Evie somewhere in the background

yell, "That was not a kiss! I saw tongues moving! If Sam had been there, I would have covered her eyes!"

My stomach tightens. "Am I on speaker?"

"Yep, sure are."

I groan. It's Sunday, so I feel the need to ask, "Who else is there listening?"

"Everyone," says Jake like it's no big deal that my entire giant family of nosy southern loons is listening in on my private conversation about sucking face with a man.

"Hi, sugar!" says Mom in a bright tone. "I wish I'd been there. Your dad couldn't have picked a worse night to get a migraine. But I heard all about it from Suzy Johnson." Just to catch you up on how fast word travels around our town, Suzy Johnson is my mom's hairstylist. "I went in this morning to get my roots touched up and heard everyone talking about how Ryan Henderson was practically resuscitating you on the dance floor! Now, catch me up to speed because, last I heard, he made you madder than a mule chewin' bumblebees."

"Which one is Ryan again?" That's my dad chiming in now.

"He's the boy from high school that June was always swearing she didn't like, but we all knew better."

I lay my phone down on the bed and walk to the kitchen to get a glass of iced tea because I know they don't really need me for this conversation. I also pop a bag of popcorn before going back to my room and picking up my phone again. ". . . no, that was Brad. You're still not thinking of the right one. We hated Brad, but I always thought Ryan was a sweetheart."

"Okay, guys, I'm going to let you go now!" I say, taking advantage of Mom's need to breathe.

"WAIT!" everyone shouts in unison on the other end, making me smile.

"What time are you coming over?" Jake asks.

My family gets together every Sunday. During the summertime, we have one long sunup-to-sundown pool party. Family comes and goes as they want, but usually, we all end up staying the whole day. It's a good time. And during the winter, when it's too cold to get in the pool, we play games and watch movies.

I know it's normal to hate your family, but mine is generally un-hateable. They are sweet, and accepting, and *completely* intrusive, but it's actually one of their most lovable qualities.

But today, I'm tired, and I just sort of feel like being alone. Or . . . maybe it's that I don't feel like being alone around them. All my siblings are married. They all have kids. Most days, I'm fine with my single life. You know, strong, independent woman and all that. But today, my best friend is married and gone, and it just feels too hard to go look at the lives of my family and feel that gaping hole.

"Actually, I didn't get home until late last night, and I'm exhausted. I think I'll just see you guys next weekend."

Everyone protests. My sisters all shout "*LAMMMEEE*" and "*BOOOO*," but Jake is the one to say, "Love ya, June. We'll see you next Sunday."

We hang up, and I toss my phone onto my bed again, eyeing the giant pile of laundry mocking me. It knows I'll never get around to folding it. It knows that I'll leave it here all day, folding a shirt here or there, and then at bedtime, I'll dump all these clothes back into the hamper so I can get under the covers. *We've been doing this dance for a whole week now, darlin'. You're never gonna fold me.* Apparently, my pile of laundry is southern too.

I stand up and meander around the house, munching my popcorn, spritzing water on my potted plants, opening and closing the fridge a few times, hoping a delicious dessert will magically appear one of those times, and then checking my phone eighteen times to see if Ryan has texted me. He hasn't. And I'm mad at myself for even caring. So what? He wants a date. He's lengthening his stay in Charleston. He kisses like freaking Casanova, and it's all I can think about. Like I said, so what?

Ugly truth is, I want to text him. I want to know what he's up to. What does a man like Ryan do on his days off?

But I can't. I can't text him, and I won't. Because we're NOT dating. He gets one date just like everyone else. *But what if I want more than one date?*

I've got to get out of my head. Or rather, I've got to get Ryan out of my head.

After turning on *You've Got Mail,* I sink back onto my couch, bundle up under my cozy Nick Lachey blanket, and wish that this was actually making me feel better, but it's not because I'm still staring at my phone, willing it to light up with Ryan's name.

But then something happens. I don't want to claim that I'm a sorceress or anything, but I've definitely harnessed some sort of mythical powers, because I hear a jingling sound at my front door, and I watch as the lock pops open.

Wait. Is someone breaking into my house?

I bolt upright, ready to grab the big knife that Ryan swears is actually meant for cutting food (but I don't agree), when the front door opens, and none other than Ryan himself walks through holding two big paper bags of groceries.

I sit, wide-eyed, under my puffy blanket as I watch Ryan step inside, kick off his shoes, and then use his foot to shut the door behind him. "You hungry?" he asks, making me nearly jump out of my skin when his brown eyes cut directly to me like he knew I was sitting here all along.

"Well, hello to you too."

He smirks, and my stomach somersaults. "I gotta get these in the fridge." And then he's gone—off to the kitchen to put groceries in MY fridge.

What is happening?! Did I invite him over and I forgot about it? And I've got to remember to move my hide-a-key.

I finally stand up and go into the kitchen. I cross my arms and lean against the counter beside the fridge. "Do you always break and enter people's houses to store your groceries in their fridges?"

He grins, puts a carton of heavy cream in the fridge, and then leans over to kiss my cheek before going right back to his task. I have decided there is only one explanation for what is happening right now: I got in a car accident on my way home last night, and I died and didn't know it. This must be heaven. Because Ryan looks too good and smells too good to be earthly.

His calm is making me twitch. "Did you just kiss my cheek?"

He looks at me like he's questioning my mental stability. *He* is questioning *my* mental stability? "Something wrong with kissing you on the cheek?"

"No. Er—yes! I mean, there is after . . ." I pause, feeling a hot blush claw its way up my neck.

"After what, June Bug?" He's smiling. He's such a devil right now.

"You know . . . after everything that happened yesterday."

What a busy little bee he is, swarming around my kitchen like he owns it. In fact, like the spot on my neck, I think he's staked his claim in here. This is his kitchen now. However, to be fair, he's used it more this past week than I have in the entirety of my living here, so it seems about right to go ahead and give it to him.

"What? The part where I saw you in your bra and panties, or the part where we made out on the dance floor?"

My stomach does a giant dip at his words. Like when you're in an airplane, and suddenly the plane drops for a second, and you wonder if it's going to level off again or if this is the end and your plane is going down. That's what being around Ryan is like for me.

But who am I kidding? This plane is going down.

"Both!" My voice squeaks. "I think we should—RYAN, oh my gosh, can you please stop putting groceries away for one second?!" Okay, yeah, it's official. I've snapped. I gave him one date, and now he's moving in. It's too much.

His brows shoot to his hairline, and he crosses the kitchen to put his hands on the side of my arms. "June, take a breath. Everything is okay. I'm just putting away groceries so I can cook us dinner later."

"LATER?!"

"Why are you yelling?"

"I DON'T KNOW. I CAN'T BRING MY VOICE BACK DOWN." Someone get me a paper bag! Or Stacy so she can slap me.

He chuckles and, oddly enough, doesn't look at me like I should be joining a circus somewhere. Ryan pulls me to his chest and rubs his hand up and down my back. "It's just dinner. Nothing serious."

"But . . . you're here. And you used a key! And you know where things go in my cupboards!"

He's soothing me, hypnotizing me with his hand, making waves of heat across my back. "Right. I put them away exactly where *you* like them, so there's nothing to worry about. Everything is the same; there are just a few extra onions in your produce drawer."

"We're moving too fast. One minute I hate you, and the next, you're filling my produce drawer. What's happening?"

He pulls me away so he can look me in the eyes. I can see that he wants to make a joke about my unfortunate filling-my-produce-drawer phrasing, but he refrains because he's a better person than me. "I'm not trying to rush you, June. In fact, this is the opposite of rushing. I want to be friends. Spend time together and get to know each other again like normal people do. And *then,* I'll take you on our date."

I open my mouth, but Ryan talks over me. "Yes, our one and *only* date. I know. You don't have to remind me."

But that wasn't at all what I was going to say. In fact, my rule keeps floating further and further from my mind the more time I spend with Ryan. It's probably for the best that he doesn't know that. So instead, I just ask, "This isn't our date, then?"

He gives me that crooked grin of his and says, "This? No. Absolutely not. Believe me, June Bug. You'll know when it's the real date."

When he sees that I'm stable again and not going to pass out on the floor, he lets go of me. I wish he didn't.

"Hey, Ryan?"

"Hmm?"

"Why did you start calling me June Bug?" I've always wondered. He did it in high school, and I hated it immediately because I felt like I was supposed to, but I never knew exactly why it was insulting.

"Because you're cute, and it sounds cute."

A short laugh falls out of my mouth. "What! That's it? I always assumed it was some sort of insult meant to irritate me."

"You know what they say about assuming . . ."

I put my face in my hands and let another layer of truth sink over me. Ryan has been calling me a term of endearment from the beginning. He really did like me.

"Are you going to have another breakdown?" he asks casually.

I ignore his question and keep my face in my hands, trying to assemble the facts. "You said you were going to cook us dinner. It's only ten in the morning. What are we supposed to do until dinnertime?" I lower my hands to find his brow raised and his charming smile dialed up to an illegal one billion.

I match his suggestive look. "I thought you said we were going to be *friends*."

One of his eyes narrows. "Friends with benefits?"

He's inching closer, but I start backing away while shaking my head. "No. That will just mess with my head."

"What if I want to mess with your head?" He says *head,* but his eyes scan down my body, saying something totally different.

I put my hand on his chest to hold him away once he backs me into the corner. "Ryannnn." My tone is a warning.

"Just one more."

"One more what?"

"Little kiss. Just a peck."

I should say no. I really should. But I can't think anymore, because my body is humming too loudly. "Fine, but just a tiny one. A *friendly* one."

He rests his hand on the wall behind me. "Last night's kiss felt pretty friendly to me." *Oh, good god.*

I swallow, and my sight zeroes in on Ryan's lips. It's not my fault. They are *right* there in front of my eyes. I don't mean to, but my hand raises, and I use my index finger to trace his lower lip, remembering what it felt like to have it pressing on mine.

"Okay, let's kiss now," I say, sounding like a twelve-year-old playing spin the bottle for the first time. I feel a little desperate for him to kiss me again. I'm on fire, and he's the extinguisher. But then again, maybe he's the gasoline.

"Actually," he says, pulling away. "Never mind. I think I'll wait."

"Excuse me?" My hands fall to my sides, pathetically limp.

"Yeah. You're right. I don't want to mess with your head." But I know he's messing with my head now from that grin on his face. "We'll wait to kiss again until our date. Keep everything simple like that."

He's walking away now, and I'm glancing around for something I can chuck at the back of his head. Ryan makes me so mad I could scream. He's always in control. Always has the upper hand. He thinks he's going to torture me by not letting me kiss him?! Two can play at this game, and I have a feeling I'll enjoy it more than he will.

We're interrupted by the sound of my doorbell.

Ryan and I both look at each other, and his brows furrow.

"You hear that?" I ask. "It's called a doorbell. Normal people use it before entering a house."

And that's one point for me, because if I've learned anything by now, it's that Ryan finds my sarcasm sexy. *Too bad, so sad, Ryan. No kisses for you.*

I give him a haughty look as I pass him, but he gives me a smolder in return that makes my knees buckle a little when I try to walk. I manage to make it to the door, though, and when I open it, I've never been more disappointed to see anyone in my entire life. Remember when I said my family's intrusiveness was their best quality? I was wrong.

"Hi, darlin'! We felt terrible about you being all alone over here, so we thought— Oh! Ryan! Look, everyone, Ryan is here!" says my mom with the least innocent face I've ever seen and a gift bag slung over her arm.

Jake and Evie (along with my dad, all three of my sisters, their spouses, and their children) are standing behind Mom, looking like the cat that ate the canary.

"Oh! Now I remember him!" says Dad.

And I guess kissing really isn't on the table today. *Wonderful.*

CHAPTER 20

Ryan

"So, Ryan, hun, what have you been up to all these years?" asks Bonnie from where she's just sidled up next to my elbow by the stove.

I would scoot to my right to get a little space, but I can't because one of June's sisters is clinging to me on that side. She has three sisters (Jennie, Julia, and Josie) as well as her sister-in-law, Evie. And yeah, they are all surrounding me. I'm completely circled by Broaden women, and it's making me sweat. I think that's their goal, though.

"After high school, I attended culinary school, and I've been working as a chef ever since."

"A chef! Goodness, boy. I had no idea. Based on how you and June used to duel back then, I would've thought you'd join the military."

I laugh and aim a smile down at her. "Oddly enough, that career path never even crossed my mind."

She uses her hip to bump me. "Probably 'cause you were never actually fighting, right?"

"Well . . ." I tap the wooden spoon against the pot and set it on the counter before turning around to face all the women. "They do say love is war."

Each of the sisters physically swoons and *awww*s in unison. Their choir alerts June that something is happening in here, because in the next moment, she's rounding the corner into the kitchen. "I should have known you guys would be harassing Ryan. He's cooking us all lunch. Let the man work in peace."

"We're not hindering his work in any way, are we, Ryan?" Bonnie turns her eyes up to me, and I see now that we're choosing teams for dodgeball. I definitely want her on mine, so I wrap an arm around her shoulder and say, "I love the company."

June rolls her eyes and turns back around. "Don't say I never tried."

The moment she's out of the room, Evie turns to me and flat out asks, "So, Ryan . . . how many women have you been with?"

Shocked does not begin to convey how I feel after that question. My mouth falls open a little, but before I can answer, Jennie steps up to the plate. "Do you have a criminal record?"

JULIA: "Why did your past relationships not work out?"
EVIE: "Are you serious about June?"

Someone help me. They are closing in. How can four small women tower over me like this?

JOSIE: "Do you want a family?"
JENNIE: "Is there a chance you already have a family that you don't know about?" *What the hell?*

I glance back to the place where June just disappeared and consider shooting a flare up into the sky for help. *Come back! I'm sorry! I'll never choose your mom over you for dodgeball again!*

But I'm a man. It's time to grow a pair and give these women what they want. I roll my shoulders once and tilt my head side to side. Then, I take turns looking around the gang of women that I would never want to face in a dark alley alone.

I point to Evie first. "I'm not going to answer that because that's a pretty personal question." Boom. Moving on to Jennie. "A speeding ticket but no criminal record." Julia. "Haven't had a serious relationship because I've been married to my job." Now I look at Mrs. Broaden as I answer the remaining questions, because I feel like her opinion matters most. "I'm more serious about June than I've ever been about anything in my life, and yes, I want a family. And no, there's no chance. I'm always *very* careful. Big fan of protection."

They all stand stunned for a full minute, glancing back and forth among one another before smiles slowly crack across their devious faces, and we all laugh. Bonnie claps me on my shoulder. "I always knew I liked you, Ryan. You're gonna fit in with us perfectly."

"I think I have to convince June of that first."

This is the part where Bonnie should smile and say something encouraging like *Oh, you've got nothing to worry about, sugar.* She doesn't. She actually looks a little apologetic. "You're right about that. And it won't be easy. She's pretty set in her ways. I love my baby girl and will support her until the day I die, but I've gotta be honest, Ryan . . . I hope you can convince her, because I'd kill to see what a baby between you and June would look like."

We've jumped from getting past date number one to wheeling June out of a hospital with a baby in her arms. Moms truly are a force to be reckoned with. But here's the thing, is it weird to admit I've been dreaming of the same thing? Last night, I pictured June in a house of our own, with a kid on her hip, singing and making pancakes. *I mean, what the hell, Ryan?* I don't even know if June wants a family—and if she doesn't that's fine with me. But I think I'd like one with her.

"Do you have any advice for me?" I ask Bonnie.

She tells the sisters to give us a minute alone and then turns to me and smiles. It perfectly resembles the sort of smile June gave me before she slipped a laxative in my Coke in the cafeteria (I didn't know it until later, of course).

"Fortify yourself," she says ominously. "June has never been one to give up without a fight. Batten down the hatches, and if you really want her, prepare to hold on in rough waters, because mark my words, sugar, there *will* be rough waters ahead."

"Not the most encouraging advice."

She pats my arms. "'Cause I like you, I'll tell you something a little more practical to pair with the metaphorical. June doesn't like jumping into cold water. Never has, never will. In the summer, she proceeds inch for inch into the pool until, finally, before she knows it, she's up to her hair."

I squint. "This still feels metaphorical."

"Don't make her jump into the cold pool, Ryan. Inch her in and let her see for herself that the water's fine." She reaches up and pats my cheek, and it makes my stomach ache from how much the action reminds me of my mom.

Bonnie walks out of the kitchen, and I lean back against the counter, trying to let her words settle into my thoughts.

A minute later, June peeks her head into the kitchen. "You still alive in here?" Her brown hair is tied into a cute messy bun at the back of her head, and little wisps are hanging loose around her temples. Her face is free of makeup, letting me see all the freckles on her cheekbones and that her lips are naturally cotton-candy pink. I love cotton candy.

A few days ago, she never would have let me see her without her makeup on. Mrs. Broaden's words poke me, and I wonder if the water is up to June's knees or hips right now.

I extend my hand toward her, and she takes it hesitantly. I yank her in close and settle my hands on her hips. Her eyes pop up to mine, and I lean down, ready to have a full serving of cotton candy. I barely brush my lips over hers before she turns her head and whispers in my ear, "Betcha wish you could kiss me. That's one point for me, sucker."

She ducks under my arm and saunters out of the kitchen, only pausing to wink at me over her shoulder.

Five hours later (yes, five), June closes the front door behind her family. After spending the entire day with the Broadens, I feel like I've just finished a triathlon that I hadn't trained for. I'm worn out, but in the best way. It's been too long since I've been around family. I almost forgot what it was like. Years of nonstop work almost had me believing that I didn't even need a family. Like my pots and pans would come to life *Beauty and the Beast* style, and I'd have all the company I needed in the kitchen.

Now I see how deprived I've been.

I'm a man who has been locked up with only bread for a decade and was just presented with an entire feast fit for a king. I want more of this. Going back to that stale bread sounds miserable.

June locks the door dramatically, puts her back against it, and sinks to the floor. The new I ♥ NICK socks Bonnie gave her are pulled up her legs, stopping midcalves. "Gosh, I thought they were going to try to spend the night."

I smile before going to sit down beside her. We're shoulder to shoulder now, and every inch of me is aware of every inch of June. I look down at her, and my eye is drawn to the way her loose sweatshirt drapes off her shoulder a bit. I slip it back up into place. "Now I see where all the swag comes from," I say, gesturing toward her socks.

June wiggles her toes, and two light-pink spots hit the apples of her cheeks as she looks down at her lap. "Yeah. Mom's been giving me this stuff for years." A chuckle rolls through her, and she looks lighter than she has all week. "It's our inside joke that Nick Lachey is my perfect man."

"Stiff competition."

"Oh, there's no competition." She looks up at me deadpan. "He wins, hands down."

Now we're both laughing. It feels good. Right.

"How much of this stuff do you have?" I ask, bumping my knee against her Nick-covered calf.

"I don't think you want to know."

"I do. But only so I can decide if you're too freaky for me or not."

She sputters a laugh. "Oh, I am, for sure. I have closets full of this sexy swag."

"You don't."

June's eyes glint when she looks up at me. "Wanna bet? My mom has been giving me these gifts almost weekly for five years."

"Five years?" I ask but then wish I hadn't because I see that June catches on to the math I just did in my head, and her smile fades.

She pulls her knees up to her chest. "I can see you figured it out. She started giving me this stuff the week I called off my wedding."

"Did you tell her Ben cheated on you?"

Her lashes fan across her cheekbones as she looks at her toes. "No. I only told her that it didn't work out. I tried to tell her several times in the beginning, but it hurt too much to talk about . . . and honestly, I just felt embarrassed."

Seeing June like this, in her goofy socks, vulnerable and open with her hurt on full display, it makes me want to go hunt Ben down and knock his teeth out one by one.

"Have you ever thought about telling her what really happened?"

June's shoulders tense, and for a minute, I think that I've just popped the intimate bubble we were in. But then she picks a piece of lint off one of her socks and says, "I have lately."

I don't know what it is about the way she said *lately*, but it's as if she's trying to tell me that something is different now. That something is changing her. Or someone. That she feels more comfortable about facing her past.

I inch my fingers across the floor until they intertwine with hers. She blinks at our laced hands and looks up at me. "You look cute covered in Nick Lachey's face."

She shakes her head, but her smile grows. "You found the note I kept, didn't you?"

"Oh yeah. Several days ago."

And then, like magic, June leans her head on my shoulder. Honestly, I'm afraid to move. She's an exotic bird that has just landed on me, and if I shift even an inch, she'll fly away.

I slowly lean my head back against the door and breathe her in. Her hair smells like oranges again today, and my hand aches to run down her smooth legs. But I don't move.

"Ryan?" I don't like her tone. It feels like she's about to take flight. "When do you leave for Chicago?"

"When I do."

"Seriously. You're going to leave soon. We need to talk about that." I can see what she's doing—trying to sabotage us before we even get going. But I'm not going to let her.

Batten down the hatches.

"No, we don't. We'll figure everything out as we go. No need to have all the answers now."

"I don't like that."

"I know." I can't resist any longer, so I kiss her head. "Trust me."

"I don't like doing that, either."

"I know that too."

She takes a deep breath, and I feel her shoulders rise and fall against my side. We sit here, in this oddly peaceful state, for several minutes until her phone buzzes. It's sitting on the floor beside her, so I'm able to see the name HUNTER FROM PARTY flash across her screen. My first instinct is to take a hammer and pound her phone into dust. But since that would make me look the tiniest bit domineering, I decide to swing heavily the opposite way instead.

"Go ahead." I nod toward the phone. It's clear by the way June is chewing the corner of her mouth that she does not want to open that text around me, so I do what I do best and taunt her. "Gone soft on me, June Bug? Surely you're not worrying about my feelings?"

She flashes a glare at me from under her lashes. "I know what you're doing."

"Is it working?"

She snatches her phone from the floor and swipes it open. "Yes."

Our eyes both scan the words, and I try very hard not to find that hammer.

HUNTER FROM PARTY: Hey June! Sorry I'm just now getting around to texting you. The past few weeks have been insane from work, but I haven't stopped thinking about you and wanting that date. Any chance you're free tomorrow night and want to go on an art crawl with me?

"Who is he?" I ask, making sure to keep my voice neutral and calm.

She shrugs. "Just a guy I met at Logan's birthday party a few weeks ago."

June isn't smiling, and for some reason, that gives me hope. So much of me wants her to text this Hunter guy back and tell him to go jump off a bridge, but then I remember what Bonnie told me.

"You should go. Sounds fun," I say, but I don't move my hand away from hers. Whether she likes it or not, this hand belongs to me now.

"Are you kidding?" She looks up to me and searches my face.

I force myself to look nonchalant. No big deal. I'm the poster child for repressed emotions right now. "Not kidding. I think you'd have a lot of fun at an art crawl."

"Well, yeah . . . but . . ." She lets go of my hand and turns to face me. Crossing her legs, she settles a scrutinizing gaze on my face. She's hooked me up to a lie detector before she begins her questions. "Have you or have you not been trying to date me this past week?"

Okay, I see. It's not a lie detector. We're in the courtroom now, and I'm on the stand. "I have. And I will date you, just not yet."

Her eyes narrow. I picture her wearing a sexy black pencil dress with a briefcase at her side, and it makes this whole thing more fun. "But you're okay with me dating other guys in the meantime?"

"Yes, Your Honor."

She doesn't acknowledge my sexy joke. "Why? This is another game, isn't it? You have an ulterior motive in wanting me to go out with him."

I smile and lift a brow. "Now why would I want you to go out with other guys if I'm into you?"

"That's what I'm trying to figure out."

I lean forward slowly and rest my lips against the shell of her ear. "Let me know when you figure it out." While I'm there, I decide not to waste an opportunity and kiss her neck before standing up.

June stays seated, eyeing me cautiously, but a faint smile hovers over her lips because she loves this. She loves the strategy. The dance. The calculation. It used to be fun in high school, but now that we know what the other person's lips feel like, the game is twice as exciting.

I stick my hand out, and she accepts it, letting me pull her up to her feet. With her standing inches from my chest, I say, "Go ahead. Accept him."

"I will if I want," she says, angling her head to the side a little and eyeing me one last time. I'm not sure if she found the answer she was looking for in my face or not, but finally, she types out a quick response accepting Hunter's invitation and hits send.

CHAPTER 21

June

D o you know what it feels like to be given a five-star prime rib from the best restaurant in town and then have it ripped away from you only to be replaced with a greasy fast-food burger off the dollar menu? I do. That's what happened when Ryan told me I should go on the date with Hunter.

There's not a chance in the world that a date with a random guy that I met at Logan's boring birthday party would be anywhere close to a date with Ryan. But let's be honest here, Hunter could show up to my house completely naked with a body like Thor, hand me a million dollars, and I would still just be like *meh, I guess that's cool*. Because Ryan has ruined me for the rest of the world.

I wanted to call Stacy and ask her what I should do, but I picked up my phone five times and set it back down because it's time I start figuring things out on my own. Stacy is married now. She's gone. The sooner I stop leaning on her, the better.

That's why, right now on Monday night, I'm sitting in an empty movie theater (except for the old man in the front row sneaking his cat out of a duffel bag, which I really don't want to concern myself with) about to consume five pounds of popcorn. Seriously. I could have gone with a hypothetical absurd number, but I'm holding the big tub that costs $30, and I would bet all my life savings that it actually weighs five pounds. And when you realize that I'm dead serious and plan to eat this entire bucket myself, it makes the five-pounds thing seem more terrifying.

So, why am I here alone about to send myself into a butter coma? Because Ryan has completely wedged himself under my skin, and I couldn't bring myself to go on another meaningless date with yet another man I know I'll never care about.

The minute after Ryan left my house last night, I texted Hunter and bailed. Why? Because I already told you, Ryan is a wrecking ball in my life. He rolled into town and crushed right through my walls. Suddenly, dates that have absolutely no chance of leading to anything permanent feel disappointing. The fun is gone.

I want Ryan in my life.

However, since I am the most stubborn human being on the face of the earth, I am pretending I'm on a date with another man, because Ryan cannot know that he's won my heart over so quickly. I need to make him sweat. Torture has always been one of our favorite games, and I'm playing it now with a smile on my face.

Just as the theater goes dark and the trailers begin to roll, my phone lights up in the cup holder. My maniacal smile grows when I see who it is. I even go so far as to chuckle evilly, but then cat-man turns around and shushes me like I'm the one with the social problem. Fine. I hunker down into my seat and try to hide the light from my phone in case the illumination offends the cat.

RYAN: On your date?

JUNE: Yep. It's going great too.

I'm smiling at my diabolical ways as I dip my hand into the buttery pot of gold in my lap and wait for his response.

RYAN: Good. You deserve a fun night out.

My shoulders deflate a little, but I'm not completely discouraged, so I trudge on.

JUNE: Fun is definitely the right word. Best date I've been on in a
    while.

And that's not even a lie! Turns out, I'm a phenomenal date. I don't even skimp on the refreshments. I've treated myself to a box of candy, a bathtub of popcorn, AND a large Coke.

Bonus: I don't even have to worry about someone with bad breath trying to stick their tongue in my mouth during this movie.

RYAN: Shit. Hunter must really be something special. Should I
    be worried?
JUNE: For sure. And he looks so good.

Still not technically a lie, because now I'm talking about the hot actor on the screen.

RYAN: I don't care what he looks like. What are you wearing?

First, I look around the theater to make sure my mom hasn't magically appeared over my shoulder to read what I'm about to text. And second, I look down at my 98° sweatshirt and black leggings that are so threadbare there's a chance they will fall off mid-movie when the extra strain of this salty popcorn bloat kicks in. *How can I spin this one?*

JUNE: A little black number that leaves nothing to the
  imagination.

Because of all the holes in the seams.

And then, just to drive the knife a little deeper, I turn my phone
on *Do Not Disturb* and focus all my attention on the movie. It's difficult, though. My mind strays to Ryan like he's telepathically pulling me to him. After what feels like the longest movie in the history
of movies, the credits finally roll.

"Thank goodness," I say in something like a groan, which makes
cat-man give me some serious side-eye as he's stuffing his furry
friend back into his duffel bag. Also, who lets someone into a theater with a duffel bag? Teenagers should not be ticket-stub rippers.

I'm so tired I just want to rush home and dive under my covers,
but I'm afraid that somehow Ryan will know I've turned in early, so
I force myself to sit here until the last name rolls across the screen
and the lights come on. A group of teenagers comes in with brooms,
laughing about something until they spot me sitting alone in the
dead center of the theater like a horror movie that's come to life.
Their smiles drop, and they all clear their throats as if they're afraid
I'm going to tattle on them for laughing.

But then, when they get closer (because I'm still sitting here)
their smiles crack again—this time at my expense.

"Nice sweatshirt, Grandma," says the one with fake bleached
blond hair, snickering as he makes his way down my aisle to sweep.

I'm the mature one, though, and don't have to stoop to his
childish level. I don't *have* to, but obviously I do, because that little
weasel needs to learn some manners. There are at least ten popcorn kernels left at the bottom of the bucket, so I make frightening
eye contact with the little rugrat before I dump the bucket over
onto the floor. "Oops," I say with a dainty shrug.

I'm feeling pretty good about my epic burn on that high

schooler as I make my way from my seat to the aisle—up until I trip on my own feet and accidentally slosh the rest of my Coke onto the front of my shirt. The teenager eyes me with a gloaty face and I can't help but feel I've brought this on myself. Fine, lesson learned. Next time I take the high road.

Despite the soda drenching my shirt, tonight was a success. I had a peaceful evening in comfy clothes, AND I still get to win my war with Ryan. Would I rather have been curled up in that theater holding his hand? Yes. But under no circumstances must he learn that information.

I pull into my driveway and finally pull out my phone to send Ryan a taunting text about how great a kisser my date is, when I notice a light coming through my living room window. A light that I specifically remember turning off before I left.

I jerk my eyes to the street, and that's when I notice what I didn't notice before. RYAN'S CAR. What in the hell is he doing here? But I don't have to think too long about that. He's moving his chess piece across the board is what. I have got to get that spare key back from him.

I puff out a sigh and get out of my car, crouching down and shutting the door softly before creeping around the house. I stay as low to the ground as possible to avoid the windows because I have no other choice. I can't just walk through that front door and laugh it off. *Ha ha, you win again, Ryan! I took myself to the movies, and some teenagers made fun of me!*

No. Half in love with this man or not, I have to crush him. Which is why I'm going around to the back door and unlocking it without making a sound. I'm Tom Cruise right now, picking a lock and ninja rolling as quiet as air through my kitchen (actually, I'm slithering like a snake because I have no idea how to ninja roll).

I make it through the kitchen, and the sound of the TV grows louder as I approach the living room. This part is going to be tricky. The hallway from my kitchen to my bedroom has a straight shot into the living room. The couch is in the middle of the living room facing the opposite way of the hallway. If I can just stay quiet and move slowly, I'll be able to get into my bedroom without Ryan knowing I'm here.

You might be wondering what I plan to do after I make it to my room. Answer: what any other desperate human being would do. Change into my sexiest black dress, apply way too much makeup, slither back out the door, and then go around the house to make a grand entrance. I'll probably smear my makeup a bit just to really sell the whole kissing thing.

It takes me five minutes to inchworm my way through the kitchen, and I don't even want to think about all the nastiness I'm collecting on my sticky shirt along the way. Worth it, though.

I'm now approaching the challenge zone. If I make it through this obstacle, I win a new car.

The glow of the TV illuminates the room, and I'm close enough now that I can see Ryan's profile on the couch. He's hunkered down, nice and comfy on my couch with his feet propped up on the coffee table. I choose not to think about how good he looks there. How I wouldn't mind seeing him there every day for the rest of my life. No time to contemplate the future, though. I must keep my eye on the prize.

Now I'm in the red zone. Carpet burn is assailing my elbows and forearms, and I think I've ripped a new hole in my ancient leggings, but none of this matters, because my stealthy moves are working. Ryan is oblivious. He hasn't so much as twitched a muscle as I continue my progress.

I make it down the hallway, and I'm two feet from my bedroom door. Ryan coughs, and I freeze. I wait until I'm 100 percent certain he is enthralled in his show again to keep slithering. And now, I've done it. My elbows are inside my doorframe, and my smile is stretching from earlobe to earlobe because I WIN, RYAN HENDERSON!

"Date go well?"

Dammit.

I pause mid army crawl and glance over my shoulder. Ryan hasn't moved. He's still staring at the TV like the villain in a movie, cloaked in darkness.

I scrunch my face up in painful defeat as I rise from the floor. "How did you know I was here?"

Ryan slowly turns his head to look at me, showing his tilted smile. "I saw your Jeep pull in. And the alarm beeped when you opened the back door. And you were breathing like you competed in a triathlon all the way down that hallway." I feel like he could have left that last part off.

My shoulders slump, and I lean on the doorframe for support. "Super."

"Why are you sneaking in?"

There is no way to answer that question that will not immediately incriminate me, so instead, I deflect.

Rounding the couch, I flip on the lights and then gawk at the man on my couch. "Better question, what are *you* doing in my living room in your pajamas?" I go over and knock Ryan's bare feet off my coffee table because I'm angry that no one in the history of sleepy men has ever worn flannel sleep pants and a plain gray tee as good as him.

He smiles, amused by my outburst. "My hotel reservation ended at ten o'clock this morning, so I'm bunking with you tonight, roomie."

My mouth falls open. "Umm, no, you most certainly are not! Go renew your reservation, pajama-man."

I can't have him here under the same roof as me for a whole night. My skin boils hot just looking at him from across the room.

"Nah, I'd rather stay here with you."

I stare at him, blinking. "No. Just no. Your opinion doesn't matter here."

He scrunches his nose up and says, "Respectfully, I disagree. Mainly because I weigh twice as much as you, and you'll never be able to lift me off this couch. So . . . fake your date?"

I scoff. "Of course not. I went on a date."

His eyes drop to my outfit, and I see the faint curl of his lips. "Little black number?"

I raise my eyebrows and widen my eyes as if to say *I dare you to admit this outfit is ugly!* "It's black."

"And the stain?"

"Soda."

He nods. "Didn't know they serve soda at art crawls."

"They did at this one."

"And Hunter? Did he have a fun night?"

Who's to say exactly what Hunter was up to tonight, but he seemed like a pretty fun-loving guy. Not the sort to sit home and sulk over a lost date. "He had a fantastic night."

"Oh, good. 'Cause I was worried when he came by about an hour ago to pick you up that maybe you guys had your wires crossed."

"What! Oh no!" I drop the act for the first time, worried that I accidentally stood the man up if my cancellation text didn't go through.

I grab my phone from my purse and frantically scroll through my texts until I find the chat between me and Hunter. I read, read, read until I get to the part where I realize Ryan just tricked me, because my *cancellation text absolutely went through.* That scheming little turd face!

My eyes snap up to Ryan, and I'm surprised lasers don't shoot out of them and slice him in half. I race toward him, grab an over-stuffed pillow from the couch, and start pummeling him with it.

"YOU JUST MADE THAT UP!" I say, emphasizing every word in between hits.

He's laughing and curled up in a ball like a little baby with his hands over his head. "And you just confirmed that you weren't really on a date with Hunter!"

"YOU ARE THE WORST, AND I HATE YOU!"

Bam. Bam. Bam.

Faster than a snake bite, Ryan reaches out and swipes my legs out from under me, pulling me down on top of him. He rolls me over so he's pinning me onto the couch. His expression is equal parts danger and amusement. My stomach twists as I look in his eyes.

"You don't hate me."

"I might," I say quietly.

"But you don't."

I swallow. "I should."

"You love the game just as much as I do."

My eyes trace a line from one dark eyebrow down his sharp cheekbone to his bottom lip and back up to his other eyebrow. I just painted a heart on his face with my gaze. "I like it a little bit."

His body is heavy on mine, and I love it so much that I consider buying a weighted blanket. Ryan smells like crisp mountain air and all my teenage desires combined into one. I think he showered here, making me wonder if his body wash is still in there.

"June." His voice is gravelly. "Why didn't you go out with Hunter?" This is Ryan's way of saying *It's time*. He's been patient and understanding with me, but he can only take so much waiting for my reciprocation.

It's time.

The last bit of fight I have left in me vanishes. "Because he wasn't you."

Everything is so still and quiet in the house. Ryan looks back and forth between my eyes and then slowly dips his head down and kisses my lips. It's a tender, I'm-in-no-hurry, melt-your-kneecaps kind of kiss, and I stay completely still. He breaks the seal of our mouths slowly only to lay another one on my bottom lip, and then the right corner, and then the left. I don't close my eyes, but Ryan does. I see the whole thing in heartbreaking detail.

I think I love him.

He pulls away with a soft, patient smile and then shifts to the back of the couch so he can wrap his arm around my abdomen and pull me in close. He's the big spoon, and I'm silent as he grabs the remote and hits resume on his show.

This, my heart whispers, *is what we've been missing.*

I relax into Ryan and close my eyes. I don't care about what's on the TV. I'm too busy healing as he holds me—sticky skin, thread-bare leggings, and all.

CHAPTER 22

Ryan

I'm standing outside of June's house, looking at the name flashing on my phone that I can't avoid any longer. Noah Prescott has been texting, emailing, and calling nonstop over the past few days. I'm afraid that if I ignore him any longer, he'll send a carrier pigeon. Or worse, he'll hunt me down himself.

"Hello?"

"There you are! I thought maybe you were dead or something."

"Not dead. Just been trying to stay off the grid for a bit." I glance at June's door, wondering if she's awake yet. I left her asleep on the couch. That woman sleeps like a brick.

When I woke up with her in my arms, I briefly thought about pretending I was asleep so I could savor the feel of her against me for as long as possible. But then I became aware of the painful sensation shooting up my arm, and I had to pry it out from under her. She didn't flinch. I think I could have rolled her off onto the floor, and she would have stayed asleep.

I got up at my usual six-thirty time and made a pot of coffee (still no sign of life from June), shaved and changed into my running clothes (she hadn't moved), and decided to go for a jog until she woke up. She could be awake in there now, and the thought has me wanting to end this call with Noah as quickly as possible.

"Yeah, no kidding. I was starting to feel like a jealous girlfriend for how many texts I sent you."

"Well, you've got me now. What do you need?"

He sighs. "I've been trying to hold the investors for your answer like you said, but they are getting restless. I can't hold them any longer. They said they want an answer by the end of the week or they offer it to Martin."

I turn my back to the house and run my hands over my face. "End of the week Sunday?"

"Saturday," he says, ruthlessly stealing a day out from under me. "Ryan, man, I can't even believe you are hesitating on this. It's the deal of a lifetime."

"I don't know what to tell you. I'm just not sold on it yet."

"Why? Do you have other offers you're entertaining?"

I glance back at June's house. "Something like that."

"I hate when you're vague. It makes me feel antsy."

I catch movement in the window and see June standing from the couch with a blanket wrapped around her shoulders and over her head like a hooded cape as she walks back toward her room. She's so dang cute. "Listen, I've gotta go, Noah."

"Ryan, don't you hang up on me ag—"

"You'll have my answer on Saturday." And then I hang up.

The heaviness I thought I escaped settles back over me, and I take another lap around the block to give June a little extra time to wake up without me around. Yeah, I'm such a nice guy that the only reason I'm delaying going inside is to give June some privacy. Not at all because my time of limbo has just ended, and I've got to make a decision I'm not sure I'm ready to make yet.

When I get back to June's house, I'm drenched with sweat and breathing hard, but I'm no closer to a decision. I want to talk to June about the job offer, but I also don't want to spring it on her, because I feel like we had a breakthrough last night.

I have a sinking feeling that saying something like *Morning, June! Hey, so I've been meaning to tell you about this job of a lifetime I was offered that will literally eat up all my time and require my undivided attention for the next three years. Think I should take it?* will only take us back three spaces. I will not pass go. No collecting two hundred dollars. I don't want to worry her with something I'm not even sure I want.

I've put my career first for so long that I'm ready to put June first now. I want to take this relationship as far as she'll allow it to go. So, for now, I need to keep it to myself. I still have a few days until I have to give Noah my answer, and I plan on using all of them to find out if June is ready for this relationship or not.

Walking into the house, I'm surprised to find her sitting at the table, still wrapped up in her fuzzy blanket, feet curled up in her chair, eating a bowl of cereal. She sees me step inside, and the spoon freezes in her mouth. Her gaze dips down and takes in my sweaty appearance and then darts back up to my face. She finishes chewing with a secret smile.

"Good morning," I say cautiously as I approach her. She doesn't respond, just holds that small grin on her face. "Are you about to dive into a freak-out and completely regret everything that happened last night?"

She slowly shakes her head no. It gives me courage to get closer. I stop just behind her and lean down to kiss the side of her neck. She makes a soft *mmmmm* sound that makes my stomach dip.

"So, I've decided when and where I want our first date to be," I say against the warm skin of her neck.

"Oh, yeah?"

"Chicago."

June pulls away, taking away my access to her neck, so she can look me in the eyes. "Chicago? Why?"

I take a seat at the table, facing her. "Because I have something special planned that can only happen there. If I only get one date, I intend on making it count."

June looks oddly thoughtful. She's hiding something behind those green eyes, and I want to know what it is. But I also know that she's not the kind of woman to spill her secrets. It's going to take time to get them all out of her, so I let it be.

"Please? I also want to show you where I live and the restaurant I've been working in." I'm basically trying to throw sprinkles on top of a broccoli sundae, hoping to make it look more appealing.

June moves her lips from side to side as she contemplates it. I'm holding my breath. "Okay," she finally says, and then a big smile cracks over her lips, and she brings another bite of cereal to her mouth. "Actually, I was going to say yes from the beginning. I just like watching you sweat." She side-eyes my torso and arms.

"Is that right? You should have said something—I've got a lot more sweat under my shirt," I say, reaching for the bottom hem of my shirt and lifting my brow.

"*Ryan.*" She says my name like she does when she wants me to behave. It only eggs me on.

I lift my shirt a few inches. "Is it hot in here or what?"

"Ryan, not the abs!" She covers her eyes dramatically with her blanket. "I'm just an innocent young woman." But she's laughing.

"Okay, fine," I say, sounding deeply disappointed. "You can look now."

June pulls down the blanket and squeaks when she finds me shirtless with a big grin. She rolls her eyes and grabs her glass of water. I only have enough time to blink before she tosses it on me to really teach me a lesson. Water goes everywhere. I, however, don't flinch because I just went on a run, and the cool water feels amazing.

June stands up abruptly and stomps into the kitchen, mumbling something about *making it worse* and then brings back a towel. I offer to let her dry me off, to which she takes the towel and pops me with it.

The rest of the morning goes on like this, with June and me doing what we do best: teasing and flirting. I end up prying her soggy cereal out of her hands and dumping it down the drain so I can make her a proper breakfast. We both eat and talk over our second cups of coffee, and June tells me little tidbits of her life that I've missed out on over the last decade. I do the same.

But I notice anytime my topic veers into the realm of work, she freezes up, so I avoid the subject like the plague. Instead of talking about my job, she learns about the hot dog vendor I swear makes a better meal than any gourmet dish I've ever had, and I tell her about the little bistro where I spent most of my off time during culinary school.

"What was it like?" she asks, leaning forward.

It's odd. I haven't thought about that bistro much since I left France, but lately, it's been sitting at the forefront of my mind. It feels good to finally let it out. "Honestly, it was nothing special. It was dark, and small, and only sat about fifteen people. But there was something so nice about it. They didn't even have many options on the menu. Everything was simple, nonintrusive, and just what I needed after a long day of overanalyzing every single spice and herb on the planet."

"Sounds nice," says June with a soft smile that I want to swim in.

"Maybe I'll get to take you there one day." But shoot, I think I spooked her. The spell breaks, and she takes in a deep breath, looking around the table before standing up.

"Wow, when did it get to be so late? I've got to get to the bakery." Suddenly, she's the rabbit from *Alice in Wonderland,* and she's late for a very important date. And I know why. I just yanked her down in the water another inch, and she wasn't ready for it.

Before she can walk away, though, I grab her hand and pull her to a stop and tug her down onto my lap. "Don't do that," I say, making her look at me.

"Do what?"

"Get weird on me again."

She avoids my eyes by looking down at where her finger is running across my collarbone. "I'm not weird. You're weird."

I grin at her attempt at a burn and bend my head to catch her eyes. "I can't help it, June. I'm trying to hold back, but it's tough. I've been holding back from you since I was twelve. I don't want to anymore." I also really need her to stop doing that with her finger, because I'm trying to move slowly and respectfully with her, but my brain is trying to erase those words from my vocabulary.

June's shoulders soften, and she slides her gaze to mine. She contemplates me for a second and then slowly bends forward to kiss me. It's short. Her lips were barely on mine long enough for me to blink, but that kiss means more to me than any kiss I've ever had, because *she* initiated it.

I'm filled with the urge to go out and buy an important leather-bound journal complete with quill and ink so I can transcribe what just happened. *November 15, June Broaden kissed me by her own accord.* That's the only thing I would ever write in that journal, because the memory deserves a monument all its own. It's progress.

She's smiling as she pulls away and then pokes me in my cheek where my dimple lives. "I'm trying. It's going to take me longer, though, because I wasn't expecting this, and I've been conditioning myself since I broke things off with Ben to believe that I can't trust anyone."

"I understand that."

"Do you?" she asks, looking like she truly wants to know.

"I do."

"Okay, good. Then don't give up on me when I get weird."

I clasp my arms around her waist. "I won't."

"Promise?"

"I promise, June." I mean it. I'll wait for her for as long as it takes.

She smiles and reaches up to smoosh my cheeks together. Not exactly the sexy turn I thought this conversation would take, but I can take one for the team if it means watching her smile.

"Stacy and I always do this after a serious conversation." Ah. I see now.

I ask if she misses Stacy while my cheeks are still smooshed together, giving me a fish face.

She drops her hands. "So much. But I'm just trying not to think about it. Or call her a million times a day. I want to give her and Logan space to get acclimated in their new life."

I laugh. "They've been together since junior high. How much acclimating do you think they really need?"

She laughs, too, and the sound lessens that weight that's always on my shoulders. "You're probably right."

"Have you told her about us?"

"Are you going to be mad if I say no?"

"I'll flip this table."

"Then YEP. She knows everything."

I shake my head and lean forward to kiss her cheek before picking her up and depositing her on the floor. "Tell Stacy. She'll want to know." Something tells me I'm not the only one June is worried will hurt her.

June and I don't broach any serious topics again for the rest of the morning. She goes into her bathroom to shower and get ready for the day, and I make myself useful by snooping through the stack of papers on her counter. I notice that they are offers to buy Stacy's half of the bakery.

My first thought is that I should add my name to the top. My second thought is to take that first thought and burn it to the ground. June doesn't need me to help her run that bakery. She doesn't need anyone's help with it. I honestly don't know why she's entertaining offers when she should buy it herself.

But when she comes out of her room an hour later in a form-fitting, black, long-sleeve top, hair braided and draped over one shoulder, and tight jeans hugging her waist with holes down the legs that do more than hint at the soft tan skin living under them, I push the papers aside and decide we'll talk about it later. She looks good. Better than good. This woman is a killer, and as I grab her jeans by the belt loops and tug her closer to me, I realize I'm dead.

I love her. I think I always have.

"June," I say, dragging out her name to let her know I'm suspicious. "Why do you smell like me?"

She peeks up at me from under her long lashes and presses her lips together. She's a kid who just got caught with a bar of chocolate smeared all over her face. "I was out of my bodywash, so I had to use yours?" She phrased it like a question, not a statement.

I shake my head at her. She used my bodywash.

She loves me.

CHAPTER 23

June

I come home from work on Friday afternoon to a note on my bed beside an empty duffel bag that reads: *Be packed by 5:00. Plane leaves for Chicago at 8:30, and we're going to be on it. I took the liberty of starting your packing for you. You're welcome.*

I peek in the bag and realize it's not totally empty. It looks as if Ryan pulled out my lingerie drawer and dumped the entire contents into this duffel bag. *Ha! You wish, buddy.*

After I've removed over three-fourths of the options Ryan and his liberty chose for me, I pack a few of the winter items I never get to wear in Charleston. Honestly, part of me thought Ryan forgot about Chicago. It's been a few days since he mentioned it, so I assumed it was on the back burner. Or not happening at all. Which was fine with me, considering how amazing our time here has been together.

Ryan has been staying with me all week, doing lots of things that feel suspiciously like dating, although he always swears it's not.

ME: *Let me get this straight. You want to take me to dinner, but it's not a date?*

RYAN: *Right. We just both need to eat, and you're out of food.* (I had plenty of food.) *And I'm going to pay for you too. Easier than making the waitress split the bill.*

And then my personal favorite is when we snuggle before bed and watch a movie.

ME: *Is this still not a date?* (He was literally lying horizontal with me on the couch while we made out off and on.)

RYAN: *Nope. I do this with all my friends. But usually Logan makes me be the little spoon.*

After I've finished packing and freshening my makeup, I have ten minutes to spare. I feel an undeniable need to keep moving, though, so I go in to clean my kitchen. Except, Ryan must have already done it earlier, not anticipating my need to stress-clean every surface in my house. How dare he be so thoughtful and clean my kitchen! That's fine. I just need to get some blood flowing (a phrase I've never thought in my life, but that I always hear Jake say when he's stressed).

So I do jumping jacks.

Now, I know I'm being absurd—that was never in question—but I have to keep moving, because if I sit still, I'll chicken out. I think that's why Ryan went ahead and booked our flights for tonight. He knew that if too much time passed between me agreeing to go with him and the actual departure date, I would pack up my whole house and move to Hawaii just to avoid taking this trip with him.

I'm very mature in relationships.

I'm midjump when my phone starts ringing. "Talk to me!" I say like one of those overly confident people on sitcoms, because I'm trying to pretend that I am one.

"Did I just . . . interrupt something?" asks my brother, letting his horrified tone convey exactly what he suspects that *something* to be. Messing with Jake is one of my favorite pastimes, so I have half a mind to say something like, *Oh, Ryan, stop it, I'm on the phone!* just to really freak him out. But I refrain because, like I said, I'm very mature.

"You interrupted jumping jacks," I say, and he sputters a laugh like I just told him a joke. "What's wrong with you? I'm serious. I'm doing jumping jacks."

"Wow. Did something bad happen?"

"Now, what about my statement would make you ask that?"

"Besides running, I've never seen you do anything close to working out. I didn't even know you knew how to do a jumping jack. Do your feet leave the ground when you jump?"

Rude. But now I'm questioning myself.

"It's where you starfish and then pencil, right?"

"Yeeeahhhh . . . something like that." He's fully laughing at me now.

"Knock it off, butthead."

His chuckles trail off. "Okay, why are you starfishing?"

I hadn't intended to tell Jake that I'm going to Chicago. Why? I'm not totally sure. I think I didn't feel like explaining myself to him or overanalyzing everything. Because it feels like I'm tightrope walking along this relationship and the slightest breeze will kick me off to my doom.

I hate that I'm this way. I hate that life has made me so scared—but knowing it and fighting it is better than going through life oblivious to my flaws, right?

"I'm . . . going with Ryan to Chicago tonight . . . for a few days."

I let that statement hang on the line between us, and I shut my eyes tight, waiting for his response. Or his warning. Or his big-brother censure.

"Pack a heavy jacket. It's freaking cold there."

Wait. What? Where's the lecture? Or the taunting? Or the million questions?

I peek my eyes back open. "Are you kidnapped or something? Where's my overly cautious brother who's always warning me to take things slow?"

He gives a short chuckle. "June. I love you. I want what's best for you. And I only had to watch you with Ryan for two seconds the other day to see everything I needed to know. Go to Chicago. Have fun and don't overthink everything. I trust him with you."

I pack Jake's words into my duffel bag and take them with me to the airport. Ryan showed up at my house with a coffee and a snack right after I ended the call with Jake, and I realized my brother was right. Actually, Jake's always right, but I will take that truth with me to my grave. I need to enjoy my time with Ryan and stop waiting for disaster ahead. *Not everyone is Ben. Not every man is going to hurt me.*

I would tattoo that statement somewhere on my body if I didn't think people would look at me funny.

And now, I think Ryan is a mind reader, because on our way to the airport, he reaches over and takes my hand and says, "When did you get your sunflower tattoo?"

I whip my head to him. "Huh? How did you know I was thinking about tattoos?"

He grins but doesn't look away from the road. "I can see your thoughts. Didn't you know?" He says it so seriously that, for a second, I think he's telling the truth. I knew he was a sorcerer of some kind. It's how he manages to wield this powerful, sexy man aura that I can't resist. "June, I'm kidding. You've been rubbing your sunflower tattoo for the past five miles."

"Oh." Why do I like the sorcerer idea better? I also don't love that I seem to put all my feelings on display when Ryan is around. Or wait. It's a *good* thing to show Ryan how I'm feeling.

It's opposite of my natural inclination, but I'm determined not to sabotage this relationship with Ryan, so I tell him everything. I tell him that after Ben broke my heart, I went straight to the tattoo parlor and had the nice man with fifteen piercings and over one hundred tattoos ink the sunflower onto my skin. It was a spontaneous decision, but I don't regret it.

"Why after you broke up?"

I look down at my hands and fidget. "Ben didn't like tattoos. Always said they looked kind of trashy. It's so ironic considering he slept with someone else a week before our wedding, which is the ultimate trashy look." I scoff. "I decided that day it was time to start doing what I wanted and not give a shit what Ben did or didn't like."

And then something amazing happens. I realize that I just talked about Ben and what he did to me, and for once, it doesn't sting. Not a bit. This is curious to me, so I force my thoughts down that rabbit trail a little further just to see if it was a fluke. I let myself remember picking up Ben's phone when he left the room and finding a text from Hallie with a photo of the two of them snuggling under the covers as if they'd been a couple for a hundred years.

Huh. No pain. No knots in my stomach. No nothing. In fact, all I can really focus on is Ryan's thumb tracing circles on the back of my hand.

He peeks at me from the corner of his eye. "I'm glad you got the tattoo. It also looks superhot on you so that's a plus."

I don't know why, but a blush creeps over my face. I think it's a combination of the way Ryan is looking at me and what his touch does to me.

"Thanks," I say quietly, but my voice betrays how much his words mean to me and it cracks.

The rest of the night goes by in a zoom. Ryan and I catch a flight to O'Hare International Airport, where we take a detour before going to baggage claim and stop at the food court. "I heard your stomach growling on the plane," he says before once again shocking me to no end by steering us toward the Taco Bell. Once was a fluke—twice is certainly on purpose.

I squeeze his arm while we wait in line. "You know, that night you got us tacos while we waited on the locksmith, I thought for sure you were stooping to fast food because you liked me. Now I'm starting to think it wasn't for me at all. Answer honestly, Ryan Henderson, is this your favorite restaurant?"

He grins down at me as we advance toward the front of the line. "I've tried to re-create the flavor of their beef. I can't match it no matter how hard I try."

A laugh rolls through me, completely delighted by this turn of events. Ryan, Mr. Michelin Chef, is a fast-food lover just like me.

After scarfing our meals in the food court, Ryan takes my hand as we both roll our suitcases behind us to the parking lot where a 4Runner truck is parked. But not just any ole 4Runner truck . . . it's a *nice* one. He's clearly had a lot done to it. It looks lifted, has big tires and blacked-out windows. It fits him. Still something I could 100 percent picture Ryan driving in high school, but with a much cooler twist. (An expensive-looking twist.) It's a simple thing, but I love that I get to know what he drives. What his guilty pleasure food is. That he wears socks with his PJs.

I'm high on delight by the time we load into his truck and make our way toward his place, feeling so joyful I could bust.

And that's why I rotate in my seat so my back is against the door and curl my legs up in the seat.

"What are you doing?" Ryan asks, glancing at me and then back to the road.

"Staring at you."

This amuses him, but I'm dead serious.

"That's creepy."

"Maybe I'm a little creepy then. Get used to it. You're too pretty not to stare at."

Ryan just shakes his head slightly as he moves his hand to my knee and keeps his focus on the road. We don't talk the rest of the drive, and he lets me stare at him the whole time. I lay my head against the seat and watch the interstate lights flash behind his head, something soft and folky playing on the radio.

I catch myself thinking something that I haven't thought in a long time.

So this is what happy feels like?

CHAPTER 24

June

"Oh, I see now! You're loaded," I say as soon as Ryan and I walk through the front door of his "apartment." And I mean *apartment* in the most sarcastic way possible, because this place is bigger than my house. And I have a pretty good size house.

He laughs. "Something like that."

I give Ryan some serious side-eye before walking deeper into the apartment. My eyes bounce from the exposed brick wall to the six-foot windows and then draw a line all the way up the enormous ceilings more fit for a cathedral than a home. There's a black slate fireplace against the exterior wall, and exactly the kind of kitchen you would expect to find in a famous chef's home just beyond the main living room.

The thing that strikes me the most, though, is his apartment doesn't smell like him. There's not a hint of his cool, spicy man scent anywhere. Maybe it's because every surface in this place is made from brick, or wood, or slate, or steel, and his scent has nothing to grab on to. I mean, don't get me wrong, this place is

INCREDIBLE. But it's the kind of incredible that makes you want to just hover by the door and snap a photo while passing by instead of going inside and getting comfy.

It's sterile and a little cold. But then again, maybe that's just because Jake was right and it's freaking cold outside here. How anyone survives with that wind chill is beyond me.

"You hate it," Ryan says without even the slightest bit of offense in his voice.

I gasp and dramatically cover my heart. "Hate it? No! I'm just . . . taking it all in, and *ohmygosh* what is this thing?!" I rush into the living room and point an accusatory finger at the couch (if you can call it that).

Ryan isn't surprised. He's smiling. "My couch."

"No!" I say, taking great offense. "This, sir, is an oversize brick covered in uncomfortable leather." I tap the metal armrests. "A couch should not be reflective."

"I agree."

"Then why do you have it?!"

"It came with the apartment. All this did. I bought it fully furnished."

I'm sure I look as if I've just witnessed a grisly murder. "Ryan. No. Tell me that's not true. How do you manage to live here with it so . . . uncomfortable?"

His smile fades a little as he walks over to drop our bags by the kitchen island. "I don't. Not really. I sleep here maybe five hours a night, and then I go to the gym, and then to work. Rinse and repeat. It's how I've lived my whole adult life."

My heart tugs for him. "That must be exhausting. How do you keep that up?"

He gives me a no-big-deal shrug and heads into the kitchen. I follow him, watching as he pours a glass of water and takes a long drink. He wipes his mouth with the back of his hand and then sees that I'm still waiting for him to expound. "I haven't had a choice. That's what it takes to be successful in my industry."

I don't know how to feel about that. Something is prickling at me, but I can't figure it out.

Ryan sees my furrowed brows and comes to stand in front of me. He takes his thumb and runs it across the area between my brows and then smiles when my face softens. "Better."

He kisses my cheek and then my jaw and then my neck. The slight scruff of his five o'clock shadow tickles the sensitive skin on my neck, and chill bumps erupt down my arms. Just as I'm ready to melt in his arms and gear up for an all-night kiss fest, he pulls away. "I'm going to get a shower. Make yourself comfortable."

He moves around me, but this time, I'm the one to catch him by the arm and pull him back to me. "Ryan . . ." I started this sentence, but I don't know the exact words to finish it. I want to tell him how I feel about him. How he scares me and comforts me at the same time. But I can't say it yet, so instead, I wrap my arms around his waist and squeeze him tightly.

"If you're going to miss me that much, you can come with me into the shower if you want."

It's like he knows I'm going to retaliate and preemptively tries to block my assault by clenching his arms down. Doesn't matter; my fingers are tiny, and I'm able to wiggle them past his muscled arms to dig them into his sides, making him laugh until he's dying for air. But I'm ruthless and don't care if Ryan breathes, so I keep going until I think he has dislocated a rib from laughter.

After I've sufficiently tortured him, he goes to get a shower, and when I hear the water turn on, I briefly contemplate taking him up on his offer. But then I shake off the thought, because I'm not quite ready to take that step with him yet. I still don't know exactly what will happen with Ryan and me, and I want to wait until I feel more secure about what we are.

The second reason I don't want to go in there is because I get a few minutes of uninterrupted relaxation (read: snooping) time without Ryan. I didn't really do that much snooping, though . . . is what I will tell him if he catches me. But really, I go through EVERYTHING. It's so ridiculously boring, though. This man has no skeletons in his closets. His drawers are empty. The desk has never been touched. Not even a single dust bunny under his bed.

Huh. He really doesn't live here. I think he left more of a foot-print at my house than in his own, and I'm not sure what to make of that.

Since playing Sherlock ended up being a bore, I go to my lug-gage and start to unpack into his guest room drawers (they are empty too). I unzip my bag, and my eyes immediately zero in on something that I know for sure I didn't pack. It's the pile of appli-cations Stacy gave me to look over. There's something new, though. A yellow note is stuck to the top of the pile.

You don't need these.—Ryan

One second ago, I was fine. Now, a knot is forming in my throat, and I think I'm going to sob.

You know that moment where you use an old hair tie, and you think you can squeeze one more loop around your ponytail, but then, out of nowhere, it snaps and shoots across the room? I'm the hair tie. Ryan's confidence has me launching across the room to my phone, tears leaking down my face.

I'm so glad he's still in the shower right now and not here to wit-ness this breakdown. Because that's what it is: my final breakdown. The one I've been putting off for five years.

I look around for somewhere private, but Ryan's whole apart-ment is like one giant co-working space where everything echoes and no one can sneak any funny YouTube videos without alerting the whole office. But I need to make this call, so I stuff myself into Ryan's closet and shut the door. After sliding to the floor and leaning back against the wall below his dress shirts, I call the one person I need to talk to most right now.

"Stacy!" I say when the call connects.

"June? What's wrong?"

"I'm in Ryan's closet!" I sound hysterical.

"Did he put you in there?!"

"What? No. I came to Chicago with him because I love him, and now I'm sitting on the floor of his closet while he's taking a shower." I say it all like Stacy is the dumbest person in the world for not assuming that first.

There's a long pause followed by Stacy starting to say something, but then pausing again, and then starting over. "Okay, Junie, you're gonna have to start from the beginning, because I tried to catch myself up, and the dots just aren't connecting. Why are you in his closet?"

Tears are streaming down my face, and I can't stop them. "Because I think I might be in love with him! It wasn't supposed to happen, but it did, and he brought me here for a first date, and I never told you because I was sad that you're moving, and I was trying to cut ties with you before you cut ties with me, but I can't cut ties because I need you, and I think I might be a fraud feminist, because I'm completely happy here with Ryan, and I don't want to be alone anymore, and I do want to buy your share of the company, but I'm too scared to run it on my own!"

"Heavens, woman, breathe!"

I do as she says, shutting my eyes and taking in a deep breath through my nose. Now that it's all out, the tears have stopped, and I feel as if a boulder has just rolled off my back.

"Okay, first of all," says Stacy, "you could never cut me out of your life even if you wanted to. Remember, we did that thing in eighth grade where we pricked our fingers and mixed our blood? So you're stuck with me forever. Second, I'm pretty sure you have no idea what feminism is, so you need to do some research. Being independent doesn't mean you have to be lonely."

Oh no, I'm going to cry again.

"Third, you love Ryan? I thought you hated him. When did this happen?"

"About eighteen years ago."

"JUNE! You've liked him all this time and kept it from me?!"

"I was embarrassed because I liked him so much, and I thought he didn't like me at all. So I just hid it and channeled all my feelings toward hating him."

"Yeah, I gathered that last part." She pauses for a minute, and I let her digest. "Okay, so, wow. How does Ryan feel about you?"

"I think he really likes me too. I mean, I would guess he does because he's been living at my house, and asked me on a date, and has been ridiculously patient with my craziness. Also, we've been making out a lot."

"I'm going to pass out. You and Ryan are making out? Would it be weird if I asked for a photo of that?"

I laugh. "Stacy, we literally made out on the dance floor of your reception. I'm betting your photographer snapped a photo or two."

"You did?! Where was I?"

"Staring longingly into Logan's eyes."

"Gross."

"Yeah, it was nauseatingly sweet."

And then Stacy and I carry on for another five minutes while she talks me down from my cliff just like I knew she would. It's what we've always done for each other, and now I feel better knowing that it's what we'll always do.

After I've filled her in on every detail of life over the past couple of weeks, she says, "So what do you want going forward?"

I press my lips together and pull my knees up to my chest. "I want Ryan. But he lives here, and I live in Charleston. I don't know how we can make it work."

"Maybe he'll move to Charleston for you."

"What? No. No way. I could never ask him to do that." Am I terrible for thinking of asking him to do that? Yes. I am terrible. I won't do it.

"Okay . . . then if you are dead set against a long-distance relationship, another option would be for you to move to Chicago. You could probably make it work running Darlin' Donuts long distance if you hired a good manager or something to run it." That doesn't sit well with me either.

At some point over the past week, my confidence has been rebuilding. I've started dreaming of owning the bakery alone. Making all the decisions. Proving to myself that I do have what it takes and forgiving myself for all the times I've given up too soon in the past.

And now my anxiety is coming back, and I just want to avoid this decision until I absolutely can't anymore. "Well, I don't have to decide tonight. I'll let you go. Sorry for waking you up, by the way. It's like, what, three A.M. there?"

She chuckles. "June, it's only ten here . . . We're about to start a movie."

"A moooovie," I say dramatically. "Right. Enjoy your MOVIE."

I jump when the closet doors suddenly fly open. Ryan is standing there, staring down at me with his hands on his hips and brow quirked.

I raise my voice. "No, sorry! I don't need any more phone books, sir, thank you!" I end the call with Stacy and smile up at Ryan, looking as innocent as a doe sipping from a stream.

"How's Stacy?" he asks, completely unfazed by my overzealous act.

"Good. Sunburned."

He reaches out and helps me to my feet. Once I'm closer to him, I smell his bodywash and take in his damp hair dangling over his dark eyebrows, and I let the truth that I just blurted to Stacy settle over me like a warm sunny day.

I love Ryan Henderson.

Now what am I going to do about it?

CHAPTER 25

Ryan

June is still sleeping in my arms. She set up camp in the guest room, so I thought that was where she was going to stay for the night. But somewhere around midnight, I heard my door squeak open followed by June's voice. "Don't get any funny ideas. I'm just coming to snuggle."

She slipped under my covers and burrowed into my side like a little bunny making a new home. And let me tell you, it's ridiculously hard to sleep next to a woman like June and not let *one* funny idea slip by. I was good, though. I rubbed her back until I was lulled into blissful sleep by the scent of her orange shampoo. *HA,* just kidding!

I lay awake the entire night, smelling that freaking shampoo and convincing myself to keep my hands to myself. Just call me Funny Guy, because I've been so *funny* all night that I want to die just to be put out of my misery. June, however, was the very picture of a sweet Hallmark movie. Her body almost immediately softened, and her breath went heavy with the telltale signs of sleep—

completely unfazed by the way our bodies were pressed together and hot under those covers.

Women are a mystery.

Now, it's morning, and I haven't slept a wink. June will sleep all day, I think. Her hair is fanned out around her, her lips perfectly pouty, and that sunflower peeking out from under her tank top is smirking at me. It occurs to me that maybe June's playing the torture game again.

She wins. Easily.

I wanted to be here when she wakes up, but now, I don't trust myself. I'm sleep deprived, funnier than I've ever been before, and her skin is like a furnace. I would try to slip out of bed quietly so I don't disturb her, but by now, I've learned that June sleeps like a coma patient and I can slide my arm out from under her and toss the covers off without her so much as twitching.

Once I'm in the kitchen and done making coffee, I check the notifications on my phone, and one in particular stands out.

NOAH PRESCOTT: Going to the restaurant this morning. Come by and see it. I guarantee you any hesitations you have will go out the window.

Noah knows I'm in Chicago, because I very ignorantly responded to one of his emails last night, saying that I was back in town and would meet with him sometime before my Saturday deadline. I don't want to go see the restaurant site, though. What I want to do is turn down the job offer and spend the rest of the morning packing my stuff out of this sterile apartment and moving it all to Charleston. Being in here after spending the week at June's house is a massive disappointment. Crushing. A physical manifestation of the gaping, echoey hole in my life the past ten years.

I never thought to compare my couch to a giant yellow marsh-

mallow, which is what June's is, but now I'm about to pour kero-
sene all over this leather brick and let the flames dance in my eyes
as I watch it burn. The vaulted ceilings are oppressive. They take
the clinking sounds of my spoon tapping against my mug and
reflect them back in subtle mockery. Emptiness surrounds me,
and I think it's funny how a place I once felt proud of now seems
repugnant.

I want yellow. Ruffled pillows. Nick Lachey's face on everything. Family-filled picture frames. Nosy siblings and parents popping in when you don't want them to.

These tall walls grow like giants around me, and I have the
strongest urge to run from them.

So why don't I just turn Noah down and start assembling moving boxes? Because June is still a wild card. I'm all in, but she's still
holding her chips. I feel like I have a wild fox in my apartment. It's
sleeping now. She'll probably eat if I carefully set out a nice breakfast and back away with my hands held up in surrender, but if she
senses any sudden movement, she'll bolt.

I hope I'm not killing any chance of our relationship before it
even gets going by keeping Bask as a plan B. There's a real chance,
though, that after our date, June will walk away. I don't really care
to be left loveless *and* careerless. Because if I go back to working in
my old kitchen, it will kill my career. In this industry, you're either
moving up or down. There's no such thing as stagnant success.

Suddenly, a scream pierces the silence, and I smile. I smile because it's June screaming, and I know exactly what has brought it
on. Thundering footsteps rumble down the hall, and I carefully set
down my coffee in preparation. Turning, I find June in her PJs,
arms folded and anger jumping from her eyes like sparks.

My gaze dips down just below her eyes to the curly little mustache I drew across her lip while she was sleeping. She can't play
the torture game and not expect retaliation.

"Morning, Sunflower. Coffee?"

"You. Drew. On. My. Face." She's practically shaking with rage.

I have to bite my cheeks to keep from laughing. "I wanted to see how sound a sleeper you are." And I'll be honest, I needed something to help me find this woman less attractive. It didn't work. Now she just looks angry and adorable.

In the next moment, June runs full tilt across the apartment, and I'm given barely a moment to brace for impact. She launches herself at me, and I'm not sure if she was intending to knock me over or knock the breath out of me, but neither happens. I catch her easily, and she wraps her legs around me. All my funny thoughts rush back.

June puts her hands around my throat and makes a face like she's preparing to squeeze the life out of me. "Any last words?"

"It's washable."

Her eyes narrow into green venomous slits, but I can see the corners of her mustache twitching. Her mind whirls with ideas of coating my toothbrush in vinegar, mixing soy sauce with milk until it looks exactly like coffee, and putting plastic wrap across the toilet bowl. I read her thoughts like a book—even the lines she wants to keep hidden.

She squeezes my neck a little and crinkles her nose like she's really going to make this strangle count. But then her shoulders drop, and her grip slackens. She brushes her thumbs slowly across my pulse points below my jaw. "You're lucky you're pretty."

"I knew you were only after me for my looks."

Her smile softens, and she tilts her head to the side. "Sometimes it's hard to remember you're not my enemy anymore."

"You'll get used to it."

I carry her into the bathroom and set her down beside the sink. She watches silently as I dab a little face wash on a rag and cover it with water. Her emerald stare is fixed on my face as I start gently wiping away the marks I left. I want to wipe away the ones I can't see below her skin too.

June watches me closely, barely breathing. The air is reacting between us. Currents are rippling. Humming. Pulling. I'm caught in the undertow of water that is not blue, but effervescent green.

CHAPTER 26

June

I need Ryan, and that scares me.

But right now, I don't want to be scared. I want to fly. I spread my wings around him and pull Ryan closer. His hands catch my waist, and I feel the tension flowing out of his fingers as they press into my sides. His eyes skate over my face, and I almost can't believe we even made it to this place.

Ryan's mouth hovers in front of me for what feels like eons. I'm dying, literally dying for him to close the gap and claim my lips.

In his eyes, I see flakes of black and gold. Hues I've never noticed before. I put my hands around his ribs and try to tug him a little closer while simultaneously inching my lips toward his. He tucks his chin back an inch, though, and smiles at his own restraint. He's drawing this out, and even my bones are aching for him.

"Ryan," I say in a quiet plea.

His hand laces into the back of my hair as his brows dip together to study me, considering something heavy behind his dark eyes. I feel dramatic—like maybe the women at the bar actually knew the truth all along, and Ryan really does hold all the world's oxygen supply. I will suffocate if his mouth doesn't touch mine.

"I don't want to be just a random date, June. I want more."

There's nothing but truth in his eyes, and I can't hold mine in any longer. As if I'm afraid he's going to disappear before my eyes, I wrap my arms tightly around his waist and hold him right here. *Me. Stay with me.*

"I want you to be more than a random date too."

Those words are a key.

Ryan cups my jaw and holds on to me as he presses his warm mouth to mine. He somehow defies physics, making time stop around us, and all that's left is Ryan rushing through my senses.

It's a slow dance, this kiss. Not a selfish act of affection, not driven by lust; but an outpouring of a man's heart like I've never experienced before. Our lips sway in graceful fluid motions, pushing and pulling, giving and taking. Ryan's thumb brushes from my jaw to my mouth, softly parting my lips and deepening the kiss. Like a spark catching on the end of a wick, fire rushes from my curled toes all the way up to my fingers threaded through the back of Ryan's amazing hair. I breathe in the cool scent of his masculine bodywash, letting it surround me as I try to etch every detail of this moment into my heart, determined to replay it every day for the rest of my life.

Calloused hands run down the length of my arms and settle around my waist, striking every nerve ending in my body as they move. Without words, he tells me he adores me, cares for me, desires me. I can feel it in the possessive caress of his lips, and in the way his fingertips slide down and press into my hips, firm yet gentle—as if he's afraid I might shatter. But actually, it's the tenderness of this moment that breaks me in half.

Ryan could be picking me up and carrying me to his room, but he's not. He senses my unease and coddles me instead. I've always struggled with the idea of my curves, but with Ryan's hands on them, they feel empowering and feminine. His fervent attention to the parts of my hips and thighs that squish and dimple makes me feel dizzy. Like they're not unwanted, but essential.

His strong arms encircle me and draw me in closer, scooting me toward the edge of the counter. The cotton T-shirt hugging his body is soft against my skin as I run my hands up his firm chest and settle them over the tense, bunching muscles in his shoulders. Part of me wants to set the restraint I feel in him free, and part of me is too scared to.

Our kiss picks up. His hands slide under my shirt to my back. I touch his hair. His shoulders. Bunch his shirt.

Ryan groans and abruptly breaks the seal of our mouths to bury his face in my neck, pressing his palms down onto the counter beside my hips. After a deep breath, his arms slide around my back until he is fully encapsulating me in what can only be described as a bear hug. My breath continues to race in my chest as I sit awestruck, held by a man I thought I'd never be able to have.

Never once in my life have I felt this safe. This . . . cherished.

Ryan lays quiet kisses on my neck, and a tear falls down my cheek. I think I accidentally sniff, because Ryan stands back up and examines my face. I turn my eyes away, but he pulls my chin back and wipes away the streak my tear left behind.

"Tears?" he asks.

I nibble my bottom lip and try to keep more tears from releasing. "Ryan, I . . . Well, I . . ." I can't get the words out. I feel them, but I can't say them.

His face is soft as his mouth tilts into a smile, and he pushes the hair back from my face. "I know. You don't have to say it yet." Again, such compassion. It disarms me.

I nod, and he lays another chaste kiss on my lips. "Want some coffee?"

I chuckle. "Not really. My mind is in other places right now."

His grin says he likes this answer, but he shakes his head. "I think we need to figure some things out first." He gives me a whisper of a kiss. "I'm not rushing you, June. We've got time."

Yeah, but the problem is his tender answer makes me *want* to rush right into it.

But he's right . . .

"Fine. You make a compelling argument," I say as he picks up my hand and lays a soft kiss against my wrist and then my palm. His warm kisses spread to each of my fingers. "Okay, but now your argument is confusing."

He chuckles against my skin. "This is one of those instances where I know what I should do, but it's completely opposite of what I want to. Basically, this is me teetering."

I eye his soft lips pressing against my thumb. "So you're leaving it up to me to say no right now? Dangerous decision."

His dark eyes shift to my hand as he raises his own, placing our palms together like two high school kids examining the differences in proportions. I wonder if this is something he dreamed of doing in high school with me? Something innocent and sweet, standing by our lockers.

His lips curl up softly as he surveys our hands pressed together before he slowly folds his fingers down between mine. "I want to get this right with you, June."

He finally looks back up, and when his gaze settles intently over my face, I melt. I'm gone. Done for. I nod my agreement because I want nothing more than to get this right with him.

We stare at each other a little longer, his hands still holding tight to mine, thumb rubbing slowly up and down mine. It's a settling moment where we let the charged air sink back to normal.

The final break of the spell is when Ryan says, "Do you think you can make do without me for an hour or so?"

I try not to frown because I'm not that girl who needs her man glued to her every second of every day. But for some reason, I feel pouty. "Sure. What do you have to do?"

"I need to go into work and check on a few things."

The vagueness of his answer pricks me. It feels familiar because I've heard it before. "Oh, okay. Yeah." I slide off the counter. "Sure thing. I'll get ready while you're gone." I'm an easy-breezy Cover-Girl now. So chipper.

Ryan catches my arm before I step out of the bathroom and hauls me back to him. I turn my eyes away from him and pretend a smile. "C'mon, let's go get some coffee."

He shakes his head slowly. "What's wrong?"

"Nothing." I force myself to meet his eyes and grin. Grinny-grin-grin.

"June, say it. We both know I'll douse you under cold water until you do."

"Rude."

"Tell me."

"Ben used to tell me that same line all the time. Now I realize he was always giving me that vague work line before he'd go . . . ya know." I shrug. "It's nothing. I was just disappointed for a minute. No big deal, though."

He dips his head so I'm forced to make eye contact again. "I'm not Ben. You can trust me."

I nod and allow my stiff posture to soften. "Okay. I'll try to remember that."

CHAPTER 27

Ryan

Later, as I'm walking toward my truck, I feel a tug somewhere deep in the pit of my stomach. *You can trust me.* The words I said to June repeat like a bad loop I can't shake from my mind. Because although I'm not going to meet a woman, I didn't exactly tell her the truth about where I'm going, either.

So far, I've been able to rationalize my omission of the truth by thinking I'm doing what's best for her. I'm probably not even going to take the executive chef position in Noah's restaurant, so why tell her about it and make her worry? Plus, we need to focus on us right now and how we want to move forward in a relationship before I dump any more changes in her lap. Changes like working myself to the bone and never having weekends off or any time to visit her. *See? Good reasons.*

But my argument feels paper thin. I need to tell June. It's cowardly that I haven't already.

I've seen those movies where the guy swears he'll tell her later and then never gets the chance and ends up losing her because of it. I refuse to let that happen. That's why the moment my truck comes to a stop in front of the address where Noah told me to meet him, I shoot June a text.

> RYAN: I meant what I said about being able to trust me. So I should have just been up front and told you that I'm on my way to check out a restaurant where I've been offered an executive chef position. I'm not sure I want the job but also not sure I should refuse it. We can talk about it later, but I just wanted you to know.

I wait five minutes for a response, and when it doesn't come through right away, I regret sending it. It was a bad idea. Now I look guilty. June is packing her bags, and she'll be gone by the time I—

> JUNE: *GIF of a woman slowly mouthing you're dead to me.
> JUNE: Just kidding. Thanks for telling me. I'll help you make a pros and cons list when you get back.

My shoulders relax, and I let out a breath. Yes. There. That was the right choice. See? I knew it all along.

There's a loud knock on my window, and I nearly jump across the console. Suddenly, I'm a fish in a bowl, and I know what it feels like to be harassed by annoying humans.

"What are you doing in there?" asks Noah loudly, like I'm on the other side of the world instead of a piece of glass. "C'mon, let's go in so I can show you around."

Once we're inside the restaurant, the first thing I think is *wow*. Like, jaw-dropping wow. This place is all glitz and glamour and next-level décor. It's designed with a 1920s theme, something straight out of *The Great Gatsby*. Everything sparkles and winks. The floor is white marble, and a magnificent chandelier hangs in the center of the foyer where guests will wait to be seated. There's a deep-red curtain that separates the wait area from the dining room, and I'm told that if a customer does not have a reservation booked at least a month out, the curtain will not open for them. They will never see inside.

Not all the finishes are in place, but I get a pretty good idea of it. It's all gold, diamond, and pearl. Nothing is gaudy, though. It's extravagant in the most tasteful way, making me feel as if I've stepped into the wealthiest society of the 1920s. I imagine drinks will flow and checks will look more like a mortgage payment. *This* will be the restaurant of the decade.

"A live band will be playing over here at all times, and the wait-staff will wear white suits and short flapper dresses." Noah's beady eyes shift across the room, and he looks downright gluttonous. "Customers will feel like they've jumped back to that glorious time when people knew how to spend money properly—letting the booze and parties take them to a happier place."

I leave Noah standing at the front of the dining room and step deeper into the place, really just wishing he'd shut up. There's something about him that grates on me.

"That's what Bask will do," he continues, raising his voice so I can hear him from across the room. "Once people step beyond those red curtains, they will enter euphoria. A place to live among the elite and dine like kings."

I can easily imagine it. In atmospheres like this, each table will be competing with the next. Drinking more and ordering more dishes even if they are too concerned about their waist sizes to eat any of it. But wasted money doesn't matter to people who come to restaurants like this. Spending a thousand or so on one meal is their spare change. Problem is, those people are never satisfied. They expect their meals to represent the money they've laid down for it, and I will break myself trying to make sure it measures up.

But I'm just cocky enough to know that it will.

Here's the problem, though. I got into cooking so I could feel closer to my mom. So I could remember her. And now, as I'm standing here, looking at this restaurant, I feel like if she were still alive, she would grab me by the jaw and say something like, *Son, just 'cause you're good at something doesn't mean it's what you were made to do.*

I feel those words in my bones.

"So what do you think? Pretty amazing, right?" asks Noah. "And let me show you the kitchen. It's not nearly done yet, but I think you'll be pretty amazed at what's already back there."

Noah's walking toward the kitchen, but I stay rooted. My scowl is deep. I'm sure that I look severe right now. In fact, I know it, because when Noah looks back, he jumps a little. It's the same fear-stricken look the lower chefs give me when I inspect a finished dish. It's that shaking, might-pass-out-or-pee-themselves look.

"I don't need to see the kitchen," I say, already turning back toward the red curtains.

"Because you're ready to sign?" I hear Noah's dress shoes clicking across the floor in a fast pace to catch me. He's afraid that if I step back outside of these curtains, the euphoric hypnotism will leave me, and I'll be crashed into reality.

"Not exactly."

"Wait." He's out of breath just from jogging that short distance. "Are you saying you're not going to take the job?"

I glance around one more time and feel lighter. "Sorry, Noah. I appreciate the offer, but it's not for me." It feels good to say it. This place may skyrocket my career, but in the words of Marie Kondo, it will never spark joy. I'm done with it.

All of it.

"No." Noah looks like he's going to hurl. It makes me think that all the talk of Martin was just to bait me into taking the position. "You have until Sunday night to decide."

"I thought it was Saturday, today?"

He gives me a desperate smile. "What week ends on a Saturday? Sunday makes more sense. Take an extra day to think about it more. I won't accept an answer before then."

"Sorry, man. My answer won't change." I turn and leave it all behind.

CHAPTER 28

June

You know what's wonderful? Holding hands with Ryan Henderson in public! I don't know why that fact is striking me more than making out with him in private. Forget the fact that our mouths have touched; Ryan lacing his fingers with mine while we walk into his workplace is the most exciting feeling in the world.

I have the greatest urge to hold our clasped hands in the air like I just won a boxing match and yell, *I'M HOLDING RYAN'S HAND!* at the top of my lungs for all Chicago to hear.

And I act on that urge.

"Shhh, you loon," Ryan says, yanking our hands back down.

He makes me promise I'll behave when we go into the restaurant, and I agree, but only because I have one hand behind my back, fingers crossed. I'll do as I see fit once we get in there.

When we step into the kitchen, a hush falls over it. It's equal parts reverence and fear. Ryan's dark eyes slide over every surface, and the entire staff waits with bated breath. I had no idea Ryan struck this kind of fear in people (clearly, they didn't know him during his saggy-jeans-and-green-leprechaun-boxer phase). But I'm not going to lie; it's sexy as all get-out holding hands with the man who's making the poor guy in the corner tremble in his stained apron.

I glance up and see the beautiful severe lines on Ryan's face and savor that I get to be on this side of his life now. The side that knows how many crinkles live beside his eyes when he smiles and that his dimple only pops when he is really and truly happy.

"Chef, you're back," says a woman stepping forward before her troop. Her eyes slide from Ryan to me and down to our hands. Her face softens a little—almost as if she's relieved to see our interlaced fingers. I like her immediately.

"Not officially," he says, the new stern quality to his voice a little shocking to me. It sends a happy little chill dancing down my spine, and I can't wait to see what happens next. "I just wanted to stop by, see how the kitchen is running, and show June around." He squeezes my hand, and for a brief moment, his severity slides away, and he's just Ryan again. "Nia, this is June. June, Nia is my sous-chef. And an incredible one at that."

Judging by the way Nia's face beams from Ryan's praise, I don't think it's a usual occurrence for him to dish it out.

For the next ten minutes, I follow beside Ryan as we walk around the kitchen. Everyone quakes, and no one escapes Ryan's notice. "Tim, you hungover? Don't let that happen tomorrow or you're out of my kitchen. Sanders, tell me you've not been scorching my sauce like this the whole time I've been gone." He's ruthless.

"You," he says, pointing to a wide-eyed young guy. "I don't even know your name, but if you keep chopping at the pace of a snail, those orders won't be out until Christmas. Don't mess it up." Actually, I cleaned up his language a bit. Turns out, Ryan has a real potty mouth in the kitchen.

It's *Top Chef* in here. High-stakes cooking, and if you're good, you go on to the next round. If you're bad . . . I don't know, maybe you just keel over and die? It feels that way by the fear radiating off these people.

As much as I'm enjoying this live episode, I can't help but notice Ryan never once smiles in here like he did in my donut shop. But I don't know. Maybe that's just the way things go in the chef world. What I do know is how happy I am to be on this side of Ryan's wrath.

A few minutes later, we follow Nia out of the kitchen, and while she and Ryan are talking shop in the hallway, I slip off to use the bathroom. On my way back, I peek my head into the kitchen again.

"Hey! Y'all are doing great! Keep at it!" I offer my encouraging speech with a big cheesy grin and a thumbs-up. I feel really good about my contribution to the staff morale until I exit the kitchen and find Ryan's lifted brow and smirk aimed at me.

"Did you just pep talk my staff?"

My eyes go wide. "Never. No. I was just giving that guy some pointers on the sauce."

"*Mm-hmm*. I'm getting you out of here before you have them all holding hands and singing campfire songs."

"Oooh, that sounds fun! Do you think they'd do it?"

He wraps his arm around my shoulder and kisses my temple. "Maybe next time. We've got a date to get ready for."

My stomach dips at his words. I have no idea what to expect. All I know is that Ryan has been dragging this out for so long that I'm sure he's got something spectacular planned. A man does not haul a woman all the way to another state for a mediocre date.

"Oh, so are you taking her to the opening tonight, then?" asks Nia.

"Opening?" I ask Ryan.

He looks down at me. "That's not the date I have planned. She's talking about a restaurant opening of one of my old friends from culinary school."

"Oh, let's go, then! If it's your friend's restaurant, you should be there to support him."

Ryan studies my face with furrowed brows, trying to find any hints of a lie. "You sure?"

I poke him in the cheek, ready for him to stop looking so serious. "Why wouldn't I be? Sounds like a fun night out."

He looks back up to Nia. "All right, looks like we'll see you there."

There's something about hearing the word *we* that makes me tingle.

They say their goodbyes, and when Ryan and I are both situated in his truck again, he leans over the console and kisses me. Just as I start to taste the mint in his mouth, he pulls away and smiles. "Are you ready for that date now?"

My heart hammers against my chest. For some reason, I thought the opening tonight would mean postponing the date. I like this option much better.

We get back to Ryan's place to get ready for this mystery date, and before we part in the hall, he says, "Wear whatever makes you feel most like a sexy woman."

1) That phrase is majorly ick and doesn't sound at all like something he'd say.
2) I have no idea what that means. It's not very helpful and leaves me more confused than before he said it.

"I'm going to pretend you never said that horrific sentence. Should I dress up or dress casual?"

But Ryan doesn't answer. He buttons his lips with a smirk and disappears into his room. Unfortunately he shuts the door; otherwise, I would absolutely watch him dress for no other reason than to get an idea of what to wear myself. NO OTHER REASON.

I open the top drawer of the dresser, where I unpacked my clothes, and my eye catches on the I ♥ NICK socks my mom bought me. My heart twists. It's time to tell her the truth. She deserves to know.

Without allowing any time to talk myself out of it, I grab my phone, flop myself back on the bed, and dial Mom. It rings three times before she answers. "Hi, sugar! I was just thinking about—"

"Mom. Ben cheated on me!" I blurt it out in one big rush, like a balloon that's had its end cut off. "I found out just before the wedding. That's why I called it off."

There's a stunned silence for a minute, and I shut my eyes, worried that she's upset with me for keeping this from her for so long.

And then I hear the three words I was not expecting. "We know, darlin'."

I peek my eyes open, my shoulders relaxing against the mattress. "You knew?"

This time, I hear the a cappella choir of my giant family. "Yep!"

I shoot up in bed. "Why am I hearing ten annoying voices?"

"Because we're all together and I had you on speaker when you called," says Mom.

"Hi, June!" That's Jake, and he's grinning ear to ear; I can hear it in his voice.

"Having fun in Chicago?" Evie adds.

"All right, y'all skedaddle. I don't think June meant for everyone to hear that declaration." *Thank you, Mom.*

"Okay, we're going. But, June, we all already knew about Ben. So there's nothing to feel weird about," says Jake, his voice slipping farther away.

I sigh. Nothing to feel weird about? Nothing other than my family all knowing my giant secret for five years and pretending they didn't know!

"Okay, baby, we're alone now. I'm sorry you were on speaker, but I had no idea you were going to blurt your heart out like that."

"It's okay," I say, feeling tired for some reason. Probably because I just dropped the heavy secret I've been carrying around for too long. "You all knew? For how long?"

"Since the day you called off the wedding."

"What!"

"Well, thank you for that. Now I'm going to need a hearing aid prematurely."

"Mom, how in the world did you know?"

She's quiet for a second, and I imagine she's scrunching her nose up in contemplation. "Are you sure you wanna know?"

"Yes."

"When we saw how upset you were but unwilling to talk about it, Jake and your dad went to Ben's house to find out the truth." *Those little prying sneaks!*

"And Ben told them everything?" I would be shocked if Ben told them the truth.

"Well . . . not until Jake grabbed him by the collar and pinned him up against the wall. Then, he was happy to spill his beans. Poor guy, though. Jake still bloodied his nose."

I let out a breath of air that's somewhere between a laugh and an exhale. I wish I had been there to see my big brother punch the living daylights out of Ben. Maybe it would've helped me heal a little faster knowing that Ben wasn't completely getting away with his shit. "Why didn't you tell me you guys knew? Why let this go on for so long?"

"Darlin', we all knew this was something you needed to feel on your own and sort through in your own time. I knew you'd tell me when you were ready. We're here to support you and love you, not smother you."

Great, now I'm crying again. "Thank you, Mom. I'm sorry it took me so long."

"Oh, phooey. It took you just the right amount of time. Some of us need to live through the healing rather than talk through it."

I smile, wishing I was near her to let her wrap me up in one of her hugs. "Have you ever thought about writing fortune cookies?"

"Are you getting smart with me?"

"Never. I love you, Mom."

"I love you too, sugar. Now, tell me, is Ryan being good to you?"

My eyes drift toward the closed door as I think back over all the tenderness Ryan has shown me. "I've never felt so happy."

"Good, because I like that boy, and I'd hate for Jake to mess up that pretty nose of his."

I sputter a laugh. "Me too."

After a few minutes, I tell Mom I've got to run so I can get ready for my date. It's hard to put into words the way I feel after hanging up with her, knowing what all my family has done for me over the past five years. I feel like someone has injected something warm and gooey into my heart of stone.

Knowing that Ryan is probably waiting on me, I quickly change into an outfit that makes me feel like a *sexy woman* (a soft cream sweater, high-waisted jeans, and my hair curled in long waves). I step out of my room and find Ryan in the hallway, wearing a suit— one that makes my mouth drop open and drag across the floor as I turn a circle and start to back up into my room to change.

"Whoa, come back here." He grabs my arms and tugs me around.

Yep. He's just as blinding the second time I see him as the first. His suit is dark gray and fits him like a glove. Underneath the suit jacket of my dreams is a white dress shirt, unbuttoned at the top, giving him a just-got-off-work-from-my-superprestigious-job look. I will dream of him in this outfit every night for the rest of the month.

"You are way dressier than me," I say, dismay drenching my tone.

His smile deepens, and he pulls me in close to him. I can smell his cologne. It's smooth like expensive bourbon, and I drink him in, getting drunk off it.

"You look perfect," he says against my cheek.

I want to say thank you, but instead, some little mouse speaks. It can't be me because the voice is too high-pitched and embarrassing.

Ryan kisses my cheek and holds out his arm for me to take. We look like a couple going to prom in this pose, but I don't care. It actually just makes me wish Ryan had been the one to take me to prom. Wearing this suit. And drenched in this cologne. Never mind, I would have become a teen mom.

In the living room, Ryan stops. I thought we would head for the door, but instead, he's turning us toward the living room. That's when I spot cheap Chinese takeout on the coffee table and *My Best Friend's Wedding* queued up on the TV. He's poured us two glasses of wine, and it almost looks as if *this* is where we are having our date.

Now, I don't mean to be a snobby person who demands a fine-dining experience for their dates, but I really expected something more captivating than fried rice and a chick flick.

"Your face right now is priceless."

Ryan's words sink in, and a relieved smile splits across my mouth. I look up at him, laughing. "OH! This was a joke. Whew. You got me. I really thought—" I break off when Ryan's grin doesn't turn into a laugh with me. "Oh, gosh. It's not a joke, is it?"

He shakes his head, and I want to melt into the earth. My face turns into lava as I begin to extract my foot from my mouth. Racing over to the coffee table, I cradle the Chinese food in my hands like it's a delicate peace offering given to me from a foreign leader. It's sacred. I will treasure it forever. "This is . . . perfect! Just perfect!"

Ryan is still standing in his same spot, wearing his same smirk, but with his hands in his pockets. Someone should take a picture of him and send it to *Vogue*. He's gorgeous, and I don't want to lose him. I plop down onto the offensive couch and manage to not even wince a little when it bruises my rear.

I pat the seat next to me with an overly bright smile. "Let's get this date going."

Now he's holding back a laugh. I'm the silliest thing he's ever seen.

Ryan walks over to me. "Set the food down, June." I wish he wasn't so confident all the time. He's the one who planned a terrible first date, and yet I'm the one who wants to crawl under the table. Ryan extends his hand, and I take it, standing up. He puts both his hands on my jaw and bends down to kiss me slowly. Smoothly. Tantalizingly.

I do melt into the floor this time.

I'm a dollop of Crisco dropped into a hot skillet. Ryan pulls away, and I see not hurt, not embarrassment, not sadness. A smile. "You don't remember, do you?" he asks.

My stomach falls like it does in the middle of a thriller movie when I thought I had the plot all figured out, and then suddenly, it shifts.

I shake my head. "Remember what?"

"Our class trip to Chicago for our tenth-grade debate."

"I remember the trip, but . . ." What does that have to do with anything?

Ryan shifts his arms around my waist. "We were all on the subway, headed back to our hotel, and I told you, Stacy, and Logan that

Jennifer Summers had passed me a note saying she liked me. You rolled your eyes, so I accused you of being jealous."

And just like that, I remember. I remember wanting to stomp across that subway car and rip that girl's hair out.

"You looked me right in the eyes and said something like, *You couldn't pay me a million dollars to date you, Ryan Henderson. Mark my words. One day, I will move to this city and date a sophisticated man and—*"

"*I'll be a sophisticated, sexy woman, and he will pick up Chinese take-out after work and bring it back to our fancy apartment, and he'll be wearing a fancy suit from his fancy job, and we will drink fancy wine and watch my favorite movie.*" A laugh bubbles through me.

"And then I told you that you could never be sophisticated like that. Or something to that extent. I can't believe I said that. Or that I remember it."

He's chuckling, too, now. "As if Chinese takeout and *fancy* wine is the most sophisticated and grown-up thing in the world."

I pull away from Ryan enough to look at our first date with new eyes. Eyes that are glistening and wet with unshed tears. "I can't believe you remembered that."

"I couldn't forget it."

I turn back to Ryan. "Wait. Did you move here because of that?" I ask.

"No. Believe it or not, I wasn't at that epic level of pining. It was a happy coincidence that the best job offer happened to be here."

"More than coincidence. Fate." I'm smiling like a fool at my cheesy line, but I don't care.

Ryan looks down at me and runs the backs of his knuckles against my jaw. "I would be lying, though, if I said I didn't hope to run into you now and then, thinking that just maybe you would move here, and we'd be reunited in some tiny coffee shop at an odd hour."

I reach up and clasp my hands behind his neck. "Such a romantic."

"Don't tell anyone."

"I'm having it printed in big letters on a billboard. *Ryan Henderson is a romantic.* It has a picture of you dressed in a cupid outfit below the words."

He leans in and whispers over my mouth, "Just shut up and kiss me, you loon."

And oh boy, do I.

The Chinese food is forgotten, and Ryan and I make out during the whole movie. That couch somehow gets even more uncomfortable, but given these new memories I'll have to associate with it, it grows on me.

"Wait," I say, ripping my sore lips away from him.

He groans and drops his head down by my neck. "What?"

"You never told me about that potential job."

"*Huh?*" he says and starts kissing my neck again. "It doesn't matter."

Au contraire, mon frère.

I push on Ryan's big chest, but he doesn't budge until he realizes I'm serious. He sits up and runs his hands through his wild hair. He takes in a deep breath and releases it. "June, please don't freak out. And before I say what I'm going to say next, I need you to know I've given this a lot of thought."

"You're scaring me."

He grimaces lightly. "The job was for a new high-profile restaurant that's opening in the area, and they wanted me to be the executive chef."

A mix of feelings tornado through my body until my mind snags on one word. "Wait . . . *was?*"

He tilts his head to fix his dark eyes on me. "I turned it down."

"What?! Why?" I panic even though he asked me not to.

Ryan scoots over by me again and takes my hand in his. "It just wasn't the right fit for me. Nothing felt right. And my commute will be too long anyway."

"How far away is it?"

"Several hours after I move to Charleston."

And now I'm going to faint.

CHAPTER 29

June

"Moving to Charleston?!" I'm screeching—panic-screeching—and Ryan's vast apartment amplifies it.

His eyes go wide, and he holds out his hands in front of him like he is trying to soothe me before I bolt. Maybe I will.

"No, don't do it, June. This is not a sudden impulse I'm acting on." He pauses, and his brows furrow. "Well, maybe it is slightly impulsive, since I never thought of moving back to Charleston until I saw you again, but . . ."

"Not helping your case."

His face softens, and he wraps his arm around my shoulders, pulling me close to him. Now I'm trapped. He's not going to let me run out of here. "June, I can't explain it right. But when I went to the restaurant today, it just felt all wrong. Not where I want to be. But back home in Charleston, it *did* feel right. I'm lonely here. I hate my apartment. I've even been hating my job."

"But you've worked so hard to get where you are, Ryan! You can't just walk away from it."

"Why not?"

I pull out of his arms. "Because you can't!"

"Actually, I can. I was serious when I told you I want more than one date. I want *us*. Or at least a decent shot to see if there is an *us*. And not a long-distance relationship. If I loved my job and this city and had a good friend group here, it would be different. But I have none of that, June. And I'm ready for a real life outside of a kitchen. I want to live where it's not so damn cold all the time. I want a comfy couch."

"I can buy you a new couch."

His face falls. "What are you saying, June?" Ryan's eyes leave me for the first time, and he scrapes his hands through his hair. "You *don't* want a relationship?"

I should let him go. I should cut him loose. *Go on, get!* He's destined for great things, and I will just hold him back.

But as I stare at the man of my dreams, elbows resting on his knees and hands in his hair, I can't bring myself to deny my heart what it really wants. "I want to be with you more than anything, Ryan."

His hands fall away, and he turns his face to me. "I don't want to do long distance."

"I don't either."

"And I think you should buy Stacy's half of the bakery. And if you do, I want to be nearby to support you through it."

"I am going to. I told her on the phone last night."

"You are?" His voice is a mix of pride and hope.

"Yes. And I want you nearby when I take it over, too," I say, feeling like the most selfish person in the world. He's willing to give up his dreams so I can have mine.

He nods like we just finished conducting an important business deal. We should shake hands now. "Then I'm moving?"

I pause, breathing deeply and considerately before I say, "I guess you are. If you truly want to." A tentative smile breaks over my mouth.

His face mirrors mine, and we both stay frozen—statues depicting two people who have made a life-changing decision, captured in the moment before they fully smile. It's beautiful. A masterpiece to be marveled at and discussed in museums across the world.

"Okay, I'm moving."

"Good."

"*Good.*"

At the exact same moment, we both crack, and unhindered laughter spills through Ryan's lofty apartment. He lunges at me, and I lunge at him, and we collide somewhere in the middle. I have so many more questions for him. I want to give him the third degree of *Are you sure?* But I don't, because everything about this moment feels too perfect to disrupt with reality.

My head falls back against the cushion—ahem, brick—again, and Ryan hovers over me, the devilish smile that I never want to forget aimed down at me. His head dips, and I intertwine my fingers in his hair so we can properly lose ourselves in kisses. His mouth is hungry against mine, tasting and exploring in a way that has me feeling wild.

Nothing in life has ever felt more right than this moment on this brick of a couch with Ryan. After frantic whispers of consent, we peel each other's clothes off and ensure we'll be very late to the restaurant opening.

"Thirty minutes and then we're out of here," Ryan promises as we're racing up the sidewalk to the restaurant. He's practically dragging me.

Ryan tried to persuade me that we should skip the opening and spend the night in his apartment instead. He made a very convincing argument, and I'll absolutely never look at his couch again (*good gracious*), but in the end, I held strong. If his friend is opening his own restaurant, Ryan should be there.

"Ah, Ryan! Slow down!"

"No. The sooner we get in there, the sooner we can get out."

I'm laughing so hard that I can't keep up now. I tear my hand away from him to bend over and adjust my high heel strap back onto my foot. "Go. Save yourself!" I say, waving a tired hand.

He turns back and scoops me up in his arms. "No woman left behind. Hold on, Broaden."

I bury my head in the collar of Ryan's dress shirt and laugh for the rest of the walk. He's being ridiculous and dramatic. I love it. I love him and this happy bubble we are captured inside. I think the bubble is filled with laughing gas, because that's pretty much all we've done since deciding Ryan will move to Charleston.

Once we approach the restaurant entrance, I make Ryan set me down. I eye the warmly lit awning over the dark-tinted glass door and watch a woman in a little red cocktail dress enter on the arm of a handsome gentleman. I send up a silent prayer of thanks that I had the forethought to pack my black cocktail dress. It's not as fancy as the dresses I see entering the restaurant tonight, but it's not too far off, either.

I lean in a little closer to Ryan as we walk under the awning and ask, "What exactly am I walking into here?"

He leans toward me, and his breath hits my ear. "A night of boring schmoozing. This is just a soft opening, meant to generate buzz. So, only those high up in the food industry have been invited."

"High up? So, people like you?"

He smirks. "Yeah. And food bloggers and journalists. Other chefs and probably a few celebrities."

"What! Like Beyoncé?"

Ryan reaches for the door and opens it. "I hope not, because I don't trust that look on your face."

I pass by him and look over my shoulder as I do. "Fun sucker."

A rush of air blows my hair as I step into Sonrisa, and it takes my eyes a minute to adjust to the low lighting. Ryan steps beside me and anchors me with his hand on my lower back. I feel instantly more at ease. My eyes grow accustomed to the dim light, and suddenly, I see everyone. I wish I didn't. It's a room full of Amazons and gorgeous Hollywood types. I'm not even sure what they're doing here. Clearly, they don't eat.

No one is seated yet, just sort of mingling around the restaurant. Well, that's what they were doing before we walked in, I imagine. Now, it seems as if every head in the place is turned to Ryan. All eyes are on him—wide, prying, searching. Am I imagining this?

I look up at him and notice that he's pulled a mask over his face. An impassive smile rests where the open one previously lived. The set of his shoulders reminds me of how he looked around his staff earlier today, but dressed in a finely tailored suit, the effect is much more intimidating.

The gravity of all that Ryan is hits me at once, and it's like I'm seeing this moment in slow motion. A few cameras flash, and I blink at the circles burned in my eyes. A new energy and buzz fills the room. In this world, Ryan is famous. These people all know him and want to be near him. Even now, they are collectively inching their way toward us. Sweat fills my palms.

In the next moment, a man in a chef's coat rounds the corner. "Ryan! You made it!" he says, crossing to shake Ryan's hand with a smile so blinding joy punches you in the gut.

"Congrats, David. This place is incredible." Ryan nods toward the room, and David beams even brighter.

"Well, that means a lot coming from you. And thanks for showing your support here tonight. I know you don't really come out to stuff like this anymore." He shakes Ryan's hand with gratitude in his eyes, confirming my suspicions that Ryan's presence here is a big deal. David then shifts his gaze to me and extends his hand. "And who is this pretty lady?"

Ryan grins and then wraps his arm around my waist. The action feels both proud and possessive. "This is June, my girlfriend."

At that title, I suck in a sharp breath. That's the first time I've heard him say those words, and yeah, I guess it's true given the discussion we had earlier, but it still shocks me. It's equal parts wonderful and horrifying. It means I'm officially done with my one-date rule.

This is monumental, and I feel like the world should stop for me so I can soak up this moment. It doesn't.

Despite the shock rippling through me, I manage to offer David compliments on his restaurant and tell him how happy I am to be here tonight. He kisses my cheek and somehow makes me feel just as important as Ryan. I like him excessively, and if everyone I meet tonight is anything like David, I have nothing to worry about.

There has been quiet music playing overhead, but when David leaves us to step out into the middle of the room and make a speech, everything goes silent. Eyes move from Ryan and me to David, and I feel like I can finally breathe. Ryan pulls me a little closer.

"Everyone! Thank you, from the bottom of my heart, for coming to the launch of Sonrisa! Translated into English, *sonrisa* means "smile," and I hope that's all you do while you're in my restaurant!" He raises both his hands to his mouth and blows a kiss to the room. "Enjoy!" And then he sweeps himself into the kitchen to the applause of the room as the waitstaff begins moving guests to various tables.

To my great dismay, Ryan and I are seated in the very center of the room. I glance over my shoulder and find a brunette with beautifully arched brows staring at Ryan. To my left, it's a blonde. I bounce my gaze all around the room and find eyes from every color of the spectrum stealing glances at Ryan. A few look at him and then scribble in a notebook. One man is secretly taking Ryan's photo from under the table. My heart rate picks up, and something feels off.

Suddenly, I feel Ryan's hand cover mine, drawing my gaze up to him. "Breathe," he says in a rich warm tone that instantly soothes me. I take a breath and let my shoulders drop. He nods his approval and squeezes my hand. "It's awkward, I know."

I lean a little forward. "I didn't know you were, like . . . *famous* famous."

He grins a little, but it still looks different from the one I'm used to. "Just in this sphere of life. It wasn't really until the *New York Times* ran an article about me. After that, I kinda blew up in the foodie world." He says it like it's the most casual thing.

I blink at him, trying not to let my mouth gape open so the man with the camera doesn't catch it and turn me into a GIF.

"What was the article about?"

He shrugs. "How I'm the youngest chef in the world to earn three Michelin stars."

I don't get a chance to respond because, in the next moment, a short man in a shiny gray suit and a woman six inches taller than him walks up to our table and clasps Ryan on the shoulder. "Well, if it isn't Ryan Henderson in the flesh. I'm surprised to see you tonight."

Ryan doesn't smile. His eyes slowly slide up to the man's smug face before he looks back to me. "Noah, this is June, my girlfriend. She convinced me we should come."

Again with the girlfriend! But this time, it doesn't shock me so much. Instead, I feel a surge of pride.

Noah reminds me of a snake. His eyes are jet black when he

looks at me—appraises me. I don't know what he's looking for, but he's definitely looking for something. "June, huh? Well, it's nice to meet someone who has actual sway in Ryan's life. We'll have to talk later." He winks at me, and then he and his date are directed to a table across the room.

I don't know how to feel. The vibe is odd in here. Ryan seems oblivious, though. He's a natural in this setting, and it shows in the confident set of his shoulders. It's not that I feel insecure, but I certainly don't feel comfortable here. Maybe it would be better if Ryan and I could actually talk, but we aren't given a chance. Important person after important person works their way up to our table and monopolizes Ryan's attention for the whole evening.

We are served the most delicious Columbian cuisine of pineapple empanadas and grilled plantains with braised beef, but Ryan is barely given a chance to take more than one bite of each food. Every journalist wants to know what he thinks of the dishes, and Ryan, wanting to help his friend, gives them all a praiseworthy quote.

Newer chefs shyly inch up to him and ask for his advice, and a few women boldly ask if he's single. He always says no and directs their attention to me, but I wish he didn't, because it makes me nervous to walk to the bathroom alone the rest of the evening.

After an hour and a half, I wish I could take Ryan up on his thirty-minute suggestion. I miss him even though I've been sitting across from him all night. Actually, no. I haven't been sitting across from him all night. I've been sitting across from Ryan Henderson, the famous chef. I'm coming to realize there's a big difference.

It's not that Ryan is offensive in this state. In fact, if I were a random girl sitting at one of these tables, I'd be drooling too. It's just that he's more . . . refined. Serious. Poised. He wears his fame well, and for some reason, that unnerves me. He looks comfortable here under all the scrutiny. Almost like it's where he belongs.

More than once, I catch myself watching him while he talks to someone important and wondering how he's going to give all this up.

Is it terrible that I'm relieved he will give it up? That this sort of schmoozing won't be a regular occurrence for us? Ryan looks beautiful and stoic and severe in this chef mask he wears, but I miss the Ryan with a teasing glint in his eye.

He tells me he wants to go congratulate David before we leave, and while he's gone, I take my cloth napkin and fold it into a teeny-tiny square. I fold to keep myself from focusing on how adrift I feel in the center of this restaurant, among all the people wondering how I got so lucky to be Ryan's date tonight.

I'm so focused on trying to turn my napkin into a swan that I almost don't notice when Ryan's seat gets taken. I look up into jet-black eyes. "So, June, right?" says the man I met earlier named Noah.

I nod and tuck my napkin into my lap. "Yep. And you're Noah."

He smiles and leans forward to rest his elbows on the table, making himself comfortable, and me the exact opposite. "You know, earlier today, when Ryan came to look at the restaurant, I was confused about why he'd turn down the job." Ah, so that's who this guy is. "But now, looking at you, I can see it all perfectly."

His words pinch me. "Oh?" I glance toward the kitchen and wish Ryan would come back out.

Noah gestures toward my face and down my body. "You're gorgeous. And he's clearly crazy about you. Those are the only two things in life that can persuade a man like Ryan to give up all his dreams." *Give up all his dreams.* I look away from Noah, wishing I could turn away from his words just as easily.

Come back out, Ryan.

"It was all his decision. He said it wasn't a good fit for him." My voice sounds quiet.

Noah makes a scoffing, guttural noise from somewhere in his throat and leans back in his seat. "Well, of course he did. Good men like Ryan will give up everything for the women they care about. But what happens in five years when all those tingly little sparks fade?" I see what he's doing. I'm not going to let his words affect me. *I'm not.* "Eh, but don't mind me. I'm just bitter because he turned me down. This restaurant was going to be huge for both of us. An *epic* career changer. But that's okay. I wish you guys the best of luck. Better than my luck, at least."

I must give him some hint that I'm curious about his meaning, because as he's standing from the table and adjusting his tie, he says, "I was married once to a woman I loved. But those sparks faded, and now, I regret waiting so long to launch my career. I hope that doesn't happen for you and Ryan."

Noah leaves the table, and when he's gone, I pick up my napkin again and *fold, fold, fold.* My hands are trembling. *Where is Ryan?* I feel lightheaded. *Come on, Ryan.* I look toward the kitchen door again and will it to open. It doesn't, and my whole body is shaking with energy now that I can't contain. I bounce my knee to keep myself from doing something more drastic, but I feel the need to run bubbling through my veins.

I hate that weasel, Noah. He's sleazy, and I'm not oblivious to it. But I also feel the truth in his words. Ryan is giving up too much for me. He's going to regret it. When we fight, he'll bring it up. If my company thrives, he'll resent it.

I can't do that to him. To me.

Before I fully realize it, I'm standing from the table and rushing toward the exit.

CHAPTER 30

Ryan

I come back from the kitchen and find June's seat empty. Thinking she must be in the bathroom; I sit down and order another drink. People have been coming to the table all night, and now is no exception. I'm forced to smile and talk with a few people, but with every minute that goes by without June returning to the table, a sense of foreboding builds.

Finally getting a break in conversation, I text June to make sure she's okay. I'm half expecting a text saying she's sick, because of how long she's been in there. Five more minutes pass and still no response.

Enough is enough.

I make my way to the women's restroom and crack the door open. "June. You okay in here?" It feels uncomfortable calling out in a bathroom like this, but what else am I supposed to do?

"Uh, no one else is in here but me," says a lady who is definitely not June.

I let the door close, feeling even more concerned now. If June is not in the bathroom, where is she?

As I'm turning a circle in the hallway and scraping my hand through my hair, Noah comes out of the men's bathroom. "Why are you hovering outside of the ladies' room?" he asks, smirking in a way I don't appreciate.

"I thought June was in there."

His eyebrows shoot up. "Oh, she left, like, thirty minutes ago. I assumed there was some sort of emergency with how quick she was moving out the door in those heels."

"What?" My voice is so stern the walls rattle.

Noah's head kicks back, and he steps away, accurately interpreting my mood. "Calm down, man. I'm sure she's fine. Come sit with me and Gazel and have another drink. Maybe I can get her to convince you to take the position at Bask."

I'm not interested in a drink.

"What did you say to June?" I say, grabbing Noah by the front of his shirt and backing him up against the wall.

"N-nothing!"

"Not buying it. I know you talked to her. Tell me what you said." I put a little more pressure against his chest.

"It was nothing. I just told her that I thought you were making a mistake by passing up the job. Because you are!"

I shove Noah while releasing his shirt and stepping away. I start to walk away but then turn back and point. "Did you imply that she was getting in the way of me taking the job?"

His eyes widen, and his Adam's apple bobs over the top of his dress shirt, telling me everything I need to know.

What I want to do is ram Noah into the wall and make him physically pay for meddling in my life, but June is more important than vengeance right now, so instead, I make my way to the front door at a clip that is sure to garner some whispers.

Before I leave, the hostess stops me. "Sir," she says, sounding awkward. I turn around. "You're Mr. Ryan Henderson, right?" I nod, and a new dread fills my chest. "Here. The lady you were with left this for you. She asked me to make sure you got it when you were ready to leave."

I take the note and nod with a polite smile to put her at ease, because it's not her fault that I'm dateless right now. Once I'm outside and away from prying eyes, I open the letter.

I'm sorry, Ryan. I had to go. You can't give up your dreams for me. I won't let you. By the time you read this, I'll already be on my way to the airport.

Please don't follow me. It's easier if we just cut things off like this.

I have loved every second of our time together and wish you the best in life.

June

I crumple the paper and jog to my truck. After checking on my phone for flights out of Chicago to Charleston, I learn that the last one takes off in half an hour. There's no way I'll make that in time, but I've got to try.

The whole drive to the airport, my anger simmers—torn between hurt and disappointment. I thought we had a good thing going. I thought June and I were finally on the same page, and she trusted me. It's disheartening that one conversation with Noah shook her so fully. But then again, maybe it's my fault. I didn't expound on my decision enough. Tell her my plans. Tell her that I've been unhappy for a long time, even before she made it clear for me what my next step in life should be.

I don't know. These thoughts all race through my head during the drive that feels like a lifetime. When I finally put my truck in park at the airport, I jump out and sprint toward the main entrance. I could probably just wait until June makes it back to

Charleston and talk with her over the phone, but I don't want to. I'm scared to let too much time pass between us.

My dress shoes are clicking over the sidewalk as I'm running toward the entrance, and all I can think of is how much I look like a bad romantic cliché of a groom chasing after his bride who split before the ceremony. I'm not the only one thinking it. Everyone I pass gives me some major side-eye and pitying glances. I should have left my suit jacket in the truck.

I make it to the main sliding doors of the airport and freeze.

Walking out of the airport, holding her heels in one hand and black clutch in the other, is June. She looks up and spots me frozen fifteen feet away from her and smiles tentatively. Her breath clouds in front of her face before she bends down to slip her heels back on. She stands up, and emeralds stare back at me.

I'm sorry, she mouths.

CHAPTER 31

June

Ryan is standing in front of me, and my heart twists. His face is hard, and it's clear how he feels about me right now. I don't blame him. Those dark brows are pulled together, and his shoulders are set for battle. He looks intimidating and angry and beautiful. My knees want to knock together, and maybe I would be running from him right now if it weren't for the fact that he's here—he came after me even though I told him not to.

I take the first step closer, but he doesn't budge.

"I'm sorry," I say again. "I shouldn't have left."

He jerks his chin toward the airport doors behind me. "Did you miss your flight?"

"Yes," I say, and I see his jaw flinch. "But it was on purpose. I never even bought a ticket." There's a brief moment where I see his face soften, but he doesn't say anything. I inch forward again. "I shouldn't have left the restaurant. Noah came over and started talking to me about all you were giving up, and it scared me. I thought if I took myself out of the equation, you would go on with your dreams, and I wouldn't get in the way."

"So you had it all figured out without me, then?" His voice is so hard it's practically thunder.

"I thought I did. But I was wrong, and it wasn't until I was walking into the airport that I could see I was just self-sabotaging." I take another step. "I saw you tonight, and you looked so cool and confident in that atmosphere that I couldn't imagine you ever being truly happy with me in Charleston. I was afraid you'd resent me later. Or I wouldn't be enough to keep you happy, and you'd leave me in the end. It seemed better to just cut you out now."

"You were wrong."

"Yes, I was. I know."

"You have to quit running from me."

I'm standing in front of him now. "I will."

"Because I want a healthy relationship with you, June. I won't keep chasing you every time you run or slam a door in my face. Eventually, you're going to have to show me that you're willing to fight for us too."

Okay, now I take a step back, because I'm feeling slightly annoyed that he's still not budging. "That's what I'm doing right now, Ryan." I say his name, punctuating every letter sound and dripping it in annoyance.

He takes a step toward me this time. "If you had looked closer, you would have seen that the Ryan from tonight is miserable. He's lonely. He rarely smiles. He hates his job and has wanted out for a long time but never saw a way. You opened my eyes, June, and I see with perfect clarity that I want you. A life with you and all the craziness we are together."

"You'll be bored with me."

He takes another step. "What makes you think I'm just going to sit around painting you all day? I wouldn't quit my job and not have thoughts for the future. I *have* plans."

His harsh tone is ripping my heart. I laid down my pride and admitted my wrongs. I think the least he could do is talk a little softer. "Well, you never shared those plans with me."

"You're right. I should have told you I bought the space across from your donut shop." WHAT! "I contacted a realtor and looked at it the morning before we left Charleston. After I left Bask today, I knew for sure it's what I want, so I called and put an offer on it. They accepted about an hour ago."

"Okay . . . W-what are you going to do with it?" I'm in shock. I need one of those shiny blankets to wrap around my shoulders.

"Open my own place. You remember the little café I told you about in France? I plan to re-create it."

I can't breathe. He has plans. Across from my bakery. Plans, people! He has plans! "A café?"

"A small one. Only a few menu options. It's the opposite of what I've been doing lately, and it's exactly what I need."

"Well, GREAT," I say, but my voice sounds harsh now, too, because I'm feeding off his pent-up anger. I take another step away, but he keeps following me. We're doing a tango outside the airport. "I think it will be a huge success," I say in the way that people do when their anger is fizzling out, but they are already prepared for a fight, so they keep their tone angry. "You should have told me about this! Stop keeping me in the dark."

"Okay, then don't freak out and run away when I tell you what I'm up to."

I throw my hands up. "I was running back to you!"

He shrugs. "You can't do that every time you're scared. You have to trust me, eventually."

"I do trust you! That's why I was on my way back to you!" I make a dramatic sweeping gesture with my hands from the airport doors to where I'm standing. People are beginning to stare, but who cares. "See?! This was me saying I trust you. I was coming back, and you were supposed to hug and kiss me! That's what happens in the movies. You ruined it, Mr. Darcy, and now we're breaking up again."

For the first time, I see a smile crack on the corner of his face. But no. I'm back to hating that smug face. I hate that grin. I hate his dimple. I want to smear a big ol' cream pie in it. "I think that's the shortest relationship in history." He looks down at his watch. "Five hours. Not even sure it counts."

"Well, it doesn't matter now, because we're over." I cross my arms defiantly. "I hope you're happy. You've annoyed me, so we're done. It was nice knowing you, Ryan. Good luck with your café."

He's got a tilted smile. "You love me."

"I hate you. H.A.T.E."

"Love."

"Loathe."

Suddenly, Ryan bends down and scoops me up and tosses me over his shoulder.

"This is the twenty-first century, Ryan! You're not allowed to do this! Stop it, you caveman." I squeal and kick my feet as he casually strides away from the airport. "ABDUCTION!" I yell while also trying to cover my butt. I'm certain I'm flashing the entire airport.

No one even pays any attention to my squeals. Ryan is nodding as we pass people, and the only ones who have stopped to note our display are *awwwwing* like kidnapping is the most adorable thing in the world.

"Put me down, you dummy!"

He pats my butt. "Not a chance, June Bug."

"Ugh. Why are you so horrible?"

I give up and go limp-rag-doll the rest of the way to the truck. My only consolation is an up-close view of Ryan's glorious butt.

We make it to his truck, and he sets me down beside it. I'm just getting ready to lay into him, but he's faster and backs me up to the truck and silences me with his mouth. I mean to push him away, I really do. But one of his hands is pressing into my hip, and the other is lost somewhere in the back of my hair, and my body wins the argument against my mind.

I give in and slide my hands up the back of Ryan's jacket and over his muscles. My eyelids roll closed as Ryan angles my face and takes full control of the kiss. His lips taste faintly of orange and bourbon, making me want more. *More, more, more.* He's never won a fight like this before, but I hope it happens this way forever. Because here's the secret: He thinks he's winning, but in this kiss, I'm most definitely the victor.

Ryan breaks away, cupping my jaw, breath as ragged as mine. He smiles. "Love."

I narrow one eye and try not to grin. "Like."

He dips his head and nips at my lip. "Stubborn, stubborn woman."

I run my finger over the top of his dress shirt collar, just barely brushing against his skin. "I told you how I felt about you all those years ago when I tipped my chin for you. It's your turn."

He pulls away now to look me in the eyes, dark pools hypnotizing me. Tenderly, he wraps his arms around me and settles me against him. "Okay, here it is, then, June Bug. I'm going to lay it all out so there's no room for confusion. I love you. I always have. Pretty certain I always will."

I breathe in his words and smile when my lungs are full. I'm not sure what right turn I made in life to get me here, but I thank every act of courage, every broken heart, and every seemingly wrong turn that got me here, encircled by Ryan's arms. Our life together won't be perfect. Far from it. We will fight every day. I will salt his ice cream, and he will draw more mustaches on me while I sleep. But I look forward to every bit of it.

I raise up onto my tiptoes to brush my lips over Ryan's as I whisper, "*I win.*"

June

One year later . . .

"I didn't come for a visit to get caught in y'all's weirdo cross fire," says Stacy, the friend from whom I will mercilessly take back the Best Friend of the Year trophy I had made for her.

Yes, it is an actual trophy I had engraved, and I gave it to her ten minutes ago. But don't think I won't pry it out of her pretty little swollen fingers if need be.

I narrow my eyes at her. "No more complaining. Snap to it unless you want to say bye-bye to that shiny little trophy." I extend the brown paper bag in front of me and twitch my head toward the bronze trophy that has a little boy kicking a soccer ball on the top. Oddly, the store didn't have any trophies with two attractive women hugging on the top, so I had to settle for this one.

Stacy gasps. "You wouldn't!"

"I think you already know the answer to that question."

Stacy eyes the paper bag and then snatches it from me. "Be right back. But when I get back to California, I'm telling Logan about how you made me do your bidding, and you will definitely receive a strongly worded text about it."

I'm undeterred by her threats and smile like an evil master-mind, because I am one. I try not to stand too close to the window as I watch Stacy waddle (she's superpregnant, so I'm allowed to say that) across the street toward Le Café, where I know Ryan will be found in the kitchen—spices and seasoning set around him like an artist's paint set. He's been itching to create a new dish all month, and last night, he shot straight up in the middle of the night and proclaimed, "I HAVE IT!"

He clicked on the lamp, searing my eyeballs with painful light, and started scribbling away in the notepad beside the bed. I've learned over the last six months of our marriage that Ryan's best ideas hit him during the night. It's horrible, and I wouldn't have married him had I known this fact.

Anyway, after he was finished writing down his masterpiece, I made him snuggle me until I fell back to sleep, but then that turned into something different, and now we're both exhausted today. WORTH IT.

However, just because I'm deeply in love with him, and he's deeply good at loving me, doesn't mean the war we began as kids has stopped. Which is why I can't resist pressing my face against the glass to see what happens next.

Stacy looks over her shoulder after she crosses the street and makes direct eye contact with me through the glass. I give her a thumbs-up and then a shooing motion, and she rolls her eyes. Now, she's inside, and my stomach has butterflies.

One minute later, the door to Ryan's café opens again, and Stacy comes out, Ryan hot on her heels, paper bag in hand. I quickly roll myself away from the window until my back is flat against the wall. Wait, *busy*! I need to look busy. I wipe my hands on my pink apron and start buzzing around like Cinderella. *La-de-da,* nothing suspicious happening here! I always sing while I tidy the bakery.

The door chimes as Stacy and Ryan step inside, and I shiver at the sight of him. He's glorious. Gets hotter every time I see him. And today, he's wearing a navy shirt that makes his eyes look like even darker pools of delight.

"Hi, babe!" I say in my cheeriest, nothing-to-see-here tone.

His smile hitches as he rounds my counter. "Stacy brought me this donut. Says it's from you." He holds up the bag.

"Yeah. We didn't have time for breakfast, so I wanted to make sure you ate something."

We're holding locked-and-loaded smiles at each other. He knows something is up. In fact, I think he's already learned the secret. "You're too good to me."

"The best." I flutter.

His smile drops. "What's in the donut, June?"

I look horrified at his implication. "Why, darling, why would you expect anything to be wrong with the donut?"

"Because I put Orajel in your toothpaste yesterday and made your mouth go numb."

"*Ha, ha, ha!* Oh, Ryan! I'm not at all upset about that. It was funny. A great prank." I might be going over the top now.

He shakes his head at me. "There's no way I'm eating this donut, June. What did you do, crush up a laxative into the flour? Inject it with ghost pepper sauce?" Ghost pepper sauce! Why didn't I think of that?

"I swear to you. There is nothing wrong with that donut."

He stalks up close to me and stares down in my eyes. I can smell his bodywash from his shower this morning, and I want to grab him by the shirt and haul him into the kitchen and tell Stacy to man the door. In fact, I would if I weren't on a mission.

Ryan leans down slowly, tantalizingly, *dangerously,* and hovers over my mouth. "What. Did. You. Do. To. The. Donut?"

I hold his bad-guy gaze, because I'm every bit the assassin that he is. "Nothing," I whisper.

His eyes grow darker, because these games we play always get him going. I think he's thinking of the back room now too.

I slide around him and pretend I'm completely unfazed by his masculine sensuality. *You can't tempt me, buddy.* I bring a fresh tray of Just Peachy donuts from the back (Ryan's favorite) and begin setting the glistening glazed treats up in the display case.

"All right then, June Bug. If nothing is truly wrong with this donut, you eat it, and I'll take one of these fresh ones."

My shoulders slump, and I flash him my most annoyed look. It's paired with a flat smile. "I'm not hungry."

"Mm-hmm."

But I hate (love) when he taunts me, so I snatch the bag out of his hand and reach in for the donut. He reaches around me, making me have to lean back as he dips his hand into the donut case and grabs a peach-flavored donut for himself.

"You're going to have to pay for that," I say, and I'm completely serious.

Stacy chimes in from somewhere behind us. "You guys scare me."

Ryan's heart-melting, sideways smile just grows. "At the same time?" he suggests, lifting my hand holding the ominous donut I tried to get him to eat up toward my face.

I look down at it, my stomach recoiling at the sight, and nod. He raises his donut to his mouth, and I raise mine.

"I'll count down," says Stacy, clearly invested in the situation more than she was leading on. "Three . . . two . . . one."

Ryan and I both take a bite, and I can barely suppress my smile when his face immediately crumples. He curses and runs to get a napkin to spit out his donut. With my mouth full of delicious, untainted chocolate goodness, I laugh like a con woman who just got away with the world's most dangerous heist.

Ryan is scrubbing his tongue. "What was that?!"

Stacy and I are both doubled over laughing, and she says, "I can't believe it worked exactly like you said it would!"

"You owe me ten dollars!" I brag.

She reaches in her back pocket and hands over a ten-dollar bill while I'm still trying to swallow my donut.

"All right," Ryan says once he sulks back over to me. "Give me your villain monologue now."

I don't waste any time. With a finger poking him in his chest, I begin. "Of course you wouldn't trust a random donut delivered to your door! And OF COURSE you would make me eat it! What do you think I am, Ryan? An amateur?" He's rolling his eyes at how over the top I am. "HA! I'm brilliant, that's what I am. I knew you couldn't resist one of my freshly glazed peach donuts, so I glazed this whole batch with a special concoction of Elmer's glue, water, and—"

"Orajel," he states.

I smile deviously. "Is your tongue numb?"

"Oh yeah. Well done, June. You won this round."

I'm so caught up in my glorious victory that I absentmindedly take another bite of my donut. It only makes it halfway down my throat when I remember how it was making my stomach recoil a minute ago. My eyes go wide, and my mouth freezes.

Ryan and Stacy both look alarmed, and they should, because I'm about to hurl on their feet. I get ready to make a break for the bathroom, but Ryan grabs a giant disposable pastry box and puts it under my chin.

Once I'm finished with it, I'm not sure I'll ever be able to look at a pastry box the same way again.

"I thought you said you didn't do anything to that donut," Ryan says while rubbing my back after I finish throwing up.

"I didn't."

"Then what happened?"

"Well . . ." I guess now is as good a time as any. "I was going to do something supercheesy and make you open a present on Christmas morning with a trophy like Stacy's. Except yours says *World's Best Dad*. But I guess this is actually more our style, telling you over a prank war."

His eyes are wide, and I can see every gorgeous flake of gold and black, and all I can think is how excited I am to pose with him in this year's Christmas photo instead of Douglas Fir.

"June," Ryan says in a firm tone while cupping my face in both of his hands, "are you trying to tell me that . . . that . . ."

I tilt my chin up to Ryan and smile. "I'm pregnant!"

BONUS EPILOGUE

Four Years Later . . .

My heart is seconds from exploding out of my chest like a confetti canon. How is this my life right now? I am a donut shop owner, not someone who belongs on television. So can someone explain to me why I'm about to go on national TV?!

When I took over full ownership of Darlin' Donuts I was honestly just hoping to keep it in business. My only goal was to not let it tank like my flower truck business had. I never ever imagined it would become this—a donut shop, turned social media sensation, turned nationwide franchise—and lead to me being a guest on the most prominent morning show in America.

And I'm going to throw up all over my hot pink outfit. (Oh no. This better be nerves and not Zoe, stomach bug.)

I'm waiting in the wings of the stage, watching Violet and Tom chitchat with their cups of coffee about what they each did yesterday, waiting for my cue to follow the woman with the headset and iPad out onto the stage. There's an entire set to the right of the cozy living room set where the hosts do their morning intro, and it's staged with a Darlin' Donuts backdrop and a worktable where

I'm going to teach them to make a donut. *Feel free to be quirky and make mistakes because our viewers love that kind of thing,* the producer of the show told me as if messing up wasn't something that was a for sure done deal no matter how hard I try to keep it from happening.

Onstage, Violet mentions how her puppy chewed up her favorite pair of heels last night, and for some reason, this very domestic statement makes my heart squeeze. I wish Ryan was here. I'd be 80 percent more calm if he were holding my hand, giving me that sideways grin that always fills me with endless confidence.

But he's home right now instead of here in New York with me because yesterday afternoon, just before we had to leave for our flight, our three-year-old daughter, Zoe, started puking from a bad stomach bug. With zero complaints, Ryan offered to stay home with her to give me peace of mind and keep my mom (who was going to babysit for us) from catching anything. Ryan is incredible at sharing the parental load, and it's one of the many reasons I love him.

As if he can feel me thinking about him, my phone buzzes from the pocket of my bubblegum pink cargo jumper. It's one of those outfits that makes me look like a mechanic if you look past the white polka dots all over it or the giant Darlin' Donuts rhinestone logo on the back.

RYAN (MR. DARCY): I'm ready for Violet to stop talking about her damn puppy.

I smile down at my screen as the world around me fades.

JUNE: It's sweet! She's being relatable.
RYAN (MR. DARCY): The heel was Prada.
JUNE: You're being snooty.

RYAN (MR. DARCY): I'm just eager to see your pretty face on the screen. I've missed you today.

How is it that after being married for three years, butterflies still surge in my stomach when he says things like that to me?

JUNE: I've been missing you! How's everything going with Zoe? I hate that I'm not around to help.
RYAN (MR. DARCY): Stop that. I've got everything under control. Enjoy your moment—you deserve it.
RYAN (MR. DARCY): And she's finally sleeping soundly after a long night, so I'm going to get a shower now and wash off all the vomit caked onto my skin.
JUNE: Sounds sexy.
RYAN (MR. DARCY): Do you need me to erase that mental image for you?

A photo comes through next that has my face turning into lava. I immediately (and suspiciously) angle my phone away from the stage crew lady beside me and ogle the ridiculously sexy photo of Ryan's mirror selfie. He's wearing black boxer briefs and nothing else. I would like to lick his abs.

And just like that, I'm no longer thinking about going on live TV in a few minutes. My brain is obsessing over my husband and how we've both been absurdly busy of late and haven't had near enough naked time with each other. Between running our two businesses and keeping up with the social life of a three-year-old (which is shockingly vibrant, I might add), we've been like ships in the night. *Happy ships, but ships nonetheless.*

It's mid ogle that the stage lady looks over at me. "Ready? Almost time to go on."

I slam my phone against my chest and no one else has ever

looked so guilty in all of history. I give a meek smile and tuck my phone back into my pocket. "Ready as I'll ever be."

She nods, and I listen as Tom announces the commercial break. This is it. I know I have roughly two minutes before I have to walk out onto that stage in front of the cameras and studio audience.

The night before flying out, as I was lying in bed and spiraling about the idea of live television, I whispered to the ceiling, "I can't believe I'm doing this."

Ryan's fingers found mine under the comforter and he whispered back, "I can. It's what you deserve."

I clutch those words to my heart as I get the final warning nod from Stage Lady and then see Violet and Tom get into position on the part of the stage that's designated for Darlin' Donuts. *For me.*

The green light flashes on the camera and Violet talks me up. "You may know our next guest as the Queen of Donuts. The woman who swept into our lives via social media and stole our hearts with her Just Peachy donuts. She has not only built her donut empire from scratch, but has catered parties for celebrities all over the U.S., and recently launched her nationwide franchising. Please join us in welcoming . . ."

Stage Lady looks back at me with saucer eyes and begins counting down on her fingers while silently miming *three, two, one!*

"June Henderson, owner of Darlin' Donuts!"

Annnnnd we're walking. But then, just as we rehearsed, Stage Lady stops just at the edge of the curtain, and I keep going without her. *Please don't face-plant, June. Better yet, please don't have toilet paper stuck to the bottom of your shoes!*

The bright lights hit as I emerge from backstage. I smile and wave out at a roaring crowd.

"It went okay, right? I think it was okay?" I ask the headset lady the second I step backstage. But she's doesn't answer. The woman standing behind her does.

"You were incredible. And after I finish my segment, I plan to stuff my face with your amazing donuts and take any leftovers back to my husband."

I lock eyes with the woman and my stomach bottoms out. *That's . . . that's . . .*

"Rae Rose," she says with a smile, extending her hand for me to shake. OMG, the queen of soulful pop is extending her hand for me to shake. *This is wild. Surreal. Unbelievable.* Is it really happening to me? The day is a dream.

I manage to pick my jaw up off the floor in just enough time to shake her hand. Am I losing it or is her hand the softest hand I've ever felt in my life? Just her presence is sweet and comforting in a weird sort of way. Like I'm fairly certain I'm her best friend in the entire world now. She's wearing an all-black sequined jumpsuit that glitters in a thousand different ways and makes me want to throw my bubblegum pink one in the trash.

"I'm Ryan Henderson," I say, and then I pause. "*No.* Sorry. That's my husband's name. I'm Rae Rose." *Oh god!* "NO! You're Rae Rose. *I* am June Henderson." Someone please knock me out and carry me away on a stretcher. I'll never recover from this embarrassment.

Rae Rose—who I still cannot believe is standing in front of me in the flesh—just smiles like she thinks I'm adorable. "It's lovely to meet you, June." She looks over my shoulder and nods at someone. And then Rae Rose lightly touches my arm and aims an earth-shattering smile at me. "So sorry to cut this short, but I've got to get out there. It was really nice meeting you. I'm going to be in touch about having you cater an event for me coming up!"

"I'd love to!" I say as she floats by me and a very stern-looking woman in a suit (her bodyguard most likely) assumes a position right at the edge of the stage. The wild cheer of the audience suddenly cracks through the studio. I thought their cheer for me was loud, but for Rae Rose, it's breaking sound barriers.

And that's when I realize how incredible my life is—because even though I'm standing here watching a pop star talk about her upcoming album, I'm thinking about how eager I am to catch my flight home to Ryan and Zoe.

The Uber drops me off outside my house and I take a minute to just stand here and smile at our rainbow Christmas lights. We're the only house on the block with them still up—and I'm not mad about it. It's only 5:24 P.M. as I walk in the house, but everything is quiet as if it's midnight. I'm used to the sound of Zoe talking nonstop and running through the house like a wild boar. But upon closer inspection, I see that the light is off in her room down the hall, and the door is cracked.

I toss my purse on the hook by the door and pad as quietly as possible down the hall. When I peek through the crack, I smile at Zoe in her bed, sound asleep under my beloved Nick Lachey blanket. And she's not alone. Ryan is passed out on the floor beside her bed with his arm up in the air, holding on to her sweet little hand.

Oh, be still my fragile heart.

I tiptoe into the room, squat down next to Ryan (who I know has to be exhausted to have accidentally fallen asleep like this), and whisper his name. He jolts awake, looking like he's not sure what century he woke up in. His hair is all disheveled, and he's wearing sweatpants with a soft dark green T-shirt. Honestly, he's never looked better.

When he finally realizes I'm the one who whispered his name, a slow smile curls his mouth. I hitch my head for him to follow me out of the room. With the precision of a jewel thief, Ryan slips his hand out from under Zoe's, and he replaces it with a stuffed animal. *This isn't amateur hour.*

He follows me out of the room and softly, *softly* closes Zoe's door behind him. Once it clicks shut, I don't waste a second before wrapping my arms around his middle and squeezing. He hugs me back, laying his cheek against my head, and I swear nothing in my life beats this.

"Hi," I say with a contented sigh against his chest.

"Welcome home, June Bug." He kisses my head.

"Zoe doing okay? I can't believe she's still sleeping."

"She's much better. But she only napped for about an hour today—she was just too worn out to stay awake any longer, even though she was dying to see her *famous mommy,* as she referred to you all day. I took a video of her watching you on TV. Cutest damn thing you'll ever see."

I laugh quietly. "I can't wait."

"For real, though, you did amazing, June. I'm so proud of you," he says, walking me backward down the hall toward our kitchen, but never breaking contact. I place my bare feet on top of his socked ones and use him like skis.

"Did you see when I accidentally puffed flour all over the front of Violet's dress?"

He grunts a laugh while stopping us beside the fridge. "Yes. It was the best TV I've seen all year."

"I think she was actually kind of annoyed by it," I say as he leans around me, my arms still locked around his waist and his hand against my back while he pulls a leftover breakfast frittata from the fridge.

He backs us toward the microwave. "Well, hey—look at it this way, if you hadn't ruined it, her puppy would have anyway." After clicking thirty seconds on the microwave, Ryan slides his hands down to my waist and props me on the countertop, stepping between my legs.

"My favorite part, though, was when you said I taste test all your new recipes." A wicked gleam sparks in his eyes and I know exactly why.

"I knew you'd like that."

Because last time I had him taste test a recipe for me, it somehow ended up with us naked in the kitchen. Best day of cooking ever.

His eyes drop to my mouth and his hands—those hands I love more than sugar—glide up my thighs. And then the annoying microwave beeps and he twists around to pull the frittata out. Ryan is very serious about food and making sure we all eat three delicious meals a day.

And this, he knows, is my favorite meal as of late.

He hovers the plate between us while grabbing a fork from the drawer beside me. He looks sleepy as he cuts an eggy bite with the side of the fork prongs and then scoops it up, blowing on it and extending it toward my mouth. I'm smiling like a fool, watching him dote on me. "You *really* missed me."

His mouth hitches up. "A little bit."

And it's these moments that make life feel so special. Yes—the big grand ones like I had this morning are incredible, but it's these micro moments in the kitchen where my husband is feeding me a gourmet frittata from a purple toddler fork that I live for.

I can't believe I ever used to fear falling in love with him.

"How was your day with Zoe?" I ask on the last bite. Ryan takes the plate from me and sets it aside, guiding my legs to wrap around his waist before picking me up off the counter. He carries me into the living room and deposits me on the couch, crawling on top of me and then wrapping his arms around my waist to flip us so I'm covering him.

"Let's just say—I didn't realize a person as small as Zoe could have so much liquid inside her."

I laugh while simultaneously feeling terrible he had to take on the brunt of disgusting parenting today. But this is what we do. Life ebbs and flows for both of us, and when one of us needs extra help, the other steps up. It's one of the many reasons our relationship works. "You think she's past the worst of it?"

He nods, smiling softly as he runs his hands through my hair. "Yeah, she's good to go now." He pauses as his eyes sweep over my face. "You look pretty."

"You look pretty," I say, touching my finger to his full lips.

He rolls his eyes, shaking his head. I love his grin. I love when the black centers of his eyes eat up the brown. I love when I feel his heart rate pick up and his skin grows hot and to know that I do that to him. *I love everything about him.*

"You know . . . it's almost the end of January," I say, scooting up his body to level my face with his.

He runs his fingers lazily up and down my arm. "Mm-hmm?"

I lower my face and kiss him. Slowly. No hurry. "We should probably take the Christmas lights down before the neighbors complain."

His hand slides down the curve of my spine, lower and lower until his big hand settles over my right butt cheek. He squeezes, and his smile is a wild thing. "I'll get right on it."

He doesn't. He kisses me over and over again, his tongue slipping into my mouth and hands wandering all over the place. After a few minutes of kissing like we have all the time in the world, Ryan shifts and settles his lips once again against my throat. "I'm proud of you, June. And I'm so damn lucky to have you as my wife and partner in life."

I think I must be sleep deprived, too, because my eyes well up with misty tears. "I think that every single day about you."

He lays his head back against the couch cushion and looks up at me, eyes searching deep in my soul for any hints of a lie before he pushes my hair behind my ear. "Even when life is like this? Hectic and mundane at the same time?"

I smile, kissing him once softly. "Especially then."

"Why especially?"

"Because even in the trenches of parenting and building a business, even when Zoe is crying at the table because she hates what we fixed for dinner, even when Stacy and Logan crash in our living room for way too long over New Year's, I have the best time experiencing it all with you—which makes me see that I'm ridiculously lucky."

And then, because I can't seem to get close enough to him, I lift his shirt and climb up through it, squeezing my head through the neck hole with him.

"You're going to stretch out my shirt, you mongrel," he says, but affection is running throughout his tone. "I have the best time with you, too, June."

I nuzzle against the crook of his neck like a cat, all but purring when he runs his hand over my scalp. "We have so many glittering moments ahead of us, Ryan. I'll love sharing those with you just as much as I love this one—living with you in your shirt."

"I love you." He kisses my head and then reaches for the remote, clicking on the TV. "Now, I've got to show you the sexiest woman I've ever seen in my life."

I groan. "Tell me you didn't record my segment."

"Oh, I did." He sounds way too excited about it. I have a feeling he's going to show it to everyone who comes over.

"Let's have sex instead."

"Can't," Ryan says matter-of-factly. "Zoe is going to wake up any second, I feel it in my dadly bones. But don't worry—I have solid plans for later tonight. I was thinking it over in the shower."

"Oooo," I wiggle a little against him, drawing a laugh from him. "Tell me more."

"You won't distract me. We're going to watch this over and over—*my god,* look how cute you are waving at the crowd."

I give up and lay my head just under his chin, closing my eyes and savoring this quiet moment with Ryan instead of watching myself on the show.

He keeps narrating his favorite moments while running his fingers through my hair, and as I drift off into a nap with Ryan's shirt as my blanket, all I can think is there's nowhere else I'd rather be but here. Confident that no matter what life throws at us, we'll always be this close.

ACKNOWLEDGMENTS

Thank you to so many people! First, thank you, readers, for making writing so rewarding! I adore every single nice review, email, Instagram message, and blog shout-out you guys send me! The encouragement never goes unappreciated.

Thank you, family, for your unending support.

Chris, my husband, just for being you. I'm a little obsessed with you and everyone knows it. Also, thank you for coming up with the Nick Lachey bit. That was all you!

Carina and Ashley, you're the best. Love you guys!

Gigi Blume, thank you for taking the time to critique this book. Some truly terrible jokes and cringeworthy scenes would have made it through without you! You're amazing.

Jen Lockwood, my editor, you did it again! Without you, a horrendous and completely plot-changing typo would have made it through for everyone to gasp at! I think you're the bee's knees.

My bookstagram community, thank you for your love, for helping promote my books, and most importantly, your friendships!

THANK YOU! Hugs to anyone who made it this far:) I'm off to write the next book now.

XO, Sarah

READ ON FOR AN EXCERPT FROM *THE OFF-LIMITS RULE*

BY SARAH ADAMS

CHAPTER 1

Lucy

I'm splayed out like a starfish ripped from the ocean and dried up on the carpet of my new bedroom. I've been here for an hour, watching the fan blades go round and round, thinking I could have turned on a show by now, but what's the point anyway? My fan friends are just as entertaining as anything on TV these days. Besides, fan blades don't fill you with romantic illusions about this crappy, *crappy* world and make you feel that you will get everything you've always wanted. No, Fanny, Fandrick, Fantasia, and Fandall don't tell me I'll get my happy ending in this life. They just—

"Oh my gosh." The sound of my older brother's voice pulls me out of my fan entertainment, and I roll my head to the side, squinting at his blurry figure filling my doorframe. "This is next-level pitiful, Luce." Drew strides into my room, literally steps over my useless body covered in candy wrappers, and mercilessly rips back the curtains.

I hiss like a vampire who's just been easily beaten in an overcomplicated plot when the light falls onto my body. *Light was the key the whole time!* My muscles are too puny and wasted away from my forty-eight-hour-feeling-sorry-for-myself binge to even throw my hand over my eyes. "Stop it, jerk. Close those and leave me be!"

He towers over me and shakes his head of brown hair like he can't believe the pitiful excuse of a human I am. I peek up through my melancholy just enough to register that I should trim his hair soon. "Look at you. Your face is covered in chocolate, and you smell."

"Rude. I never stink. I can go weeks without deodorant and still—" I lift my arm and wince when I get a whiff of myself. "Oh yeah, shit, that's bad."

His brows are lifted, and he's nodding his head with a humorless smile. "You need to get out of this room. I gave you a few days to pout that things didn't turn out like you wanted, but now it's time to get up and get moving."

"I don't *pout*."

"Your lip is actually jutting out."

I suck the offending lip back into my mouth and bite it. Drew extends his hand, and I take it, only because I really have to pee and not at all because I secretly know he's right and I've wallowed long enough. When my world went south a few days ago, the first thing I did was call Drew to come get me and my son, Levi—not like, come get us from the restaurant, but come get us from Atlanta, Georgia, where I was paving my own way, making my life happen for myself, living the dream, and failing miserably at all of it.

Drew didn't even bat an eye when I asked him to come help me pack up my dignity and haul it back home. From the beginning, he wasn't thrilled about my decision to move out of Tennessee and away from our family, so without hesitating, he said, "Be there tomorrow, Luce. I'll bring a truck." And he did. He spent the whole next day helping me pack everything in that dinky (very smelly) apartment, and then he drove me back to his house in Nashville where my son and I will be living (rent-free, *bless him*) for the fore-seeable future.

The only reason I've been able to spend the past few days inter-viewing my fan blades is because my amazing parents took my four-year-old for a few days while I get unpacked and settled. I don't think they meant for me to settle my butt into the carpet and lie here for the entire weekend making excellent fan friends, but it's what I've done, and no one is allowed to judge me because judging isn't nice.

Once I'm standing, Drew sizes me up, and let me tell you, he does *not* like what he sees. "I think you have a bird's nest in your hair. Go take a shower."

"I don't feel like showering. I'll just spray some dry shampoo to kill the stink. And maybe the birds."

He catches my arm when I try to turn away. "As your older brother, I'm telling you . . . get in that shower, or I will put you in it, clothes and all, because honestly they could use a wash too."

I narrow my eyes and stand up on my tiptoes to look more frightening—I think the effect would be better if I didn't feel chocolate smeared across the side of my face. "I'm a grown, adult woman with a child, so your older-brother threats aren't effective anymore."

He tilts his head down slowly—making a point that he's, like, nineteen million feet taller than me—and makes direct eye con-tact. "You're wearing dinosaur PJ pants. And as long as you call me, pulling that *baby-sister* card when you need my help with some-thing, the older-brother threats count."

I raise an indignant chin. "I never do that." *I definitely do it all the time.*

"Take a shower, and then put on a swimsuit."

I make a disgusted *ugh* sound. "I am *not* going swimming with you. All I want to do is eat disgusting takeout, fill my body to the brim with MSG, and then crawl under the covers until next year rolls around with shiny new promises of happiness."

He's not listening. He's turning me around and pushing me toward the bathroom. "Get to it, stinky. Like it or not, you're putting on a swimsuit and coming with me. It's been too long since you've seen the sun, and you look like a cadaver." I'm feeling blessed that he didn't mention I smell like one too.

"I hate the pool." I'm a cartoon now, and my arms are long droopy noodles, dragging across the floor as I'm pushed toward the bathroom.

"Lucky we're not going to one then. My buddy and I are taking the boat out to wakeboard for the afternoon. You're coming too."

I'm standing motionless in the bathroom now, eyebrows-deep in my sullen mood as Drew pulls back the shower curtain and starts the water. He digs under the sink and pulls out a fluffy towel, tossing it onto the counter. He's giving me tough love right now, but I know underneath all this dominance is a soft, squishy middle. Drew has one tender spot in life, and it's me. The tenderness also extends to Levi by association and because my son's cheeks are so chunky and round you can't help but dissolve into a pool of wobbly Jell-O when he smiles at you.

"Isn't it, like . . . frowned upon to skip work on a Wednesday?" I ask, trying to needle him so he'll leave me alone with my candy bars and sadness.

"Yes, but it's *Sunday*." The judgment in his voice is thick. "And unless one of my patients goes into labor, I have Sundays off."

I blow air out through my mouth, making a motorboat sound because I'm too lethargic and wasted on chocolate from my pity party for snappy comebacks. Which is sad because snappy comebacks are my thing.

"Lucy," Drew says, bending to catch my eye like he knows my thoughts were starting to wander back down the dark tunnel to mopey-land. He points behind him to the steaming water. "Lather, rinse, and repeat. You'll feel better. Promise." He leans forward and gives a dramatic sniff. "Maybe even repeat a few times. Then move on to the toothbrush, because I think something crawled in your mouth and died." *Siblings are so sweet.*

I punch him hard in the arm, and he just smiles like he's happy to see me showing some signs of life. "But seriously, thank you," I say quietly. "Thanks for taking me in too. You're always rescuing me."

The day I realized I was a week late for my period, Drew was the one who drove to the store and bought my pregnancy test. He's the one who held me when I cried and told me that if I wanted to keep the baby, I wouldn't have to go it alone because I'd have him (and then my parents quickly hip-checked him out of the way and reminded me I'd have them too). This is part of the reason I moved to Atlanta a year ago—not because I wanted to get away from them, but because I wanted to prove to myself I could stand on my own two feet and support my son.

Spoiler alert: I can't.

I'm a twenty-nine-year-old single mom and an unemployed hairdresser (I got fired from the salon I was working at) who's having to live with my older brother because I don't have a penny in savings. Turns out, kids are mega-expensive. And when you choose to live away from your support system as a single parent, you have to put your child in daycare (which costs your arm), and hire babysitters when you want to go out on the weekend (which costs your leg), or hire a full-time nanny (which costs your soul).

Although Levi's dad, Brent, pays child support, it's just not quite enough to help me get ahead of bills and debt. Brent is not a bad guy or anything, and he's even offered to pay extra to help give me a financial cushion, but for some reason, I'd rather start wearing tennis shoes without socks and selling them to people on the

internet who want them *extra sweaty* before I take money from
Brent. He's always had too much emotional pull in my life. At one
point, I might have dreamed of us actually becoming a family one
day—but not anymore. Those dreams have long since evaporated,
and now, any time he texts me after midnight saying something like
Why don't we ever get together, just the two of us?, I know better than
to respond.

Drew gives me a soft smile and really doesn't have to say anything because we have that sibling telepathy thing that lets me see
inside his head. He speaks anyway. "You'd do the same for me."

"Yeah. Of course I would." But I'd never need to because Drew
has his life together 100 percent of the time.

He pulls me in for a hug. "I'm sorry you're bummed, but I'm
glad you're home and you and that jackass broke up."

And just like that, our sibling comradery vanishes and I'd like to
kick him in the shins. I settle for pushing out of his hug. "He wasn't
a jackass!"

"Yeah, he was. You just need some space from him to see it."

"No, *Andrew,* he just wasn't smooth and *super cool* like you assume you are, and that's why you didn't like him. But he wasn't a
jackass."

I really don't know why I'm defending Tim so much. I wasn't in
love with him or anything. In fact, that's why we broke up. There
was no spark, and we were basically friends who kissed (and not all
that often). I'd never even introduced him to Levi because somewhere in the back of my mind I always knew our relationship
wasn't going anywhere.

I'm a little ashamed to admit it, but I only dated him because he
was *there* and available. I was new to Atlanta, having taken an open
position at a new salon, and he was one of my first clients. We hit it
off, started dating (if you can even call it that since we barely saw
each other due to me not having any friends or family around to

help babysit), and, for a few months, fell into a comfortable pattern of going out on Saturday nights when I could afford to hire the sixteen-year-old down the street. She had a more active dating life than me, though, so I had to book her weeks out and pay her a fortune.

Then, the roommate I moved to Atlanta with got engaged to her boyfriend and asked to break our lease agreement early so she could move in with him. I, being a woman deeply afraid of confrontation, agreed wholeheartedly before remembering that I didn't trust anyone else to live with me and my son. I tried to make it work financially on my own for a while, but then the burden just got too heavy. I was two months behind on rent, and then I lost my job at the salon because I continued to cancel on too many clients.

Did I mention it's super hard to be a single parent without a nearby support system? Turns out, most bosses really don't give a crap about your child at home with a stomach bug, and unable to go to daycare. They really only care that you didn't show up to work and earn them the money they were counting on.

So, I got fired, and then the next week, Tim and I broke up, and *then* I got the official eviction notice from my landlord. I didn't need any time to think about what to do. I called Drew and told him to come get me, and then I cut Atlanta off like a bad split end.

Now, I'm sad, but not because I miss Tim. I'm sad because I *don't* miss Tim and my life feels like way more of a mess than it should at age twenty-nine. It's like I'm mourning something I hoped could happen but didn't.

"No," says Drew, "I didn't like him because when I came to visit and the three of us went to dinner, he said he was cold and accepted your sweater when you took it off and gave it to him."

I feel a familiar defensiveness boil in my chest. "He has a *thyroid problem* and gets cold easily. And I told you, I wasn't even cold!"

"Then why'd you take my sweatshirt after he took yours?"

"Because . . ." I drop my gaze, so he hopefully doesn't catch my defeated look. "It had been six months since I'd seen you and I missed you?" I can't let Drew know I also found Tim annoying at times or else he'll add it to his ongoing list titled: Drew Knows Better Than Lucy. *It is a solid list, though.*

He doesn't comment on my blatant lie. Just lifts a brow and points to the running water. "Stop stalling and take your shower. But make it quick or we're gonna be late."

Well, joke's on him, because I don't even want to go out with him and his *buddy,* and I don't care one bit if we're late. In fact, I feel like teaching my brother a lesson, so I take an extra-long time, reenacting every sad shower scene I've ever seen, letting the spray of the water rush over my face as sad music plays on the speaker in my bedroom.

Bang, bang, bang.

I jump out of my sopping wet skin and press myself back against the tile, certain I'm about to be murdered by a polite killer who likes to knock before he enters, but then Drew's voice booms through the door. "I swear to God, Lucy, I will cut off the hot water if you don't get out soon. Also, that's enough Sarah McLachlan." He turns off my *Super Sad Mix* and blares "Ice Ice Baby" as an overt threat.

Ah—so nice living together again.

I want to be furious with Drew, but instead, I'm using all my willpower not to laugh.

I'm a whiny baby all the way to the boat dock. *The sun is too bright. My head hurts. There's nothing good on the radio.* Honestly, I'm surprised Drew didn't unlock the doors, pull the handle, and push me out on the interstate. That's what I would have done if the roles were reversed, because even I don't want to hang out with me right now. Even so, he took my annoyance in stride, turning off the radio, giving me his sunglasses, offering to stop for Advil. Really, it's suspicious how syrupy sweet my brother is being.

At the last minute, I even asked him if we could make a pit stop at our mom and dad's house so I could check on Levi. Let's be honest, Levi is with his two favorite people in the world, so he's not missing me. My mom has probably fed him so many sugary treats he's completely forgotten my name.

When the door opens and I see my little cutie, blond hair all askew in various cowlicks, eyes bright with sugar overdose, and white powder mysteriously coating his lips, my suspicions are confirmed.

I glance down at my child and then up at his grandparents standing at attention behind him, mischief written all over their faces. "This is a surprise drop-by . . . you know, to make sure everyone's following the rules," I say, drawling out the last word like I'm a detective tilting her aviators down, completely on to their tricks.

Both grandparents make a show of gulping nervously, and I abruptly drop down to get eye level with Levi. I reach out and run a finger across his top lip, bringing the powdered sugar close to my eye for inspection. "Mm-hmm . . . just what I thought. Donut residue." He giggles and licks his lip nearly up to his nose to get every particle of sugar he can. *I taught him well.*

My mom puts her hand on Levi's shoulder and squeezes. "Stay strong, buddy."

I narrow my eyes up at my mother (also my favorite person in the world) and shoot to my feet, getting in her face like a drill sergeant. "How many?" My voice growls menacingly. Levi giggles again, and I glance down at him. "Do you think this is funny, little man?"

"Mom, you're so silly."

"How many?" I repeat again to my mom, undeterred by the

adorable chunky-cheeked boy. She lifts her chin and makes a show of pressing her lips closed. "I see . . . that's how it's going to be? Fine. I know who to go to when I want the truth."

"Luce, come on, we gotta go," Drew says, sounding a little impatient behind me. *Someone has lost his funny bone.*

I hold up my finger behind me in his direction and shush him before taking a slow step directly in front of my dad. His eyes widen, and I know he'll be an easy crack. "So, Mr. Marshall, are you going to talk, or are we going to have to do this the hard way—"

"THREE!" he blurts, and then my mom shoots him the stink eye.

I grin and push my imaginary glasses back up the bridge of my nose. "Thought so. Sir, ma'am, do you happen to know the effects too much sugar has on—"

I don't get to finish my sentence because Drew picks me up over his shoulder and starts carrying me away. "Bye, guys," he says with a smile and wave. "We'll have our phones if you need us."

"WAIT! Let me at least kiss my child goodbye, you oaf."

He pauses and backs up a few steps, bending down so I'm lowered to lip level with Levi. He laughs and laughs at the sight of me on "Uncle Drew's" shoulder, so much so that I'm barely able to plant a kiss on his sugary cheek from all his giggling.

"Love you, baby. Be good for Grammy and Grandad," I tell him, feeling my heart squeeze a little painfully at the thought of leaving him again. Other than the times I had to work, Levi and I haven't spent much time apart this last year. Although I'm happy to see him reunited with family, I also have this strong desire to stay close to him. Plus, stuffing my face with donuts sounds infinitely better than going out with Drew and his buddy on the boat.

"Have fun, you two," say my parents, breaking character to wrap an arm around each other and wave as Drew walks us away and deposits me in the front seat of his car.

After our twenty-minute drive, we pull into the marina, and I take my sweet time getting out of the car. Maybe if I move slow enough, he'll leave me behind and just let me curl up in a depressed ball under a tree somewhere.

He can see right through my shenanigans. "Dammit, Lucy, do I have to drag you onto the boat too? You're going on the lake, because you need this whether you can see it or not. Quit being a pain in the butt and get moving."

"What happened to Mr. Congeniality from the car ride?" I ask, getting out and slamming my door shut.

He pulls a cooler out from the trunk and grins at me—his eyes a darker blue than mine, filled with sibling exasperation. "I was hoping you'd get it all out of your system so Johnny Raincloud wouldn't follow us out on the water."

"You didn't have to bring me, you know. If you wanted a happy companion, you could have just invited some of those fun women who love you."

"I didn't want to bring a fun woman. I wanted to bring you. My annoying little sister."

I narrow my eyes and cross my arms.

He jerks his head toward the back seat. "Grab the towels and let's get on the water."

"One hour," I say, following behind him with the towels like a stubborn puppy that doesn't want to walk on a leash but knows it doesn't have a choice. "I'm staying for one hour and that's it. Then, I'm going back to my candy bar babies."

"Just get in the boat, Eeyore," says Drew, fighting a smile as he extends his hand to help me over the railing.

Once in the boat, I run my palms along the bright-white upholstery. It's hot to the touch, and I can't help but smile at my brother's dream come true. He's always wanted a boat, and he finally made it happen. He's been working his butt off the past several years, completing medical school and then enduring his residency and whatever else doctors have to go through. Now, he is an ob-gyn in a small private practice, and this was his official "doctor" present to himself.

Other than a partner feeling slightly uncomfortable with him working closely with women's bodies all day, I can't help but wonder why he's still single. He's good-looking, funny, and outgoing. Most women love him, yet he won't have it. He dates (a lot) but has never been interested in settling down.

Taking my towel, I lay it across the boiling-hot leather before sitting so I don't sear my butt cheeks. I settle in, begrudgingly feeling like Drew was right; it really does feel good to be outside with the sun tickling my skin. "So, which buddy is coming out with us? Farty Marty or Sweaty Steven?" Oddly, all of Drew's friends have terrible flaws, so much so that I'm beginning to wonder if he has a beauty complex and refuses to associate with anyone prettier than himself.

"Cooper," he says while shoving the cooler into a little side compartment.

Ah, yes, the recently moved-out roommate. I haven't met this one yet. He moved in with Drew about a year ago, right after I left town, and they apparently became besties right away. Drew won't let me refer to them as that, though, so I make sure to do it as often as I can.

"Hmm . . . Cooper Pooper."

"Don't do that."

"I have to. How will I remember his name otherwise?"

Drew doesn't look at me as he secures the boat canopy. "Repeat it to yourself five times."

"Cooper Pooper. Cooper Pooper. Cooper Poo—"

"Not what I meant, and you know it," Drew says, looking over his shoulder with the same look the actors on *SNL* get when they try not to let the audience see them laugh. *He missed me.*

I shut my eyes and lean my head back, feeling the sun singe my eyelids and trying to imagine what terrible flaw of Cooper's I will have to endure all day. Bad B.O.? Snaggleteeth? Greasy hair? Probably a heavy combination of each.

I don't know, and it doesn't matter anyway. I'm just going to lean back against the warm leather and sleep the day away. Drew forced me out here, but he can't force me to smile or pretend I'm enjoying life with Pooper Scooper Cooper. *See?* I'll never forget his name now. My method works.

I hear footsteps approaching on the dock, but my eyes feel too heavy to open. Probably all that MSG really settling into my bloodstream and trying to embalm my body.

"Hey, Coop," says Drew, and I can feel my whole body stiffen with dread. He's here. What's it going to be? My money is on the B.O. "Just throw your stuff over there by Lucy. Oh, by the way, that's my sister."

I guess that's my cue to open my eyes and try to act like I don't see the nasty hair-sprouting mole on the tip of this guy's nose.

ABOUT THE AUTHOR

SARAH ADAMS is the author of *The Rule Book, Practice Makes Perfect, When in Rome,* and *The Cheat Sheet.* Born and raised in Nashville, Tennessee, she loves her family and warm days. Sarah has dreamed of being a writer since she was a girl but finally wrote her first novel when her daughters were napping and she no longer had any excuses to put it off. Sarah is a coffee addict, a British history nerd, a mom of two daughters, married to her best friend, and an indecisive introvert. Her hope is to write stories that make readers laugh, maybe even cry—but always leave them happier than when they started reading.

authorsarahadams.com
Instagram: @authorsarahadams

ABOUT THE TYPE

This book was set in Hoefler Text, a typeface designed in 1991 by Jonathan Hoefler (b. 1970). One of the earlier typefaces created at the beginning of the digital age specifically for use on computers, it was among the first to offer features previously found only in the finest typography, such as dedicated old-style figures and small caps. Thus it offers modern style based on the classic tradition.